SEDONA STORM

SEDONA STORM

Barbara Scott and Carrie Younce

THOMAS NELSON PUBLISHERS

Nashville

Published in Nashville, Tennessee, by Thomas Nelson, Inc.

Library of Congress Cataloging-in-Publication Data

Scott, Barbara, 1948—
    Sedona storm / Barbara Scott & Carrie Younce.
      p. cm.
    ISBN 0-7852-8266-1
    1. Women journalists—Arizona—Sedona—Fiction. 2. Occultism—Arizona—Sedona—Fiction. 3. Murder—Arizona—Sedona—Fiction.
4. Cults—Arizona—Sedona—Fiction. 5. Sedona (Ariz.)—Fiction.
I. Younce, Carrie, 1959— .   II. Title.
PS3569.C595S43   1993
813'.54—dc20   93-30667
                                                 CIP

Printed in the United States of America

1   2   3   4   5   6   7 — 99 98 97 96 95 94

DEDICATION

This book is lovingly dedicated to our devoted husbands, Michael Scott and James Younce, who believed in God's call on our lives and were faithful to cover us with prayer. In those last weeks, they cooked, cleaned and baby-sat with Carrie's daughter, Anna Michele, as we worked day and night to finish this book. May the Lord bless them all the days of their lives.

Also, special thanks go to Carrie's parents, Rev. Dr. Gary and Millie Heniser, for their hospitality and for giving up so much of their time, as well as to Stephanie Vallas and Janet Clark for also corralling Anna.

We also would like to thank Donald Brandenburgh, our literary agent, and the wonderful editorial staff of Thomas Nelson, all who believed in the project.

And may God continue to bless the "real" Joshua Intercessors from St. Anne's Episcopal Church, Oceanside, CA, who regularly went before the Father on our behalf.

We give all the glory to God!

PROLOGUE

Against the arid azure sky, darkness was gathering. Seen by no human eye, making no detectable sound, the culprits of hell assembled above the red desert floor of Sedona.

Humtah, Lord of the Place of the Lizards, paced the hot air. His agitation was made obvious in the folding and unfolding of his hideous bat-like wings.

"Here I am, moments away from one of the greatest alliances in history—a moment of highest honor among my peers—and all I have in attendance are a wandering exile, a constant thorn, and a wretched scavenger." He spat a dustball upon the rocks below.

Hearing their names, the demons Nod, Koz, and Piteous-Cull drew near to their captain.

"Premier Humtah," Nod gushed and bowed, "do not be disconcerted. All is in readiness."

"It is, it is." Koz scuttled up alongside Nod, scraping the ground as he tucked in his scaly, emerald-colored wings. "There is but to wait."

"WAIT," spat Humtah, spreading his pinions wide and flattening Piteous-Cull, who had forgotten to bow. I am the Lord of this place. I am the prefect of this region. "Who am I to wait?" He puckered his lips and raised a clenched fist into the air. "I demand the respect owed to me. I am the host. . . ."

Humtah's tirade dropped like lead from his lips at the sound of the thick, purring voice behind him.

"I believe then, that we are your guests."

Nod, Koz, and Piteous-Cull fell prostrate as Humtah spun around and bent in a low servile bow. Before them, in full demonic regalia, stood the Legion of Commanders.

Time ceased, and all present held silence, until the most wretched Regent Commander Vaizaitha clapped his talons on each side of the bent Humtah's pointed head and jerked him to full height.

"I did not come here merely to hold court, you worthless son of a snake." Vaizaitha shoved Humtah backward with a growl. "Where shall we meet where no light can find us?"

"We have prepared the underground cavern for your comfort, your Excellency." Humtah gestured and then led the way. As Nod and Koz rose to follow, Vaizaitha slapped them aside.

"No riffraff." His glare sent the two minor demons scampering, with Piteous-Cull closely following.

✝✝✝✝✝

From behind a blind of pure light, the angels watched the unholy assemblage file underground. The two, garbed in spotless white, knew the danger of being seen too soon. To provoke the battle now would surely mean defeat. They waited silently until the hierarchy had disappeared and only a few minor demons were left visible. Then Goyo, the larger of the two angels, spoke.

"There will be carnage here. I saw Desmodus, the Drinker of Blood."

"And a great war against the faithful," added Goyo's companion, Sandor. "I saw among their number Quench-Bersha and Mibzar." Sandor turned his back and leaned against a large boulder. "Zethar-Zebah, the master of abortion, was there also. There was only one whose name I do not know."

"Yes, Yoko-Sharuhen," Goyo mused. "She is the demon who is also called the Female Abode of Pleasure." He strode over and laid a consoling hand on his friend's shoulder. "Do not despair, brother Sandor. The Lord our God is one, and His name is above any other. At the name of Y'shua, every knee will bow, in heaven, on earth. . . ."

"And under the earth. Yes, I know," finished Sandor. "Thank you for reminding me that we are servants of the Most High God." He straightened up and threw his arms wide. "What a mighty God we serve!"

"Who was, and is, and is to come, glory to His Name." Goyo joined in the praise. After a few moments, the angels felt their joy alight. As praise filled their mouths, God's glory filled their veins, and His joy returned to strengthen their spirits.

"Come," said Goyo. "We must report all that we have seen."

Sandor turned once again to face the direction of the underground cave. Raising his fist, he shouted to the invisible throng of planning devils. "I look with relish to the time when we will show you that it is a fearful thing to fall into the hands of the Living God."

"Amen, and amen," answered Goyo, and the angels disappeared.

Regent Commander Vaizaitha addressed the company of hellish chieftains with empty wit and incompetent wisdom as he laid out the plans for the battles ahead. He leaned on the stone table before him as he spoke.

"And so, you can see the possibilities that are before us. If we win. . . ." He grinned in great satisfaction. "*When* we win, it will bring to a close this present age. We will rule again." He edged forward and stared around the room, meeting every eye. "We cannot afford even one error. You must remain true to the plan. No improvising. Stay in rank. Do not, at any time, underestimate your adversaries." He slammed his fist onto the stone table for emphasis. "You may not see them, hear them, or even smell them, but do not be deceived, they are there, watching all the time."

A hand shot up from the back of the room. It was Mibzar, the ranking demon over Sedona's New Age religions. "Are they not weak in this area, Commander? I don't mean to brag, but we have moved in such a large number of our own that—Christians," Mibzar spat out the word with disgust, "are almost paralyzed in Sedona."

"Have you forgotten that just one of them can put one thousand of us to flight?" quivered Quench-Bersha, who led the fight against the entire body of Christians in Sedona. "The number of them is not as great a worry for us as is the strength of their faith. I fear there are some who could stop us before we've even begun."

Desmodus, the drinker of blood, stood and addressed the entire assembly.

"My fellows, have we forgotten that the groundwork is already laid for us? Mibzar and his cohorts have done a fine, subtle job of injecting their followers throughout the region. Quench-Bersha has eliminated all but a small core of the faithful, who were not so easily lulled into apathy. Zethar-Zebah and the whisperers of pro-choice propaganda have spilt enough blood that many rifts are now open. Thanks to the now present lady, Yoko-Sharuhen, we will soon abolish all rule save the rule of our Lord Satan."

A cheer arose from the demons in the cave room. Vaizaitha cleared his throat and clapped his talons together, regaining control of the meeting.

"Let us not celebrate prematurely, good fellows," he reminded them. "Although we have been successful up to this point, we must not forget the danger of the tasks at hand."

Humtah smirked. "But Commander, why should this be any more dangerous than the previous missions? Our numbers increase daily through the openings to our kingdom. In this century alone, we have seen Hitler's monumental blood-spilling which almost eradicated God's chosen and opened many rifts around the world."

"And let us not forget Vietnam and the killing fields of Cambodia," Mibzar cackled. "What a victory!"

Vaizaitha unfurled his black, scaly wings and pinned his generals with a penetrating stare. "You forget one thing."

"What's that, Commander?" Desmodus asked.

"Though many of this generation have been deceived by our New Age religions, those who are left have been taught spiritual warfare," Vaizaitha spat. "They know who we are. They recognize us. They gather in prayer groups to come against us. We must divide them! Isolate them. Inject them with doubt and depression. Sow strife and fear among them. Hound them with past sins. Not one is to be spared."

Vaizaitha's rapid-fire instructions had sobered his troops. "Yoko, you are dismissed to begin your part. The rest of you, gather your ranks, for tonight we will sacrifice." A murmur of anticipation rippled through the crowd. Vaizaitha raised his talons, "So mote it be."

In a hillside home just outside of Sedona, a group of women gathered to meditate in a dimly-lit chapel. They sat on overstuffed pillows atop a colorful medicine wheel which had been worked into the tile of the floor. Behind the altar on a stone throne in front of the room sat a slender woman, with long blonde hair billowing out behind her. She sat with eyes closed, holding the hands of a young Indian woman on her right and on her left, an attractive woman in her forties. The women chanted:

> Mother Earth, we bow to you.
> Nah nah, hiya, nah nah, hiya.
> Source of life, source of seed.
> Nah nah, hiya, nah nah, hiya.
> No life higher, no life lower.
> Nah nah, hiya, nah nah, hiya.
> In your circle all is one.
> Nah nah, hiya, nah nah, hiya.

Suddenly, the blonde woman's eyes snapped open, and she began to channel the voice of the demon Yoko-Sharuhen.

"My daughters, how lovely to be with you again. It is I, Mother Earth, whom you know by many names. I am Gaia, she whom you have worshipped, and I am Isis, wife of Osiris, and I am Seydna, Diana, Demeter, Hecate, Cubele, and Coatlicue. I am the Virgin, Great Mother, and Crone. I am all that is. I am the light divine. I am love. I am will. I am perfect design.

"Tonight, I speak to you in the personality of Coatlicue, the Earth Mother of the Aztec. There are many things I want to share with you. Up until now, you were not capable of perceiving my infinite source because of your level of existence. But the time is now right.

"I have been in pain for many years, years of birthing children who turn on me like a pack of wild dogs and devour me. I am the Great Lady Coatlicue, who lives under the earth and makes the plants grow. I am fertility. I am life. But you have abused me, and now my energies must be revived. Now is the time for the healing of the land. We must renew the life force to strengthen my fertility, and I have come to you, you who are woman and the source of all life, to help me accomplish this task.

"To achieve this end, there must be a sacrifice, an offering of life's blood. There is power in the blood of the innocent. The blood cleanses the land, allowing it to open like the petals of a flower so that I might come forth and once again take my place as the source of all life.

"You have been faithful, and I am blessed to call you my children. You have always worshipped me in spirit and in truth. In the coming days, you may be asked to do things that up until now would have seemed violent to you. But there is no escape. I have given you life, and I demand a certain portion of life in return. It is time to release your past beliefs and inhibitions that have kept you bound. It is time to receive the truth and usher in the dawning of a new age. I must have a sacrifice. For this is my chosen path of power."

Before the demon departed, leaving its channeler a limp, rag doll, it gave specific instructions: times, places, and rituals. The women were ecstatic at their excellent fortune. And so began the plan.

CHAPTER
1

The newsroom was organized chaos—phones ringing and keyboards clicking and the editor shouting orders through the thin walls of his paper strewn office. But like all reporters, Christine McKay had the uncanny ability to tune out the noise and focus on the task at hand. As she scanned the daily headlines from around the world on her computer, a seemingly unimportant story from the back pages of the *Los Angeles Times* caught her attention.

In disbelief, she reread the headline: TEENAGER FOUND CRUCIFIED IN ARIZONA DESERT. The image of an upside down cross flashed through her memory, and in self-defense, her mind clamped down. It was gone, but her ulcer burned with the next sip of coffee.

Her intercom buzzed. "Front and center McKay."

"Right boss."

Christine grabbed a notebook and placed her favorite chewed-up pencil hurriedly behind her ear. As an afterthought, she snapped off her terminal before striding confidently through the maze of desks and aisles. Knocking as she entered, she plopped down in the cracked vinyl chair in Jack Garth's office.

"What's up?" She leaned forward and snatched the last bite of chocolate donut out of his hand.

"Hey," he yelled. Christine grinned and popped the whole thing in her mouth, chewing it slowly with a smile. "That was my last one, Chris."

"I'm just paying you back for your french fry escapade at Nick's Pub yesterday," she replied.

"Payback, eh? Then this takes care of the donut," Jack quipped as he handed her a copy of the same story she'd just read in the *Times*.

"Yeah, I read it," she shrugged. "So what?"

"So catch a flight to Phoenix and check it out."

"You can't be serious," she said. "This is probably just some crazy who thinks he's on a mission from God. It'll be buried in the unsolved mysteries file tomorrow."

"I don't think so. Look at this."

Jack handed her a worn manila file, which she slowly opened and leafed through articles from the *London Times*: two more teenagers had been murdered, one in Machu Picchu, Peru, and the other at Stonehenge in England. Both had been crucified— upside down. Her stomach acid continued to gnaw, and she automatically pulled the Tums out of her skirt pocket and popped one into her mouth.

"You're the expert on this stuff, Chris," Jack said. "Does it look like *one* crazy could be responsible for it all? Maybe it's some new kind of devil worship, but on an international scale."

"This is a little too public for ordinary Satanists," she said. "Anyway, they're more interested in the blood of animals—and what's the point of crucifying a cat?" she grinned mischievously.

"Come on, Chris," he admonished. "I'm serious. I want you to see what you can find in Sedona. Call Scotland Yard, then check with the Peruvian Embassy in Washington. There's got to be something tying these murders together."

"Hey, remember the story I covered in Sedona a couple months ago?" she recalled. "That old couple who was buying blood off of high school kids?"

"Yeah, vaguely, why?"

"It turned out they were just dabbling in Satanism, but I made some pretty good contacts with the locals. I've kept in touch with one of the gallery owners. I'll make a few calls and see what I come up with."

"Great," Jack replied. "Give Barry a call downtown too. Maybe he's been alerted by other juvenile departments around the country. Then see if Joanie can get you on the first flight out tomorrow morning."

"Jack!" Christine objected. "What about my vacation? You promised me I could take the next two weeks off. I'm already booked on a flight to Miami Friday night. I need a break."

"Look, I promise I'll give you an extra week off. Just get me this one last story."

"I promise . . ." Christine snorted.

"Really," Jack said. "This could be something big. Just as soon as you're back, I'll put you on a plane to Florida myself. Deal?"

Jack was smooth, but Christine knew him too well. Though it was hard to say no to his little boy smile, she wasn't falling for it this time. She opened her mouth to say no, when Jack clenched the deal. "Of course, I can always turn this over to Candie."

"No way!" Her temper flashed. "That twit couldn't write an original recipe." Christine was hooked, and she knew it. "I guess the story's mine," she sighed resignedly.

"Call me when you get to Sedona," Jack chuckled.

✛✛✛✛✛

In the blackness of the throne room of Hell, Commander Vaizaitha stood trembling before Satan himself. His former air of superiority had vanished. The walls shook as Satan, Prince of Darkness, lambasted his general.

"This girl must be important to the enemy, otherwise, she wouldn't have been sent into our territory. She smells like danger to me, and when I smell danger, the Lord of Hosts is near."

"But, Master, she's so insignificant," Vaizaitha whimpered. "She's practically ours. We've known her since childhood. There is no escape from us now." Vaizaitha smiled, feeling some of his pride returning.

"There is always escape when the Lord of Hosts is involved," Satan pointed a gnarled talon at his general. "She's caused us too much trouble in the past, and I won't have her meddling now. I care not what it costs. Stop her!"

"Your will be done, Master," Vaizaitha declared, bowing low and backing away from the throne.

As he turned to leave, Satan growled, "Commander, do not fail, lest you be cast into the pit—before your time."

Vaizaitha raised one arm in salute as he disappeared through the ceiling of fire.

Scudding black clouds seemed to chase Christine as she turned onto Highway 40 and headed home to pack. The traffic was bumper to bumper through the 270 interchange, but then it thinned out after she crossed the bridge into St. Charles County. Thunder rumbled ominously in the distance as what appeared to be an April storm rolled toward her. After turning off the main highway, lightning continued to flash intermittently across the newly tilled corn fields on Bryan Road. The whipping wind made steering a challenge. Finally, Christine turned onto Great Warrior Drive and parked her VW Rabbit in the garage of the tiny tract home she had bought last year. Entering the house, she immediately switched on the television to catch any weather warnings. There was only a snowy screen where the Channel 5 weatherman should have been. She scanned for any clear signal, but every channel was off the air. Checking the cable connection, Christine confirmed that it was in perfect order.

Maybe lightning struck a transformer, she thought. In disgust, she clicked off the TV and tossed the remote control onto the sofa.

✝✝✝✝✝

Above Christine's house, Tartak, the Hero of Darkness, and his comrades Rosh-Rot, the Chief of Decay, and Shashak reviewed the plan created by their Lord and High Commander, Vaizaitha.

Rosh-Rot spoke first. "At any cost? Any cost to whom? Seems to me we have been sent to kill a cricket and make our Lord Vaizaitha look good in the eyes of the Master."

"Watch your tongue, brother, or you may find it tied to your tail by Satan himself," Tartak warned. "Nothing was said of murder yet, only rendering her useless."

"Is not death the best form of uselessness?" Shashak, the assaulter, smirked. "I say we separate her head from her shoulders and offer it to Vaizaitha as a trophy."

"Who asked you?" Rosh-Rot spat at Shashak, reminding him of his place. "You're here to take orders!"

"Enough! Enough!" Tartak slapped his talons together and grabbed them by the scruff of their scaly necks. "We're here to neutralize the human, not one another."

Shashak bowed humbly to his superior. "Yes, Lord Tartak."

Rosh-Rot turned his seething yellow eyes on his equal. "I take orders from you this day, and this day only, Tartak."

From inside the dark cloud, the shrieks of a hundred demons joined the wailing wind, creating a cacophony of pure evil, thirsting for the taste of blood.

"Assembled hosts, be still!" Tartak roared, raising his massive forearms into the fetid air. Silence rippled slowly through the throng until only the wind was heard. "Tonight, we will crush the enemy's first attempt to thwart our plan. You have been entrusted with a great task, an important victory, but beware. The enemy may attempt to intervene. Be vigilant and watch your backs."

Tartak turned to Rosh-Rot. "Wait for the word to be given before you strike."

Rosh-Rot leered and grinned, the saliva dripping from his sharp yellow fangs. "Yes, Lord Tartak," he mimicked Shashak sarcastically.

✠✠✠✠✠

Christine snapped on the dining room light and paced once more to the sliding glass door. She watched as the approaching storm blotted out the last light of sunset. Mysteriously, the wind had died, and there was a heavy stillness in the air.

Tornado weather, she thought, debating whether to sleep in the basement tonight. Behind her, her guardian angel Miklos, who had been with her since birth, put a steady hand to his sword, casting an uneasy glance at the storm.

This bears the mark of the enemy, he thought. "Basement," he whispered into Christine's ear. "Basement."

Christine responded to what she thought was her own fear of storms and gathered up her blanket and pillows before heading down the stairs into her musty basement. As she made up the old hide-a-bed, the sump pump clicked on and began its incessant sucking noise.

"I hate basements," she groused to her big yellow cat, George, who nearly tripped her as he wound himself around her legs. As she bent to pick him up, the bare ceiling bulb, which was the only illumination, flickered and went out.

"That's just great!" She had forgotten her flashlight, and she wasn't about to start hunting for the fusebox. Her eyes finally adjusted to the darkness, and she was relieved to see that the street light down the block shone through the tiny window above her, giving her just enough light to distinguish the outline of the sofa.

"Guess it's bedtime, George," she said, pulling back the covers and rolling onto the creaky mattress. George jumped up and curled next to her as she heard the rain begin to pelt the basement windows. The air was heavy and sultry, but Christine soon fell into a restless slumber.

Alert, Miklos waited for what he sensed was coming, cloaking himself in the dim light from the window. His head turned, watching every corner of the room. Soon, fiery eyes stared back at him as through the walls, under the door, and through the windows a stench of decay filled the air. The cat sensed the evil presence and hissed. Growling deep in his throat, he stood bolt upright and backed away, tangling himself in Christine's long, dark chestnut hair.

"Lay down, George," Christine mumbled, rolling onto her back and pushing him away. He began to meow. Suddenly, something heavy landed on her chest. She reached up to pet the cat and felt instead the hard, hairy leather wing. Her eyes flew open, and she was face to face with Shashak, the Assaulter. She tried to scream, but his taloned claw gripped around her throat, paralyzing her. Christine thrashed under him, but he only laughed and licked his slavering lips.

"You're mine now!" Shashak chortled. Above her, Christine could hear furniture crashing and glass breaking as the demonic storm ripped through her house.

Without even drawing his sword, Miklos intervened, knocking the demon Shashak aside. The angel covered Christine's body with his own and challenged the demon.

"Not this one, you scaly worm!" Miklos then drew his sword and pointed it at Shashak, but his arm weakened as a voice from the blackness addressed him.

"He's not in your league, Angel," grated the sinister voice of Rosh-Rot. "Remember me?"

A fiery red sword struck a stinging blow to Miklos' left cheek, knocking him off of Christine and leaving her unprotected. Shashak chirped in glee as he leapt on her again and resumed his foul attack, growling and whispering vile things into her ear as he choked the breath from her body.

Outlined in stark blackness against the basement wall, the massive demon Tartak, with bull-like head and bulging fiery yellow eyes, watched gleefully. He was delighted by the destruction of the girl after all. He thrilled as Shashak's claws tightened on her windpipe. Why not just eliminate her completely?

Miklos could feel Christine's terror and her life ebbing away. He bravely fought his old enemy Rosh-Rot, as Tartak stood by watching and laughing. The angel's strength was flagging.

Christine was dying, and she knew it. With the renewed energy of the damned, she bit down on the leathery arm, but the demon only squeezed harder. With her last breath, she squeaked out, "God, help me!"

Her call for help was answered immediately; Miklos pushed his advantage on Rosh-Rot as the joy of the Lord sang through his veins. Suddenly, through the concrete wall above Christine's head, a blinding light flashed, filling the basement with the glory of the Lord as Kerestel, Captain of the Hosts of Heaven, emerged into the room. Kerestel's sword slashed and sliced in a billion streams of white light as he challenged the princes of darkness.

If Kerestel was here, Jesus the Christ was near! In terror, Tartak called, "Retreat! Retreat!"

The darkness fled, and Christine sat bolt upright in bed, gasping. Shaking, she huddled against the back of the musty sofa, but could see no one in the room, neither demon nor angel. The rain had stopped, and the silence was deafening. The light from the window was brighter, as the full moon spotlighted her castaway teddy bear who stared glass-eyed at her from atop a wicker chest.

Meowing, George jumped up on the bed and rubbed himself against her arm. She hugged his velvety body close, but he squirmed away and lay down on the pillow next to her, licking his paw. It was all just a nightmare . . . and yet. . . . She rubbed her throat.

Listening intently to the creaking house, Christine hid under the sheet just like she had when something had frightened her as a little girl. Tomorrow would be soon enough to survey the damage upstairs. It was dawn before she finally drifted back to sleep.

The next morning, Christine ached all over as she stiffly padded across the bare floor to the stairs. *What a night!* With the morning light, her tough exterior was back in place. Sedona would have to wait if her house had been blown away in a tornado.

Slowly, she mounted the stairs and peered into her once beautiful living room. Furniture had been smashed, and the sliding glass door had blown in, leaving slivers strewn across the dining room. She slipped into a pair of running shoes before assessing the rest of the damage. Deep even scratches had destroyed the wallpaper she had searched for so diligently, and her drapes were shredded.

Must have been tree branches, she thought as she gingerly touched her throat again, remembering the taloned demon of her nightmare. The phones were working, so first she called the airline and changed her flight. Then she called the *Sentinel* and left a message for Jack to call her ASAP. Thank God she had insurance.

Finally, the worst of the mess was cleaned up, and Christine turned the hot water on in the shower, then laid out her clothes on the bed. Returning to the bathroom, she stripped off her nightshirt and stepped cautiously under the steaming flow. As the water struck her throat, her skin stung like fire, and she once more reached up to touch the welts.

George, what'd you do to my neck?

Carefully, Christine soaped her weary body and then stood under the pelting spray as it loosened the stiffness from her muscles. *I feel like I fought off Hulk Hogan last night and lost*, she thought as she bent to turn off the water. Stepping from the shower, she grabbed her towel and wearily wiped off the steam from the mirror. She gasped at her reflection. Her throat was covered with ugly purplish bruises, and there were bloody scratch marks, the same kind of even scratches she had seen on her living room walls. Suddenly, her teeth began to chatter and her body to shake. Her knees buckled with the shock. She sank to the toilet lid, wrapping her towel around her body protectively, and began to cry.

What in the name of God is happening to me?

The insistent ringing of the phone finally broke into Christine's consciousness. She dashed to the bedroom and picked up the receiver.

"Hello," she answered, clearing her throat and sniffling.

"Hey, Chris, you should be on a plane by now. What gives?" It was Jack.

"You should see what the tornado did to my house last night," she exclaimed. "It imploded my sliding glass door, rearranged my furniture and tore my wallpaper and drapes all to heck."

"What tornado?" Jack said slowly.

"What *tornado?* Criminy, Jack, you should see this place. It's a disaster!"

"Honest, Chris, there've been no tornadoes reported that I know of." He sounded genuinely puzzled.

"Jack, I'm telling you, something tore up my house, and it wasn't my cat. It had to be a tornado. What else could implode a sliding glass door?"

"Chris, it didn't even rain last night," he countered.

"Then what was hitting my basement windows last night!" she cried. "I spent the whole night in the basement . . . there were storm clouds . . . thunder . . . lightning . . . and something tried to kill me!" She was now weeping hysterically.

"Kill you! Chris . . . Chris," Jack yelled. "Hey, calm down. I believe you already. Something obviously happened, but honest hon, there was no storm, at least not downtown."

Christine wiped her eyes with the back of her hand and sat down on the bed. "There's got to be some explanation for this! My neck looks like somebody used me for a scratching post. It's bruised and shredded and I hurt all over."

"I'm coming over," Jack said. "You need me."

"Wait," Christine moaned. "I can't stay here any longer. Can we meet at Nick's in about an hour?"

"You're sure you're alright to drive?" Jack asked.

"Yeah, I'll be alright as soon as I get out of here."

"If you're not there by noon, I'll come looking for you."

"Thanks, boss," she said gratefully.

Christine threw on her favorite jeans and a pink sweatshirt and hurriedly packed a suitcase. Then she grabbed up George and put him in his kitty taxi for the ride to the kennel. As she took out her keys to lock the door, she chuckled.

What's the use? Might as well leave the front door open, too, she thought, shaking her head. She picked up her cat and the suitcase and loaded them in the backseat of her VW and backed out of the driveway.

✠✠✠✠✠

A tired Miklos rode on the roof of Christine's car as she dropped off George, then sped down Highway 70 to Nick's in downtown St. Louis. Soon, he was joined by Pesach, the angel of the Passover, and Wardar, the Protector of the Soul.

"How goes the battle, brother?" Wardar laid a comrade's hand on Miklos' drooping shoulder.

"I've never fought so hard without the coverage of prayer, and I didn't even see it coming," Miklos puzzled. "What was the sense of it all? What do they want with her?"

"The Lord High God has put His hand over her," Pesach answered. "She will be instrumental in exposing the deeds of the enemy in future days."

"Why didn't anyone warn me?" Miklos asked.

Kerestel's brilliantly lit form appeared next to Miklos.

"No one should have to warn a guardian, Miklos," Kerestel reminded him gently. "I am here to tell you that your work will be increasingly difficult in the near future. Your charge is embroiled in a holy battle that will not only include her soul, but the souls of *many*. I have assigned Pesach and Wardar to accompany you until such time as the human Christine becomes a believer: Pesach, so that death will continue to pass over her, and Wardar, to guard her soul. You, Miklos, shield her spirit." With that, Kerestel vanished.

Miklos' strength was renewed as Pesach and Wardar began to sing praises to God! Slowly, he joined them, raising anthems of worship to the Most High. The entire atmosphere, both inside and outside the car, radiated well-being.

✛✛✛✛✛

Christine felt her spirits rise the closer she got to Nick's. Her panic had lifted. Everything seemed like just a bad dream after all. By the time she met Jack, she was calm. Her boss told her not to worry about the repairs on her house. He'd have it taken care of while she was gone.

As they discussed Christine's experience, they agreed it must have been a freak atmospheric disturbance, like those mysterious circles in a wheat field. And the scratches on her neck, well, they must have been caused by George when he panicked at the sound of the implosion of her door. It all seemed perfectly logical . . . now.

The early morning light filtered through the bougainvillea as Star White sat staring blankly across the stone-paved patio. Huddled miserably in the corner of the sofa, she pulled her bare feet up underneath her thick pink robe. A half-empty glass of carrot juice dangled from her right hand as she absently raised her left hand and ran her fingers through her sleep-tangled blonde hair. At the sound of footsteps on the stairs, Star turned as Libby Brinkman entered the room.

"I suppose *you* slept well," Star snapped, slamming her glass down on the table.

"Why don't you go ahead and break something," Libby said calmly through clenched teeth. "You're being such a child about all this."

"You are so cold," Star gasped. "How can you live with yourself?"

"Easily," she replied flippantly, "and you never had any problem with what we're doing before last night." Libby changed to a more conciliatory tone, hoping to sidetrack her sensitive roommate's accusations. "Can't you see how important you are to our cause? You're the special channel for our Earth Mother. You're the one she's chosen for a higher purpose."

Star shuddered and pulled the robe more tightly around her neck. "I'm not so sure it's a higher purpose anymore."

"How can you say that?" Libby said astounded.

Star White began to cry again. "Libby, it was murder!"

"Shut up! Do you want Heather to hear you?"

Remembering her daughter sleeping upstairs, Star lowered her voice, "I didn't like Gary Knox. I didn't like anything he stood for. I certainly didn't want him involved with my daughter, but nobody deserves to die like that!"

"According to the Earth Mother, *who spoke through your mouth*, it was an honor to die like that." Libby's face radiated with awe. "To be instrumental in the dawning of a New World, that's how I would choose to die."

"I don't care why we did it!" Star exclaimed. "We're both guilty of murdering Gary Knox."

Slowly, Libby's face took on a hardness of scorn, and its master Tilon rose up in her. The demon spurred her on to anger. "Strike out," he whispered. "Keep her in line. Who does she think she is, calling you a *murderer?*"

But the word struck a chord in Libby's soul. She crossed to the curved bar and drew her brush from the expensive leather bag sitting there. Staring at her reflection in the mirror, her voice was cool and even: "What do you think I do for a living? I'm an abortionist. I 'murder babies.' " Irritated, she briskly brushed her short auburn hair.

"It's not the same thing," Star whispered hysterically. "Abortion is legal. Murder isn't!"

"Not murder . . . sacrifice," Libby corrected.

"No, *murder*," Star got up off the couch and faced Libby's reflection. "Gary didn't sacrifice his life, *you* took it!"

Libby whirled. "I *took* it and *gave* it to your goddess! Unfortunately, she wasn't satisfied with the sacrifices from my clinic any longer."

"I don't want to do this any more!" Star buried her face in her hands, sobbing.

Tilon coiled tightly around Libby's heart and whispered again, "How dare she question your authority! What a feeble vessel our goddess has chosen."

"Grow up!" Libby was disgusted with Star's predictable display of emotion. "You're perfectly satisfied with the power of the sacrifice, but you don't want to do what's required to receive it. You're just like all the rest . . . weak, whiny, and useless."

Stunned, Star raised angry, snapping eyes to meet Libby's cold flint stare. "And you're nothing but a cold, calculating, murderess witch."

Like the deadly strike of the rattlesnake, Libby's hand found its mark on Star's left cheek, knocking her back. As if nothing had just happened, Libby slipped her brush back into her purse and strode to the door, ignoring the shocked and weeping Star. She stopped and turned with steely calmness.

"Get hold of yourself before your daughter hears you," Libby directed, "and don't do anything stupid."

Tearfully, Star rose as the door closed and slowly paced to the cathedral window. Dropping her robe to the floor, she sank down and assumed the full lotus position for her morning meditation. An unnatural peace settled over her as she was surrounded by Satan's angels, softly stroking her body. Finally, the soothing harmony of her mantra filled her being as she escaped earth's bonds and floated toward the light.

CHAPTER
2

Once on the plane, Christine managed to avoid conversation with the obnoxious sales rep sitting next to her by pretending to sleep. But for some reason, the closer she got to Sedona, the more anxiety gnawed at her stomach.

It was always the same. She hated these stories, but she was compelled to investigate them. During the short commuter hop from Phoenix to Sedona, she went over her game plan again. First, she'd talk to the sheriff, of course, and the attending physician, family, friends. She wanted to know everything about Gary Knox, even down to the kind of cereal he ate for breakfast.

Who would want to murder an 18-year-old kid, especially like that? She unconsciously stroked her throat.

Deep in thought, she was unaware of the passage of time until the small plane began its banking maneuver over the Sedona airport. Red rocks rose like sentinels out of the high desert floor, their color changing moment to moment with the shifting of light and clouds.

What a great place for a vacation, and here I am chasing the boogie man again. Curse Jack anyway! I should be sipping margaritas in the Florida Keys right now. Oh, well, maybe I can wrap this up early and hang around here for a few days, play some tennis and soak up the desert sun.

As they were landing, Christine spotted a church that seemed to rise out of the red rock itself. Once on the ground and in her rental car, she checked her watch and decided she had enough time to explore it. She found the Chapel of the Holy Cross, one of Sedona's most famous landmarks, on the tourist map and headed south. She'd drop by Pat Fisher's gallery later and save the sheriff for tomorrow. In truth, she was just plain tired. She hadn't had a vacation in two years. And her sleep hadn't been exactly restful lately.

Christine turned the white Taurus left at the road which led up toward the church. Cars lined the driveway, so she parked on the road below and walked up the steep drive to the chapel.

The sign on the outside said that it had been designed by sculptor Marguerite Brunswig Staude, who worked with Frank Lloyd Wright on her idea for a cruciform church. Inside, the simple benches in the small restful sanctuary invited Christine to sit down a moment and gaze out the enormous windows surrounding the cross. All you could see for miles were brick-red buttes and an endless intense blue sky. A young Indian woman lit a candle and sat down to pray. How peaceful it was to just let her mind drift, listening to the recording of a Gregorian chant.

The two impish demons, Koz and Nod, had crept into the sanctuary with Christine, hiding in her shadow. Koz, the smallest of the two, attached himself around her shoulders, whispering his litany of destruction.

"You don't belong here, Christine. What are you doing in a church? God turned His back on you a long time ago. Where was He when your parents were divorced? Where was He when Laura was raped and murdered?"

Christine shook her head as she tried to ignore the voice, but it kept on. "There's no God, and even if there were, He hates you for all you've done. You don't belong here. Get out!"

The demons cackled as Christine nearly leapt to her feet and turned her back on the light streaming through the window, but they quickly screeched in terror as Wardar, the tall golden-haired protector of her soul, grabbed them by the scruff of the neck and tossed them aside. They spun into the air, blowing sulphurous smoke, and took off for safer territory. They were no match for an angel like that!

Miklos followed Christine to her car, his wings protectively shielding her.

"Christine, God loves you!" he said, but she could not hear. The demons had stopped her ears with their blackness, and although they were no longer present, the tape of their lies played endlessly in her mind.

Tiredly, Christine pulled into a parking stall at Tlaquepaque, an authentic recreation of the little Mexican town on the outskirts of Guadalajara. Before renting a motel room, she was anxious to talk with Pat Fisher. Pat had been invaluable in pointing her to the right sources last time. She ought to drop in on Sheriff Anderson, but she'd fence with him tomorrow morning. He hated reporters.

Christine walked leisurely past the shop windows filled with fine pottery, Indian jewelry, and Southwestern art, all for the more discerning buyer. Some of the paintings in Pat's gallery sold for as much as $20,000, way out of her league, but it was fun to window shop.

The sound of splashing water greeted her as she pulled open the heavy redwood door of Pat's art gallery, The Phoenix. A tiny fountain created a soothing backdrop for the red rock scenes depicted in the paintings of one of Sedona's most famous artists,

John Delarosa. Pat was busy with a customer, so Christine browsed through the gallery, running her hand over the bronze figure of a Remington, admiring its detail. The famous landmarks of Sedona, especially Cathedral Rock, had been painted in all their moods of light. The artist obviously spent much of his time outdoors in all kinds of weather. There were snow scenes, spring scenes and stormy scenes, all evoking the grandeur that was Arizona.

"So you made it!" Pat's voice startled her. "How was your flight?"

"The food was terrible as usual, but we didn't crash," Christine quipped.

"I told Mom before you called that you'd be back after what happened," Pat said as she warmly embraced an uncomfortable Christine.

"I was hoping we could have dinner and you could fill me in on what you know about Gary's murder," Christine smiled, somewhat embarrassed by Pat's open display of affection, but strangely drawn to her.

"Everyone has their suspicions, but we're all in shock I think," Pat offered. "Gary was such a great kid—straight A student, active in church. He had a scholarship to MIT next fall."

"Had he been dabbling in the occult?" asked Christine.

"Gary? No way!" Pat seemed shocked.

"It's happened to other bright kids," Christine explained.

"Not this one," Pat assured her.

The front door opened, and a group of tourists oohed and aahed their way in.

"Listen, Christine, why don't you meet me here at six, and we'll give you a home-cooked meal at Mom's house." Pat raised her hand to let her customers know she'd be right with them.

"It's a deal," Christine accepted. "That'll give me time to check into a motel."

"Mom really wants to meet you, plus my brother John is coming home tonight. We'll make a party of it."

"I didn't know you had a brother," said Christine.

Pat proudly waved her hands at the paintings around her.

"John Delarosa is your brother?" Christine exclaimed. "I'm impressed."

"Yeah, he got all the talent in the family," Pat laughed.

One of the tourists was attempting to pick up a bronze statue of two stallions in battle.

"I'd better go," Pat motioned with her head toward her customers. "I'll see you later."

After checking into a room at the Welcome Inn, Christine spent the rest of the afternoon wandering through the quaint courtyards of Tlaquepaque, with their splashing fountains and galleries. At 5:30, she was at loose ends and walked back to The Phoenix, where Pat was ready to depart early.

During the drive out to Mrs. Delarosa's home, the two women renewed their acquaintance. Christine had immediately liked this tall, athletic blonde the first time they met. She had expected Pat to be a snob; she was wrong. Pat was one of the warmest, funniest women she'd ever known. Their friendship picked up right where they left off. Christine was soon laughing as Pat regaled her with stories of the "winkies" of Sedona.

"Winkies?" Christine giggled, stopping at a red light. "What's a winkie?"

"That's what we locals call crystal gazers," Pat explained. "You know, New Agers. Well, anyway, there's this one guru with a shaved head who lives out in the country somewhere with about ten of his followers. One day, they come into town in this broken down old school bus, all of them dressed in robes like Hare Krishnas. Then the guru steps out into the middle of the street and starts walking down the center line. All these nuts fall in behind him in a 'V' formation like he's the head goose or something and start making all these scooping motions with their hands. Traffic is at a dead standstill."

"You're making this up," Christine said.

"No, really," Pat continued. "Sheriff Anderson goes up to this guy and yells, 'What do you think you're doing?' You remember how the red creeps up his neck when he's mad.

"Well, this guru says, 'I am blazing an energy path, so my chelas can bathe in my power.'"

"What a weirdo!" Christine was amazed.

"Keep your eyes on the road!" Pat went on. "Oh, *he's* nothing. I'd rather know what they're doing out in public than wonder what they're doing in some of these canyons."

At the mention of the canyons, they both thought of why Christine had come to Sedona.

Clearing her throat, Christine asked, "Did you know Gary Knox personally?"

"Sure," Pat answered solemnly, staring out her window at the setting sun. "He was in my Sunday school class when he was a freshman. He had a zeal, you know? He knew exactly where he was going. He was so gifted." She paused. "Turn right at the next corner."

Pat directed Christine up a long, curving driveway to a rambling Spanish adobe. The front door was thrown open by a smiling plump matron, and Christine immediately knew she was welcome.

Molly Delarosa, her short blonde hair swept back from bright blue eyes, held out her arms and unexpectedly hugged Christine, who automatically stiffened at the familiarity. Molly was sensitive enough to notice and gracious enough to hide it.

"Welcome, Christine. Pat's told me so much about you."

"You have a lovely home," Christine said politely.

"Thank you. Would you like something cold to drink?" asked Molly as she led them into the house. "Iced tea? Soda?"

"Iced tea would be great," Christine said, sad that she had not been able to receive the abundant affection of this woman. It was difficult for her to trust others immediately, a hazard of her profession.

Pat's heels clicked on the tile floors as she followed her mother into a comfortable family room, its walls decorated with John's paintings. The Southwestern decor, with its muted sand colors and turquoise, was both clean and soothing. Pat kicked off her shoes and curled up on one of the curved sofas as her mother handed her an icy glass of tea.

"Thanks, Mama," Pat said, as she took a sip.

Christine liked the informality of this obviously wealthy family. Others may have been pretentious, but not the Delarosas. They were real and honest people—the "salt of the earth" as her grandfather would have said. Despite the comfort of their home, Christine was beginning to sense some of the loss they felt from Gary's death.

Funny, she hadn't thought about Gramps in a long time.

"Pat, there's something I've wondered ever since we met," Christine began. "Why on earth did you open your home to a reporter? Most people would resent the intrusion."

Pat threw back her head and laughed. "That's a reporter for you—always looking for a story behind everything."

"I suppose so," Christine smiled and took the offered glass of tea from Molly.

Molly smiled and patted Christine's shoulder. "Because you're not like most reporters, Christine. Don't you know that?"

"What do you mean?"

"Pat told me that when you came to Sedona the last time, you didn't sensationalize or trivialize," Molly answered. "You were polite, you didn't intrude, you didn't push. You asked thoughtful questions, you verified your facts, and you took the matter seriously. Simply put, you told the truth. That's rare these days."

Molly's comments were sincere, and Christine found herself warming up to this lady. This was one sharp cookie.

"I'll take that as a compliment to my first boss," Christine explained. "He must have been seventy-five at least. His family owned a little newspaper in this backwater town along the Mississippi. He said everybody already knew everybody else's business, so if you were going to report it, you better get your facts straight. He was a stickler for the truth. Sometimes, he'd make me check my sources four and five times until he was satisfied I'd gotten it right."

"When you were here last time, I got the impression that you knew more about the occult than most garden variety reporters," Molly said. "I've read several of your magazine articles since then. All of them had occult themes. What's your interest?"

Christine felt the tiny knot of anger that never left her.

"It's personal," she said, swirling the ice in her glass. In the uncomfortable silence, she decided to tell the truth. "When my little sister Laura was just fourteen, she was raped and murdered by a boy who claimed 'the devil made him do it.' They'd gone to school together since kindergarten." Her clipped tone revealed her bitterness.

"How horrible!" Molly exclaimed, placing her hand on Christine's arm. Christine withdrew.

"It was a long time ago," she continued, shrugging her shoulders. "Maybe one of these days I'll be able to write a book about it."

"It's a shame, but even in the church most people don't perceive Satanism as real," Pat commented. "Maybe a book like that might open some eyes to the danger facing young people. At least I believe it would."

"You're a definite minority," Christine said.

"Christians always have been," Molly smiled.

Christine was uncomfortable with the direction the conversation was taking. She didn't want to get into some big religious confrontation. Her agnosticism brought out the Bible thumpers in droves. Their next question would be, "Do you know Jesus?" So she changed subjects.

"Pat tells me you are a friend of Gary's mother, Molly."

"That's right," Molly answered. "I've known Elaine since our days at Arizona State. We were roommates. In fact, I dated her husband before she did."

"Then you probably knew Gary as well."

"I practically raised him," Molly remembered. "He was her youngest and my godson. Oh, how I miss him! This was his second home. He loved my cinnamon rolls." Molly paused, and her eyes glistened. "He was so very bright, a real genius when it came to computers. His room was wall-to-wall equipment."

"Had his behavior changed at all in the months before his death?" Christine asked. "Did he seem worried about anything?"

"He did seem a little anxious about something, but he wouldn't say what," Molly recalled. "We all assumed he had the usual pre-college jitters and was apprehensive about leaving."

"Do you have any theories about who killed him?" Christine turned to Pat.

"There are plenty of theories," Pat offered, "but nothing you could prove. We do know that Gary and his Christian friends were being harassed at school."

"By whom?" Christine moved to the edge of her seat.

"Elaine said Gary was invited to a party for the senior class last Halloween," Pat continued. "When he got there, they were playing with a Ouija board and setting up for a seance, so he told them they were playing with demons and left. That's when the trouble started at school. He got a few crank calls in the middle of the night, then it stopped. Elaine thought it was all over. I don't think she could have even conceived of an evil that could do this to her son."

"Do you think one of those kids could be capable of murder?" Christine wished she was taking notes.

Their conversation was interrupted when the front door opened.

"Mom?"

"We're in here, John," Molly called out.

John, in blue jeans and a striped shirt with rolled-up sleeves, seemed to fill the air with his exuberance as he strode into the family room.

"Hi, squirt," he said, rumpling Pat's hair, who in turn glared up at him. It was obvious this was a family who loved each other and was used to good-natured kidding.

"John, this is Pat's friend, Christine McKay, from St. Louis," Molly introduced them.

John Delarosa extended his hand, "Hi, Christine."

"Hello," Christine replied, as his hand engulfed hers.

Always the writer, she searched mentally for the perfect one-word description of him. Charisma. Definitely, it was charisma. Tall, at least 6'2", with deep blue eyes, shining black hair, and a dark olive complexion, John Delarosa would stand out in any crowd. A simple gold and turquoise cross hung around his neck.

"I've admired your work for a long time," Christine said. "I had no idea you were Pat's brother."

"Fisher is my married name," Pat injected. "Robert died two years ago."

"I'm sorry. I didn't know," Christine's cheeks colored bright pink.

"Don't feel embarrassed," Pat smiled. "Robert's with the Lord Jesus."

Sensing Christine's discomfort, John quickly changed the subject. "What's for dinner, Mom?"

"Chicken fajitas," Molly replied proudly.

"Ah, the specialty of the house," John exclaimed. "I'm starving. When do we eat?"

Dinner was filled with good-natured teasing between Pat and John and lots of laughter. Christine was reluctant to bring up Gary's murder again. Just for this one night, she wanted to be part of a family like this—a family that had no dark secrets to hide—a family that was whole and loving.

Too soon, it was over, and Christine drove through the Arizona night to her motel. It was after eleven when she emerged from her car in the parking stall in front of her room. Automatically, she checked the shadows for movement before she unlocked her door and made a dash for the room, quickly inserting the key in the lock. *It pays to be cautious when you're a woman travelling alone,* Christine told herself. She could not see the three massive angels, who surrounded her watchfully, swords drawn.

After a quick shower, she settled into bed, and quickly fell asleep. The angels took up their posts as her breathing slowed to an even pace and she entered the dream world.

She was walking through a dark forest. The creaking redwood trees towered over her, blocking the sun. A sense of dread filled her being, but she felt compelled to continue down the rock strewn path. She tripped and skinned her hands, and blood began to stream from holes in the center of her palms. Directly in front of her was a cave, and a voice inside beckoned, "Christine. Christine."

Inside, she walked slowly toward a stone altar, behind which was hung an upside down cross. She watched as a black hooded figure poured a silver chalice of blood over a little girl's body. It was Christine's blood, the blood that had come from her own hands. She screamed, and it echoed over and over and over again.

Christine awoke abruptly to the pounding on her door. "Are you alright in there? What's going on in there?" Pound, pound, pound.

Still shivering, she stumbled to the door and peered through the peephole. It was the potbellied night clerk. Leaving the chain on the door, she cracked it just a fraction.

"I'm alright," she assured him. "It was just a nightmare." Miklos moved unseen behind her, the point of his sword just under the clerk's nose.

"Well, you woke up half the guests. Are you sure you're okay?" he said suspiciously, trying to peer around the door. The demon of lust inside him leered and licked its lips.

"I'm fine, really," she said, beginning to close the door.

"You want some company?" he asked, eagerly. Just then Miklos pushed his sword through the man's head, dispensing with the lustful demon who disappeared with a screech.

"No, thanks," Christine answered sharply, and slammed the door shut. Miklos smiled at his companions and returned to his post.

Leaving the light on, Christine lay back down and pulled the covers up to her chin, staring wide-eyed at the ceiling. The dream was so real . . . so very real.

Wardar placed a protective hand on Christine's forehead. Turning to his companions, he shook his head. "This one's memories are more like nightmares from hell."

"As she is able, the Lord will cleanse her," Miklos smiled down at the now peacefully sleeping Christine. "But for now, her memories will have to remain as dreams. She is not strong enough to remember and stay safe."

Pesach nodded in agreement. "Death has passed over her many, many times because of her grandfather's intercession on her behalf."

"And has she been dedicated?" Wardar asked.

"As a child," Miklos answered. "But not yet baptized with water or with fire . . . not yet."

"As long as she's been dedicated, there's always hope," Wardar declared, raising his sword. "His mercy is everlasting!"

CHAPTER
3

After black coffee and a blueberry muffin at the Roadrunner Cafe downtown, Christine headed for the Yavapai County Sheriff's Department where she was admitted to Sheriff Anderson's office.

"It's nice to see you again, Sheriff."

"Miss McKay," he drawled, waving his hand at a chair for her to sit. "Why is it that I am not surprised?"

Apparently the battle lines are already drawn, Christine chuckled inwardly as she sat down in his sparse office. She pulled out her notepad and composed herself. "I'd like to ask you some questions about the Gary Knox murder, Sheriff. What can you tell me about the case?"

"You must have read the paper by now," he said sarcastically. "Why else would you be here."

"All I read in the paper could be put down to speculation and hearsay," she answered sharply. "I want facts."

"Exactly," the Sheriff snorted.

"There's always another story," Christine probed. "What did the media leave out?"

"Most of the truth, to start with," he responded.

"Like what?"

"Such as the location. He wasn't found on some ancient Indian burial ground. That was a lot of mumbo jumbo. He was found hangin' upside down on a crude cross on Cathedral Rock."

"He was actually nailed to a cross?" she verified.

"Yep," Sheriff Anderson rose to look out the window. "I've seen a lot of things in my time, but I've never seen anything like what that kid suffered. It made me sick all the things they did to him."

Christine steeled herself against the image. The overweight Sheriff turned and leaned forward, taking the lid off a glass jar of red licorice.

"Want one?" he offered.

"No, thanks."

Fishing out a handful, he sat down and began chewing on one long red whip, rocking back in the squeaky chair which threatened to topple at any instant. Christine glanced at her notes.

"Could he have been killed elsewhere," she continued, "then nailed on the cross for effect?"

"No, ma'am, he died on that cross, just like St. Peter."

"St. Peter? You mean Jesus, don't you?"

"Didn't you ever go to Sunday school?" he asked. "I mean St. Peter. That's how he died. They crucified him upside down."

"Who do you think did this, Sheriff?"

"I couldn't say," he dodged. "We're still investigating."

"But, you've got a gut feeling about it," she pushed. "I can tell."

"Now, Miss McKay, I thought you'd gotten all the speculation and hearsay you wanted," he quipped. "We just don't have enough evidence to make a concrete call on this one."

Christine continued to push. "You said *they* crucified him. Then you don't think it was someone acting alone?"

"That cross weighed a ton," he declared. "There had to be more than one person involved."

"Any idea what the motive was?"

"Beat's me," he shrugged. "I can't think of any reason for killin' somebody that way."

"Do you believe Satanism or some occult group is involved?" Christine was tiring of his evasive answers.

"I couldn't say. . . ."

"I know," Christine muttered. "Not enough evidence."

"Now you got it, Miss McKay," the Sheriff smiled with a patronizing grin.

"How long had he been dead before he was discovered?" she tried a new angle.

"At least a day." The Sheriff, tired of the game, stood and paced to the door, opening it for Christine to leave. "Look, it's all in our report, which I'm sure you've read."

"I just like to verify the facts," she said, closing her notepad.

"Our investigation is ongoing," he sighed, "and when we have anything else to report, I'll let you know."

Christine could tell she wasn't going to get anything more from him. She stood up and extended her hand.

"Thanks, Sheriff. As usual, you've been very helpful."

"It's my pleasure, Miss McKay," he drawled. "We don't get too many big city reporters up this way. And not near enough pretty women."

Holding her tongue, Christine left his office without a backward glance. Sheriff Anderson knew more than he was telling, but he wasn't about to let her in on it. There had to be another source. Christine asked the on-duty officer to see the official report again, which she scanned quickly, going over the same details Anderson had just given her. There were no discrepancies. The man followed the book.

Two hikers had discovered the body, a vacationing couple by the name of Jerry and Lisa Vance, who returned home to San Diego the next day, leaving their forwarding address. She'd already jotted down the information and planned a phone call later in the day. Almost unconsciously, she pulled a Tums from her pocket and popped it in her mouth.

Pushing through the front door of the station, Christine glanced at her watch. It was half past nine, still a little early to call San Diego, so the attending physician was her next stop. He was more cooperative, but she found out little more from him than she had the Sheriff. Gary Knox had died at or near midnight on Good Friday, April 17, and his body was discovered on Easter Sunday.

The symbolism here is a little too deliberate, Christine thought, absently touching her throat.

Christine had no idea she was driving a fully loaded car back to her motel. Miklos rode up front next to her, and Pesach and Wardar sat in the back. When they drove into the parking lot, Pesach noticed a familiar glimmer in front of Christine's motel door. "Look, brothers," he cried, "our numbers have increased." Goyo, the Watchful, and Sandor, Defender of Men, emerged from their cover of glimmering light. Pesach zoomed through the roof of the car and joyfully enfolded his brother angels who stood waiting for their return.

"Greetings from the Lord Most High," Goyo raised his hand in salute to the angels guarding Christine. "We have been sent to strengthen the forces here in Humtah's territory."

"Thanks be to God!" Miklos praised.

The warriors stood aside as Christine entered her motel room. She pulled open the drapes and turned on the air conditioner before sitting down on the bed and opening her notepad.

"Kerestel has called an encampment for tonight," Goyo turned to Wardar. "There is much you do not know yet."

"We've been scouting in the desert, shielded of course," Sandor related, "and we have observed the assemblage of Hell's Legion of Commanders headed by Vaizaitha, Son of the Atmosphere."

"Once again, the forces of Hell have laid a plan to bring about the close of the age," Goyo continued. "This time, there is no Hitler, no Grand Inquisitor, no human at which to point the finger. They have so intertwined their plan with local false religions that they are almost invisible. They have cloaked themselves in social services, local culture and the political arena so well that even the most diabolical demons have hands with which to work."

"Christine is here to expose this?" Miklos enquired.

"Not only expose, but to destroy the enemy, Miklos," Sandor said, placing a comforting hand on his comrade's shoulder.

"My Christine?" Miklos was somber.

"No," answered Goyo, "the Lord's Christine."

"What was this you said about an encampment?" Wardar queried.

"Yes, when do the others arrive?" Miklos asked Goyo.

"By this afternoon, they'll gather at Immanuel Faith Chapel," Goyo answered. "Molly and her intercessors have called for a prayer vigil tonight. They are mighty prayer warriors."

"Indeed, it is because of them that we have been sent," Sandor smiled. "We have waited a long time to reclaim Sedona from the New Age demons. With the help of these people through the power of the Holy Spirit, we will!"

"Praise to the Lord Most High," they all shouted in unison, their hands lifted toward heaven.

Dialing the Vances' phone number in San Diego, Christine could barely hear the recorded message because of the interfering static on the line.

"I'm sorry," the recording crackled, "the number you have reached is no longer in service. Please check your number and dial again or call an operator for assistance. Thank you."

Why wasn't she surprised? Christine called information, but there was no new listing for a Jerry and Lisa Vance anywhere in San Diego or Orange Counties. Next she tried the area codes in L.A. and San Francisco. The Sheriff's material witnesses had vanished without a trace.

As much as she hated to bother Elaine Knox, she was Christine's next logical interview. A quick phone call confirmed that Mrs. Knox was at home and had been forewarned by Molly Delarosa that Christine might call. Christine checked the batteries in her tape recorder and opened the door to leave when the phone rang.

"Hello?"

"Christine?"

"Yes."

"This is John Delarosa."

Christine felt an unexpected warmth at the sound of his voice.

"Hi, John. What can I do for you?"

"I thought I might persuade you to go exploring with me this morning."

"Exploring?" Christine's interest was piqued.

"Mom thought you'd probably try to find the place where Gary Knox was murdered on your own," John explained, "so she asked me to take you out there myself."

"Great!" Christine exclaimed. "But first, I have an appointment to meet with Elaine Knox."

"You mind if I tag along?" John asked. "She might be a little more at ease with a family friend around."

"I know the media has a reputation for being bloodsuckers when it comes to interviewing families of the victim, John, but I'm not like that," Christine assured him.

"I believe you."

"Thank you," Christine answered with relief.

"How about I pick you up in my Jeep in about half an hour, then after seeing Elaine, we can drive out to Red Rock

Crossing," John asked. "We'll have to hike to Cathedral Rock, so wear your boots."

"Will tennis shoes do?"

"Not quite," he laughed. "What size do you wear? I'll see if I can borrow a pair. We're going into some pretty rough country."

"Size eight," Christine relayed, trying to hide the smile in her voice.

"I'll see you soon, Chris," John said as he hung up the phone.

Christine started at the familiarity of the nickname and decided she liked it.

For an artist, John was prompt and well organized. Not only had he found a pair of boots, but he brought along a picnic lunch for later.

Accompanying John was his guardian angel, Aaro, the Enlightened. Miklos extended a welcoming hand.

"Nice to see you again, brother," Miklos greeted. "We could use your good company."

"Your words are truer than you know," Aaro replied. "If they are venturing into the enemy's territory as John has indicated, then you indeed can use my 'good company.'"

"Onward then!" Wardar and Pesach raised their swords.

The Knoxes lived in the same upper-class neighborhood as the Delarosas. John pulled the jeep up the long circular drive and parked in front of the Spanish-style house, a riot of red bougainvillea almost covering the white stucco walls. Before John could come around and open her door, Christine had already jumped to the ground and was striding toward the front door. He quickly closed the distance between them and rang the bell.

A tired-looking, but still beautiful woman opened the door, welcoming them with her gracious smile. She hugged John and then turned to Christine. "John, who's your lovely friend?"

"Hello, Mrs. Knox, I'm Christine McKay."

"I've been expecting you," she said with a faint Southern accent. "Please come in." Elaine Knox had been raised in Atlanta and came to Phoenix twenty-five years ago to attend Arizona State. She had met her husband, Gerald, there and had never gone home. "I'm afraid the house is still in a bit of turmoil. I've been sorting through Gary's things, deciding what to keep and what to donate to the church thrift shop."

She led them into the formal living room.

"I apologize for putting you through an interview," Christine offered, "but I was hoping you might shed some light on the mystery surrounding Gary's death."

Although her face was still pinched with pain at the loss of her son, still there was a peace about Elaine Knox.

"You don't have to do this, Elaine, if you don't want to," John interjected.

"I know, but if it will prevent this happening to someone else's child, I'm glad to help."

"Do you mind if I record our conversation?" Christine asked, as she laid her tape recorder on the white brocade sofa and pushed the record button.

"No, not at all," Elaine said graciously.

"Perhaps you can just tell me about those days leading up to Gary's murder," Christine began. "Was there anything unusual about his behavior?"

"Not really. Oh, he was a little nervous about finals coming up and going away to college, but nothing out of the ordinary."

"Pat Fisher said that there was some trouble at school last Halloween and that you'd gotten some crank calls," Christine continued.

"That's right," remembered Elaine. "But there hadn't been any problem since then. The calls had stopped."

"Was he still being harassed at school?"

"He never talked about it if he was," Elaine answered.

"Would he normally have told you about something like that?"

"I would hope so," Elaine replied. "We had a very trusting relationship. I suppose if he thought it wasn't important, he wouldn't have said anything."

Christine thought about her own sister's involvement in the occult. None of them suspected until it was too late.

"Did Gary keep a diary or a journal of some kind?" Christine queried.

"Why yes, he did," Elaine offered.

"Would you mind if I read through it?"

"Sheriff Anderson has it now," Elaine replied. "But I don't think it'll be of much help. Several pages were missing."

"Do you think Gary tore them out?"

"I don't know," Elaine mused. "I can't imagine why he would do such a thing."

"What did Gary do in his spare time, Mrs. Knox?" Christine changed the tone of her questions.

"Well, he spent most of his time doing homework, but he was very active in the senior high group from church. He was president this year," Elaine said proudly. "They meet every Wednesday night, and on most weekends, they plan some activity together. They're all close friends."

"Did you notice any deviation from his normal routine that week?" Christine probed. "Did he bring home any new friends, or stay out late at night?"

"No, nothing like that," Elaine said.

"Mrs. Knox, this is a hard question to ask," Christine began. "It's hard on kids to be outsiders. After the incident last fall, could Gary have gotten mixed up with kids who were dabbling in the occult or in Satanism?" Elaine looked shocked at the suggestion, and Christine hurriedly added, "Maybe even for the altruistic purpose of trying to help them."

"Of course not!" Elaine exclaimed. "He loved the Lord, and he knew he couldn't help someone by compromising with the devil."

John frowned and shook his head at Christine. He was right. She wouldn't learn anything if she antagonized Elaine Knox.

"I'm sorry, Mrs. Knox, I didn't mean to imply that Gary would actually practice any of these things."

Elaine nodded, accepting the apology. "You'd just have to know Gary to understand how ludicrous that sounds."

"Tell me about the last time you saw Gary alive," Christine went on.

The question brought quick tears of remembrance to Elaine's eyes. "He was really excited. He was going to meet Cory Jensen and some friends who were driving to a Steven Curtis Chapman concert in Phoenix on Thursday night. My husband and I had Bible study until about 10:00. Gary wasn't home yet, but we hadn't expected him, what with the drive and all."

"So, when he didn't come home that night, you weren't concerned," Christine prompted.

"We knew it would be late, so we went to bed," Elaine recalled. "We trusted Gary. After all, he'd be going away to college in the fall."

"Of course."

"I woke up sometime around 3:30 in the morning and the kitchen light was still on," Elaine remembered. "We always left a light on for him. I checked his room and saw that his bed hadn't been slept in, and that's when I started to worry. I called Cory's house and woke up his father. He said that Gary had never shown up at all that night! They got a call from someone they thought was me, who told them Gary had the flu." Elaine reached up to wipe away a tear. "That's when I called the police."

The strain of telling the story was taking its toll on Elaine. Her sorrowful voice wavered with emotion. John reached into his pocket and handed her a handkerchief.

"Elaine, you don't have to talk about it anymore," John interjected, taking her hand.

"No, it's all right." John put his arm around her, and Elaine buried her head in his shoulder. "If only I'd called sooner," she cried.

"It's not your fault, Elaine," John soothed. "There was nothing you could do."

"Would you mind if I had a look at Gary's room?" Christine asked quietly.

Elaine blew her nose. "No, of course not. It's a mess though. I just started to clean out his closet this morning."

"What are you looking for?" John asked Christine as he helped Elaine to her feet.

"Nothing specific," Christine answered, "but it might help me to understand Gary a little better."

Elaine brushed the damp hair back from her face and led them down a hallway to a spacious bedroom, the walls covered with memorabilia from a happy childhood—pictures of Little League teams, swimming trophies, and award certificates for academic achievement and Sunday school attendance. His senior picture hung over a cluttered computer desk. A calculus text was still open as if he had just left to get a snack from the kitchen. He was a serious-looking young man, with blue eyes that seemed to be looking at something no one else could see.

From the corner of the ceiling, the tiny demon Piteous-Cull, the Wretched Scavenger, skulked quietly. He had come to feed on the leftover grief and guilt that filled Gary's empty room. Immediately sensing the stench of death, Pesach drew his sword and pinned the squeaking demon to the wall, dispatching him into oblivion.

"Tell me what Gary was like," Christine said as she surveyed the room.

Elaine smiled. "He was so good," she said, running her fingertips across his picture. "And funny. You can't tell by this picture, but he had a great sense of humor. He could mimic any sound he heard. I remember one day when he was about thirteen, I kept hearing this bird in the house. I thought it had flown in through the patio doors when we weren't looking. I went from room to room, and it seemed like it was just in the next room. Well, it was Gary!" She laughed. "He was always doing something silly like that."

"But he was a workaholic too," she continued. "Many a night, I'd get up at midnight, and he'd still be bent over his books studying or programming the computer. He'd just forget about the time. I'd ask what he was doing, and he'd launch into some detailed explanation about hard drives and Turbo Pascal, and my eyes would glaze over." She smiled, remembering fondly. "He was so bright!"

A Bible lay open on Gary's bedside table, and when Christine opened it, a small piece of paper fluttered to the floor. It was a list of names.

"What's this?" she asked, handing it to Elaine.

"A prayer list of some sort, I imagine," Elaine answered.

"Do you know any of these people?"

"Sure, they're kids from school," Elaine read the list aloud. "Heather White was the one who gave the Halloween party. Chad Lawrence was one of the boys who was harassing him. Gary said he really felt sorry for Chad. His mother is an alcoholic, evidently."

Christine turned to a passage Gary had marked with a ribbon. He'd used a yellow marker to highlight Ephesians 6:10–18 (NIV): "Finally, be strong in the Lord and in his mighty power. Put on the full armor of God so that you can take your stand against the devil's schemes. For our struggle is not against flesh and blood, but against the rulers, against the authorities, against the powers of this dark world and against the spiritual forces of evil in the heavenly realms. Therefore put on the full armor of

God, so that when the day of evil comes, you may be able to stand your ground, and after you have done everything, to stand."

The words made Christine uncomfortable, and the specter of the demon of her nightmare rose up in front of her. She quickly dismissed it. Even though she reported on the occult, she didn't really believe in the devil, only in human beings who were capable of unspeakable acts of evil.

John looked over Christine's shoulder. "Looks like Gary was engaged in spiritual warfare."

Christine looked up sharply. "What do you mean?"

"He was waging a battle for the souls of those names on his list," John explained.

Elaine interrupted, "Now I remember what this list is all about. His youth group decided to pray daily for the salvation of all those kids who were at that party."

"The Halloween party," Christine verified.

"That's right."

"Did it do any good?" Christine was sarcastic.

Elaine smiled. "Heather accepted Jesus the week before Christmas. In fact, she and Gary had been dating. He even asked her to the Senior Prom."

Christine was a little skeptical at Heather's sudden transformation. She made a mental note to interview the girlfriend.

"Was Heather a regular visitor?" Christine asked.

"Yes, she had become active in the church youth group and was over here almost every week," Elaine continued. "She hated staying at home with her mother."

"Why was that?" Christine inquired.

"Mrs. White didn't approve of Heather becoming a Christian," Elaine stated coldly.

Christine's instincts told her she was onto something.

"Why would that bother her?" Christine asked.

"Star White owns a New Age bookstore in town," John answered. "She sells crystals and miniature pyramids. There's a huge painting of the Earth goddess Gaia hanging over her door."

"Heather says her mother thinks she's a 'good witch,'" Elaine remarked. "But now that Heather's a Christian, the girl can barely sleep in that house anymore without having nightmares."

Christine made another mental note to pay a visit to Star White. She picked up a picture of Gary and his dad fishing.

"That was taken in Oak Creek Canyon last summer," Elaine said.

"Gary seems like a special young man," Christine smiled.

"Yes, he was."

"I really appreciate your letting me ask you all these questions, Mrs. Knox," Christine drew their meeting to a close. "You've really been helpful. I'd like you to call me if you think of anything else that might be important. Maybe your story can prevent this from happening to someone else."

"I hope so," Elaine sighed. "I want to find out who did this to my son. I pray for them every day."

"You must hate them very much," Christine remarked sympathetically.

"No, I only pray that God will forgive them."

Christine couldn't understand that reaction at all. Even though the kid who murdered her sister was locked up for life, whatever that meant in today's judicial system, she would gladly see him fry in the electric chair. Every year that he came up for parole, she was there making sure he never saw the outside world again.

Elaine hugged John and shook hands with Christine as they left the Knox home. They drove in silence. While John concentrated on his driving, it gave Christine a chance to observe him closely. There was a solidness, yet a gentleness about John Delarosa that she found herself attracted to. It was as if she could just relax and be herself when he was around. He turned and smiled, catching her staring at him.

"Do I have dirt on my face?" he laughed. Blushing, Christine found herself uncharacteristically speechless. "Thanks for being sensitive with Elaine," he continued.

"She's in a pretty fragile state right now," Christine said, finding her voice. "By the way, how do you know so much about Star White?"

John shifted the jeep into second gear and slowed to make a left turn onto a dirt road. The sign pointed to Red Rock Crossing.

"I used to be a 'winkie'," he turned and grinned at her.

"You mean a New Ager?"

"Yep."

"I can't imagine you sitting in a Lotus position, contemplating your navel," she teased.

"Worse than that even," he rolled his eyes heavenward.

"Like what?"

"I've done everything from astrology, to past life regressions, to transcendental meditation, Eckankar, rebirthing, channeling. You name it," John shared. "I meditated often at Sedona's psychic vortexes."

"That's hard to believe," Christine laughed.

"You doubt my veracity?" he said in mock indignation. "Ask my mother. She wore out a pair of knees praying for me."

"What happened to change you?" Christine ventured cautiously.

"I was sitting on Bell Rock during the Harmonic Convergence in 1987, chanting '*OM*' and supposedly channeling cosmic energy into the earth," John explained, "when I looked around and saw a bunch of desperate people searching for meaning in their lives. Then I realized I was just as desperate as they were.

"If this was the meaning of life, sitting on a rock and chanting at the sky, I wanted no part of it. So I stood up and hiked down into reality."

"Then what happened?" Christine prompted.

"I went for a three-day walk in the desert by myself, fasting and praying," John continued, pulling the Jeep into the parking lot of the picnic ground. He cut the engine and turned to look at Christine. "All the stupid things I'd done, all the time I'd wasted, came flooding in on me. I asked for God's forgiveness, and I asked Him to prove to me He was real. The morning of the third day, I felt His presence and this tremendous love. It was as if I'd taken a warm bath in honey. This wonderful, gentle peace just seemed to settle around my shoulders. I asked Jesus to come into my life, and He did."

"Just like that," Christine said skeptically.

"Just like that." He seemed so sincere, and yet Christine just didn't believe life was that simple. "I found out later that Mom and some of her friends were holding a prayer vigil for me at the same time."

Any serious talk of religion made Christine want to run, and she felt herself drawing back, despite her attraction to this man. She opened the door, and John reached over to take her arm. Instinctively, she looked up at him in distrust, and he quickly let his hand fall.

"Chris, I'll never push you into anything. I just wanted you to know who I am." He smiled, and Christine thought he had the kindest eyes. "Now let's see what Mom packed for lunch. We've got a hike in front of us."

As they unpacked their lunch, they were unaware of the protective angels around them.

"Well, brother Aaro," Miklos said with a smile. "It looks as if we might be seeing a lot of each other from here on."

"That," answered Aaro, "depends upon the will of the Lord."

"*And* the choice of Christine," Wardar reminded them both.

Pesach pulled some manna from his pouch and broke it, distributing it among his fellow warriors. Aaro produced a chalice and raised it to heaven.

"Here's to her choice of life!" he toasted, and they dined.

CHAPTER
4

Christine's breathing sounded loud in her ears as she struggled to keep up with John's grueling pace across the rough sandstone terrain, her vision narrowed to the few feet of ground in front of her. After his warning about rattlesnakes, she gingerly skirted every shrub and spiny bush where one could hide. She hated snakes! The screech of a red-tailed hawk riding an updraft overhead caused her to look away from the trail, and she ran into John's back just as he stopped unexpectedly.

"Sorry," she mumbled.

"Watch out for the crucifixion thorn," he said, pointing to a wicked looking bush.

"What an appropriately gruesome name," Christine shivered, steering a wide path around it. "Can we stop a minute?" Her heart was racing from the unaccustomed exercise. John offered Christine his canteen, and she gratefully drank the cool water, wiping her mouth with the back of her hand.

"It's not much farther," he encouraged her. "You want to rest for awhile? Sometimes I forget that not everybody hikes just for the fun of it."

"Maybe we could just slow down a little."

For the next half hour, they climbed steadily through a small woodland of pinions and junipers. Sweat trickled down the back of her neck as the sun blazed hotter. Scurrying across a hot boulder, a lizard sought the relative coolness of its shade.

"Smart lizard," she commented, and John laughed.

Christine liked the sound of his laugh: deep and gentle, not crude like a construction worker laughing at a dirty joke, but honest and straight from his heart, as if he really enjoyed her company. She decided that if she ever could trust a man, then John Delarosa just might be the one. But trust was so hard. First her father left her mother for another woman, when her mother was pregnant with Laura. Then Laura was murdered by a boy with whom they'd shared a sandbox. It would take an act of God for Christine McKay to truly trust a man.

Then there was Randy. Amazing that after all these years, the memory could still hurt. Automatically, after years of practice, she forced him back into her subconscious.

Christine slipped on loose shale, and John caught her just as she went down on one knee.

"Are you alright?"

"I think so," she winced, brushing off her jeans, and they continued to climb. "Tell me more about these supposed vortexes."

"A psychic by the name of Page Bryant claimed that she had channeled a spirit entity by the name of Albion who pinpointed the exact locations of the vortexes on Cathedral Rock, Airport Mesa, Boynton Canyon, and Bell Rock," he explained. "Cathedral Rock is supposedly female or magnetic, Airport Mesa and Bell Rock are male or electrical, and Boynton Canyon's energy is both male and female, electromagnetic. Then along comes Jose Arguelles who said he got the idea for the Harmonic Convergence while driving down Wilshire Boulevard in L.A."

"No doubt," Christine commented cynically.

"Right," John said wryly. "Anyway, he claimed that on August 16, 1987, 144,000 people would come together around the globe to commit 'ritualistic surrender' to the Earth by chanting at these vortexes. It was supposed to be a great turning point for mankind, and there would be massive UFO sightings as extraterrestrial intelligence would finally be able to communicate with us."

"Sort of like tuning in to a giant antenna in the sky," Christine added.

"Something like that," John laughed. "Arguelles claimed that date coincided with the date the Aztecs circled for the return of their god Quetzalcoatl, the god of peace. He said that according to Hopi Indian legend these 144,000 would 'dance awake' the rest of humanity. Then by 1992, we would shift civilization from a centralized military state of terror to a de-industrialized, decentralized, post-military society."

"Sounds kind of spooky, actually," Christine remarked, "especially with the break up of the Soviet Union."

"I wouldn't give Arguelles the credit for that," John continued. "Even then, there was a lot of disagreement among New Agers about his validity." He went on to explain the rest of the theory. "On the date of the Harmonic Convergence, there was a grand trine: nine planets were aligned in the heavens. Arguelles claimed it was only the beginning. It all was supposed to coincide somehow with the Mayans' great cycle which will end in 2012."

"Weren't the Aztecs descendants of the Mayans?"

"In a 'round about way," he said. "In the tenth century A.D., the Mayan culture just vanished, but some of the Mayan people were living for some time under the domination of the Toltecs, from whom the Aztecs descended."

"Did you believe in Arguelles' theory?" Christine wondered.

"I'm not sure if I actually believed in his theory, or just hoped he had some answers," John admitted. "There were some people who paid shysters 150 bucks a ticket just to sit on Bell Rock and wait for a spaceship to beam them up to a better life."

"Did you?" Christine asked, scuffing the toe of her hiking boot on one of the many rocks littering the trail.

"I wasn't that gullible," John quipped. "Almost, but not quite."

John froze, and Christine heard his gasp. Moving up to his side, she had the same reaction. There stood a crude cross of tree trunks, at least eight feet tall, with dried blood where Gary's hands and feet had been nailed. Dried blood stained the ground underneath. The reporter in her took over, and Christine shut her mind to the images of torture. Adjusting her Nikon camera, she methodically photographed the cross and the surrounding area. Yellow police tape roped off a small area around the base. Standing unseen at either side of the cross, Goyo and Sandor waited for the group.

"My God, why would anyone do this?" John finally spoke.

"My God, why would anyone do this?" Miklos and Aaro echoed.

Christine scoured the nearby area, looking for other markings which might have been left, but if there had been anything, it was obliterated now by footprints.

"The police have probably been through this place with a fine-toothed comb," Christine commented. "If they found anything, they're keeping it to themselves."

The entire group of angels surrounded John. Crystal tears fell from each angelic eye. They were not mourning the passing into glory of one of God's saints, but rather the sickening victory of the enemy.

Christine looked over at John and saw anguish etched on his face as he bowed his head in prayer. He was crying! Christine had never seen a man cry.

"I'm sorry, John. I forgot you knew him."

"Why? Who would do this?"

"It's obviously someone who thinks these psychic vortexes have some kind of power," she theorized. "I don't think it was Satanists though. Did you ever hear of any other New Age group who believed in sacrifices?"

"No," he sighed, wiping his eyes. "They may have been weird, but I've never heard any of them advocating human sacrifice."

"Well, somebody has just started a new religion," she observed matter-of-factly.

"Or a very old one," he said wearily.

"Didn't you say Arguelles believed that the Aztecs had predicted this Harmonic Convergence?" Christine asked.

"Not specifically, but their mythology alluded to it," John replied.

"Didn't the Aztecs sacrifice people?" Christine tried to recall what she had learned in her world history class.

John's eyes lit up. "Yes, but the priests only sacrificed virgins, didn't they?"

"I'm not sure, but I think I'll make some calls and check it out," Christine stated.

✛✛✛✛✛

Miklos and Aaro unsheathed their swords as a hissing black horde of minor, but aggressive, demons surrounded them. Pesach, Wardar, Goyo and Sandor moved into defensive positions around the couple. Nearby, an ugly fissure in the rock spewed forth a stream of black creatures released from the bowels of the earth by the blood of the human sacrifice. The air over Sedona was foul with their sulphurous presence. Desmodus, the Drinker of Blood, perched his vulgar vulture-like body on top of the cross, licking the blood from his clawed toes.

"Well, if it isn't the 'fearless' ones from heaven," Humtah taunted, strutting up to Sandor. "What brings you to my territory?"

"The Lord Most High as you well know, Humtah," Sandor stood his ground. "If you dare try to harm one of these humans, you will have Him to answer to."

"Really," the demon drawled. "He has been of little trouble to me these last days. Why should I be concerned?"

Humtah belched fire at them, rolling his yellow, bloodshot eyes to heaven and laughing fiendishly.

Aaro's hand tightened on his sword as his wings enfolded John, who sat dejectedly on a boulder, silently crying out to his God. Aaro could feel his strength building because of John's prayers.

"Give notice to your master," Wardar challenged. "His day is coming. Then we will cast you all into the lake of fire forever."

"Ha! I'm so frightened," Humtah shivered mockingly. "Look around you."

The angels, not taking their eyes off the demon prince or their human charges, edged cautiously around the clearing until they could look behind them. A slimy, seething black ooze flowed down Cathedral Rock, its stench clinging to everything it touched. On closer inspection, it was actually a demon mass so thick it appeared to be one putrefying body. The fissure in the rock widened with each moment, belching forth even more demons, like an unending lava flow.

"We could possess the female now with little trouble and make her our own," Rosh-Rot bragged, stepping from the shadow of the cross.

Miklos' temper flared when he saw his old enemy. As he drew his sword, Pesach laid a restraining hand on his arm. With the threat of the sword still in his voice, Miklos addressed the strutting demon. "You have to get through me first, Rosh-Rot, and I don't think you've forgotten the last time we met."

Rosh-Rot roared his anger, pointing his gnarled taloned finger at Miklos. "I have not forgotten, Messenger! But your Captain Kerestel is not here to save you this time. Beware that I do not send *you* to oblivion. Now take your humans and get off *our* mountain while you still can!"

John's spirit was uneasy as he finally noticed the late afternoon light. Dark clouds were massing on the horizon. Suddenly, he felt as if someone had dropped him off in the middle of a graveyard at midnight. Glancing at his watch, John couldn't believe it was almost 5:30. How could he have been so distracted that he forgot the time? He knew better. He might be able to find his way back in the dark, but the hike was difficult enough for Christine in full daylight. Besides, there was something evil about this place now. Standing up, he quickly brushed the red dust off his jeans and found Christine copying a curious drawing on the rock wall into her sketchpad.

"We'd better go, Chris. We want to make it to the car before dark."

"Yeah, okay," she said distractedly, erasing a line in her notebook and redrawing it. "Look at this rattlesnake painting. Look at the way the two heads face each other. Have you ever seen anything like it before?"

He studied the red and black rock painting. "No, I don't think so. Does it mean something to you?"

"No, but . . . it just doesn't look like the normal graffiti around here. I think I've seen it somewhere before. It looks more like some kind of ritual symbol."

John's uneasiness was growing as, unknown to him, Aaro and Miklos urged them to leave *now*. Sinister black clouds had swallowed up the blue sky. Unconsciously, John edged closer to Christine in a protective stance, scanning the fast moving weather front rolling over them. A gust of wind preceded the first crackle of lightning. Christine finally seemed to notice as thunder rumbled nearby.

"Chris, we really need to head back."

She shivered, despite the oppressive heat. "This place gives me the creeps."

They had only hiked a few yards down the trail when the sky opened up, the slashing rain blinding them. Christine slipped, and John almost pulled her shoulder out of the socket when he caught her in mid-fall. Lightning struck a nearby pinion tree, its sap exploding with ear shattering thunder as the air was rent in two. John and Christine were knocked to the ground.

"We can't stay out in this," he said, catching his breath. "We're like human lightning rods in the open."

"What are we going to do?" Christine gasped, as she shoved her precious camera under her t-shirt. Her hair was already plastered to her head.

John took her by the arm as another bolt of lightning struck nearby.

The band of angels slashed and fought their way to clear a path for the couple, sending demon after demon back to the pit of hell.

"Aaro, ask John to pray for help!" Miklos shouted over the raging torrent as his sword cut the head off a murderous demon, who disappeared shrieking in a puff of smoke. As Christine and John stumbled on the slimy clay trail, their guardian angels whirled and flashed in all their glory, lighting up the darkness which threatened to overwhelm them. There was a cave. If only Aaro could get through to John.

In the language of angels, Aaro began to beseech John and God, communicating spirit to spirit. "Bashida shadogonda ramayetha!" "Lord God deliver us!"

As John leaned up against the cliff face, shielding Christine with his body from the worst of the pounding rain, he sent up a plea to God Almighty. "Lord God deliver us! Holy angels make haste to help us!"

Then he remembered. The cave. Really, just a depression under a giant overhang, where he had once camped overnight as a teenager. It was an old Indian dwelling, whose walls were black with the soot of ancient campfires.

"Come on," he shouted, grabbing Christine's elbow and pulling her along.

John's words were lost in a clap of thunder, but she didn't protest. Somehow she knew John would take care of her. This was his element. The darkness was almost absolute, and it seemed as if he moved more by instinct than by sight. Christine cried out as she fell again and blood spurted from a gash in her arm. John tore a strip off the bottom of his t-shirt and wrapped it.

"Hold on to me," he yelled. "It's not much farther."

Then he was pulling her down into deeper darkness. Her ears rang with the sudden muting of storm noise. Breathing raggedly, she dropped to the dry floor of the cave, all thoughts of rattlesnakes driven from her by the battle with the storm. She heard John unzip his backpack, and then a beam of light momentarily blinded her before it darted over the floor of their cave.

"Thank you, Jesus!" he exhaled. "No snakes." Thunder crashed, drowning out his words. "Are you okay?"

"I think so," Christine said cautiously. "My arm is really killing me though."

"Let me take a look," John said, unraveling the blood-soaked bandage.

The bleeding had slowed, but there was a deep gash which needed stitches. Dragging the backpack closer, he rummaged around until he pulled out a small first-aid kit.

"You're a regular Boy Scout," she declared, trying to laugh.

"I've got the first-aid badge to prove it," John said, smiling in the dim light.

Funny, it didn't hurt so much when he held her hand. As he efficiently cleaned the wound with antiseptic, Christine winced and bit her lip. Soon, her arm was rebandaged with gauze and tape.

"We need to get you to a doctor, but that should keep out any infection," he observed. "Are you cold?"

"A little," she shivered. "You wouldn't happen to have any dry clothes in that magic bag of yours?"

"As a matter of fact." John drew out a lightweight aluminum-like blanket. "Earthquake supplies," he explained, pulling out another one for himself.

Amazingly, Christine was warmer, the space-age fabric trapping her own body heat. John flopped down beside Christine and leaned against his pack. Rain poured in sheets off the cliff face, making it seem as if they were trapped behind a waterfall.

"I wonder how long it'll last." Christine shifted positions, trying to get comfortable on the hard ground.

"Even if it stopped, we're stuck until morning," John replied. "It's too dangerous at night, and now there's the danger of flash floods."

"I can't believe this," she fumed.

"Are you hungry?"

"I'd kill for a cup of hot coffee."

"How about a ham sandwich and a granola bar?" he smiled.

Once again, John had thought of everything.

"You're a pretty resourceful guy," Christine declared, munching on her sandwich.

"When you're out in the desert," he explained, "you learn to take precautions. It's an unforgiving place. I think about Jesus, fasting and praying in the desert for forty days and forty nights: no flashlight, no first-aid supplies, no food."

"No granola bars," she grinned, crunching into one. "You really think He could survive that long without eating?"

"Don't you?"

"I suppose Gandhi survived," she remembered. "But he was so weak by the end of that time, they thought he would croak."

"Gandhi wasn't Jesus," John countered.

"They were both great teachers," she said.

"Jesus was more than a teacher," John replied. "He was God."

Christine leaned her head back on the cave wall, sighing. "I wish I could believe it." For the first time ever, Christine found herself letting down her defensive shield with a man who was almost a stranger. But he didn't seem like a stranger. "I wish I could have a faith like yours."

"You can, Christine," John said gently. "All you have to do is believe."

Running the dust on the floor through her fingers, Christine shook her head no. "Too much has happened in my life. Too many people I love have been hurt. I've been hurt. If there really was a God, He wouldn't let so many people suffer: not my God anyway."

"Nor mine," John spoke. "Let me explain it like Billy Graham did. He said that man was like the ant. God created the ant, and He loved it and took care of it. But one day, this little ant headed toward a cliff and certain death. What was He to do? First of all, the ant wasn't capable of thinking like He does. He couldn't hear Him. He couldn't see Him. The ant couldn't understand God. Because God was so much greater, if He reached out and touched the ant, He might kill it. If He put His hand down in front of the ant, it would just walk over Him without knowing it and keep marching toward the cliff."

Christine smiled. "So God accidentally stepped on it, right?"

"No," John laughed. "Remember, He *loved* that little ant. No, God had to find a better way. So the only thing to do was leave heaven, give it all up, to become an ant. That way, in ant language, He could tell him, 'Stop. Don't go that way; you're going to die.' Jesus was like that ant. He went over the cliff for us, so that we don't have to."

Christine wrapped her arms around her knees under the blanket. "I've never heard it explained quite that way."

"Think about it," John said, stretching out on the dirt floor. That was all he said. No pushing. No pressure. Christine contemplated the little ant.

"But why do people have to suffer?" she asked. "If God is so great, surely He could put an end to all the evil."

"Satan's days are numbered," John explained, "and he knows it. Then Jesus will reign forever."

Sitting beside them in the cave, Miklos and Aaro raised their arms and clapped hands in the air, celebrating John's words.

Christine just couldn't buy it though. "I wish I could believe you, John, but it's so much like any other myth. Every civilization has a great prophet somewhere in its history."

John stayed calm. "But Jesus is the only one who claimed He was God the Son."

There wasn't anything else to say.

Sometime during the night, they fell into a restless sleep as Miklos, Aaro, Pesach, Wardar, Goyo, and Sandor kept watch, their swords still at the ready. They were safe for now. But that didn't keep the enemy from prowling at the perimeter of the cave. The demons had been routed, but they would attack again.

The next morning, Christine awoke to find John exploring their shelter. He ran his hand across the rough surface of the back wall, shining his flashlight on some crude writing.

"What is it?" Christine asked.

"The Lord is my shepherd . . . Gary K . . ."

She gasped, a chill running up her spine. "They must have held him here until the sacrifice!"

"I think you're right," John agreed as he touched the writing gently with his fingers.

Christine felt as if a slimy hand had ruffled the back of her neck, as indeed a tiny imp had attacked when the angels turned their backs for a moment. Miklos knocked it off with the tip of his sword, sending it shrieking into the abyss.

"Let's get out of here," Christine shivered.

Damp and exhausted, the couple hiked in silence back down the trail to the Jeep. John called what he thought would be a worried Molly from his mobile phone, only to find that she was at perfect peace. She informed him that he and Christine were bathed in intercession at the prayer vigil the night before.

After having Christine's arm stitched up at an emergency clinic and notifying the Sheriff of what they'd found, they drove back to the motel silently. For once, Christine couldn't think of anything clever to say. All she wanted was a nice hot shower and about twelve hours of sleep.

Heronim, the Bright and Powerful, awaited the exhausted angel band as he perched on top of the Welcome Inn sign. Spying the weary company approaching, he raised his sword in salute.

"Hail, good fellows!" Heronim cheered. "The Lord's peace be upon you!"

At the sight of their joyful brother, their spirits lifted and their battle-worn bones were strengthened.

"What news have you for us, Heronim?" Goyo enquired, making haste to join him in midair. As they clasped hands affectionately, the others surrounded them, eager to hear what Heronim had to report.

"The prayer vigil, called by the saint Molly Delarosa, was filled with God's power!" Heronim shared enthusiastically. "The faithful came out in great numbers, and their prayers enabled God Almighty to dispatch our legions to encamp around the entire perimeter of Sedona."

"Glory to God!" Wardar exclaimed, spiraling skyward.

"When do we move?" asked Sandor, eager for the battle.

"Patience, brother," Heronim smiled at the younger Sandor. "There will be plenty of time for you to wield your sword. For now, we must remain hidden. Goyo, may we withdraw to the interior of this building?"

"Let us go," Goyo said. The assembly followed him as he slipped through Christine's motel door. Inside, the angels hovered cross-legged above the floor, listening intently to Heronim's report.

"Kerestel has laid a ceiling of celestial protectors over Immanuel Faith Chapel to deflect the onslaught of Quench-Bersha and his cohorts," explained Heronim. "Similar ceilings are planned for every other body of believers. Every guardian has been put on alert. We have at least two cloaked scouts at every New Age demon's door. We have already received word that Mibzar is nervous." A cheer rose from the group.

"As well he should be," Pesach added.

"Your post has not changed," Heronim continued. "The girl Christine is too important to leave unguarded now."

"We know this to be true, brother," replied Miklos, "after last night."

"Last night?" Heronim inquired. "Were you just returning from engaging the enemy when we met?"

"Indeed," Miklos answered, "and it was a close call. Before we were aware of it, we were surrounded by Rosh-Rot and his allies."

"We were covered on every side, but we prevailed!" Sandor declared exuberantly, thrusting his fist into the air.

"We prevailed *only* through the prayers of the saints," Goyo reminded his little brother.

Sandor looked downcast. "Forgive me my pride, brothers."

"You are forgiven," Heronim said, slapping him gently on the back. "Victory is so sweet, that sometimes we forget whereby the victory comes. 'But thanks be to God, *He* gives us the victory through our Lord Jesus Christ. Therefore my brothers, stand firm. Let nothing move you,' as it is written in Paul's first epistle to the Corinthian church."

Miklos looked up as Christine stirred, and Heronim rose to depart. "When I saw you returning," Heronim addressed them solemnly, "there was no joy about you. It is crucial to retain our Lord's joy. Therein lies strength. Without joy, there is no hope. Without hope there is only despair, and in despair, there is only defeat."

"Well spoken," Goyo agreed, standing to embrace the messenger. "Give our greetings to Kerestel, and the peace of the Lord be with you."

"And also with you," Heronim said as he passed through the wall into the sunlight.

CHAPTER
5

The next day, fully rested, Christine called the research department of her paper.

"Good morning, this is Jan," the familiar voice answered the phone pleasantly.

"Hi Jan, this is Christine."

"How's your vacation in Arizona?"

"Vacation . . . right," Christine groused. "I hiked across the desert in a thunderstorm yesterday afternoon."

Jan laughed. "Hiked? You?"

"Listen, I need you to look something up for me."

"Sure," Jan said, all business. "What do you need?"

Christine plumped up a pillow behind her and propped herself against the headboard of her motel bed, reviewing her notes. "First off, I need anything you can find on Aztec human sacrifice, especially in goddess worship. Oh, and check if there were any ceremonies where rattlesnakes were worshipped."

"Rattlesnakes," Jan said, shivering. "Yuck. You always pick the grossest subjects for research."

"Yeah, I know," Christine said matter-of-factly. "Oh," she added, "and see what you can find on the Harmonic Convergence of August 16, 1987, especially as it relates to Sedona."

"That all?"

"For now," Christine finished, scratching a note on her pad.

"Okay," Jan replied. "I'll get right on it."

"You're a lifesaver, Jan. Just one more thing—connect me to Jack in the newsroom?"

"Sure," Jan answered. "See ya when you get home."

Christine hummed along to the canned music on hold until Jack finally picked up.

"Garth here," he answered sharply.

"Hi, Jack, this is your star reporter."

"How's it going, Chris?" he asked.

"This one is really bizarre. It gives me the heebie-jeebies, Jack."

"Really, what have you found?"

"I've seen some pretty grisly stuff," she continued, "including an upside down cross covered with dried blood. I even spent the night in the cave where the Knox boy was held before his murder." Christine flipped her notepad to a clean page. "Any more crucifixion reports?"

"As a matter of fact," Jack said grimly, "a young boy was found at the temple of Delphi in Greece."

"Crucified upside down?"

"You got it," Jack confirmed. "Only, they didn't use a tree. They painted an upside cross on the stones, then drove spikes through his wrists and feet. Pretty gruesome."

"Has anybody made the connection yet with Sedona?"

"Not that I can tell," Jack answered. "I found the story in one of the English tabloids. The local authorities are treating it as an isolated case."

"Just like the others," she said, slipping into her shoes. "It's like the authorities are blind. Listen, Jack, I've got to run, but keep me posted."

"Okay," he said, "but try to wind it up soon. You're spending a fortune."

"So when did you become an accountant?"

"The brass upstairs is suddenly on a cost-cutting witch hunt."

"I'll try not to eat lobster too often," Christine quipped cynically.

Christine nosed her rented Taurus into a space at the side of the small flagstone library. After checking the card catalog, she pulled the few books available on the Aztecs and Mayans, then sat down to scan their indices. After an hour, she finally found a tiny reference to Coatlicue, the Earth goddess worshipped by the Aztecs, who was said to demand blood sacrifice. It said her skirt was made of braided serpents, and she wore a necklace of alternating human hands and hearts, with a human skull pendant.

Accompanying the text was a small black and white sketch of the goddess.

As Christine studied it, a bell sounded inside her head.

Quickly, she flipped to the sketch from the rock wall at Gary's murder site. It was the same drawing! She was staring at the face of Coatlicue—formed by the same two rattlesnakes facing one another—just as it was drawn on the sandstone cliff.

Suddenly, Christine's ears began to ring, and she felt like the room was spinning. A wave of nausea enveloped her, and it felt as if her head were being squeezed between two muscular hands.

Pocheroth, the Binder, stood behind Christine's chair, cheered on by a chattering crowd of demons, as he attempted to crush her skull between his massive talons. From behind him to the right, Pocheroth heard the metallic song of a sword being drawn. The demons let out a warning shriek, and before Pocheroth could turn to face his enemy, the angel Miklos drove his sword between the Binder's protruding shoulder blades. Drawing down with all his strength, Miklos split him in two. The crowd of minor demons fled yowling through the floor of the library.

A warmth flooded through Christine from the top of her head to the soles of her feet as the pressure on her head dissipated. Still flushed and a bit nauseated, Christine copied the one reference to Coatlicue, then spoke to the librarian, a friendly woman in her mid-forties.

"No, that's all the books we have right now," the librarian answered her question softly. "You might try Phoenix."

"No, that's alright," Christine said, leaning against the counter.

As she turned to leave, the librarian said, "Wait! They have a *wonderful* Aztec exhibit in San Diego right now. I was just there last month. It's breathtaking."

"Did they have a bookstore?"

"I believe so," the librarian said, checking her watch.

"It might be worth a trip to San Diego," Christine thought out loud.

"Are you researching a book?" The librarian peered suspiciously over the top of her glasses.

"I'm a reporter," Christine explained. "I'm just filling in some background material on Gary Knox's murder."

The librarian appeared shaken. "Terrible, wasn't it! He was such a good boy. Not like most teenagers these days."

"So everybody says," Christine commented, observing the librarian's reaction. "Did you know him?"

"No, not really," the librarian stated quickly. "I know his mother worked on last year's Walk for Life. I hear she's a lovely woman. I know she must be devastated. I can't imagine losing a child, especially that way."

"Yes, it was terrible," Christine sympathized. "Well, thank you for your suggestion about San Diego."

"You're very welcome," the librarian said, following Christine to the door. "If you need anything else while you're here, just give me a call."

Christine smiled as she pushed open the glass door into the blinding sunshine. The librarian hurried to the phone on the desk and dialed.

"Hello, Libby?" she said urgently. "This is Joan. I think we may have a problem."

Christine scooted her plastic lawn chair closer under the shade of the table umbrella. The mid-morning sun was already hot. Taking a long drink of iced tea, Pat dabbed at the sweat on her brow with her terry cloth wristband.

"You didn't tell me you played tennis like a pro," Christine groused, leaning wearily back in her chair.

"You didn't ask," Pat laughed. "I was state champion in high school."

"I feel like hanging up my racket for good."

"You're not that bad!" Pat assured her. "I could give you a few pointers while you're here."

"You could give me lessons for a year," Christine grumbled, "and I'd never play tennis like that. This bandage doesn't help much either."

As the waiter in white shorts and crisp blue shirt approached, Christine scanned the slick, laminated menu emblazoned with the gold fox emblem of the tennis club.

"Have you decided yet?" he asked politely.

"I'll have the Spanish omelet and a side order of strawberries," Christine ordered.

While Pat gave her choice to the waiter, Christine soaked in the atmosphere of this high desert setting, the magnificent red monoliths rising toward heaven. It was like another planet compared to St. Louis. Right now, it was peaceful and the sky was a bright sapphire, with only a few patchy white clouds, but she knew how quickly that could change. Remembering the horror of the storm in the desert, she shivered involuntarily. There had been something so evil about that place, and the storm brought back memories of her more recent brush with the fury of nature. Christine's fingers played over the now-healed scratches on her throat.

"Christine? Christine?" She started back to reality. "Where were you all of a sudden?"

"Just thinking," Christine hedged.

"I asked when you're going home."

"Maybe sooner than I want," Christine answered. "Jack told me to wind things up, but I just don't have a story yet . . . at least nothing different than what's already been written." She took her straw and idly stirred the ice in her near-empty glass. "It's like something inside me is burning to find out who did this and why. The problem is, the paper won't pay my motel bills forever."

"You could stay at Mom's house," Pat offered. "She has tons of room."

"They'll expect me back if I don't come up with something," Christine said, dodging the offer. "The real problem is how to get to San Diego. I know Jack won't spring for another plane ticket."

"That's easy," Pat brightened. "John's flying to San Diego on Tuesday. He has a show there, so I thought I'd tag along and pick up a few new pieces for the gallery. There's plenty of room in his plane. What's in San Diego anyway?"

"A museum exhibit on the Aztec civilization," Christine explained.

"Aztec!" Pat was puzzled. "What's that have to do with anything?"

Christine leaned on her elbows, excited by her idea. "Something's been bothering me the whole time about this," she shared. "It's not like the normal satanic ritual. It's more sinister.

These people aren't afraid to leave their victim as a warning. That makes them extremely dangerous. And there seems to be a worldwide network."

"But what do the Aztecs have to do with it?"

"Suppose there were a group of people who believed they had the answer to all the world's problems," Christine talked out her theory. "A group who wanted to bring about the New World Order that everyone's talking about. And suppose they believed that if they sacrificed to an Aztec god or goddess that they would be appeased and raise us all up to a glorious new era."

"I'd say that it sounds pretty weird," Pat said. "Not that I'm doubting you. I just can't believe that someone would actually kill people in order to bring about a 'New World Order.'"

The waiter set a steaming soft yellow omelet covered with picante sauce in front of Christine.

"It's more than possible," Christine went on, taking a bite of her eggs. "Pat, I have seen more evil than you can imagine: dogs turned inside out, cannibalistic murders, children who have been ritually abused and sacrificed."

Pat slowly lowered her English muffin, no longer hungry as the images flashed across her mind.

"I don't know how you can stand it, Christine."

"Sometimes I can't," Christine stated matter-of-factly. "But somehow my mind filters it out. I remember once arriving at a house just as the police entered and found a double murder—parents who had been hacked to death by their son. There was blood everywhere, and he had smeared satanic symbols and filthy slogans all over the walls. It's funny. I remember it, but I don't. It's like I receded down a long, black tunnel, and I only saw it through a narrow telescope, as if I were looking at a tiny TV screen."

"Oh, Christine!"

Suddenly, Christine was no longer hungry either and pushed her plate away as the memories surged upward—all the victims crying out for justice.

"It must be what happens to soldiers on the battlefield," Christine explained. "The mind can't handle that much horror, so it shuts down."

"Why do you even stay in the newspaper business? Why don't you get out and do something else?" Pat urged.

"What else could I do?" Christine shrugged. "This is all I know. This is what I'm good at. If I don't expose this stuff, who will?"

Pat said nothing, but leaned back and studied Christine compassionately. "Christine, sooner or later, even soldiers go home, unless they're killed in battle. I worry for you and what it's doing to you."

"I'm fine," Christine brushed off Pat's concern, surprised that she had shared so much. "Really." She pushed her chair back and picked up her racket, signaling that the conversation was over.

✚✚✚✚✚

A ceiling of angels covered the roof of Immanuel Faith Chapel as the brown stucco church gathered in its Sunday worshippers. Miklos raised his hand in salute to Kerestel, as he accompanied Christine in the wide open doors. Aaro led the way with John, watchful as they scanned the outside perimeter. The skies over Sedona were dark with the demons spewing like molasses from the opening at Cathedral Rock.

"How can they not sense it?" Miklos asked. "The stench is suffocating."

"Molly knows," Jeremio, Molly's guardian angel, informed them, "as do many others. They are well prepared for the task before them, but it will be painful. This remnant is the strongest I've ever seen."

"Indeed," chimed in Sandor. "The more they are persecuted, the stronger they stand." He looked across the congregation, most of whom were wearing the spiritual armor of God.

The angels rejoiced as the saints gathered to praise and worship the Most High God, lifting their hands to heaven and joining in the singing.

Miklos stood behind Christine, his wings enfolding her as she sat without any armor, vulnerable to attack. Here, the forces were strong, and she was safe. But outside, it was becoming more difficult, even with the assistance of Pesach and Wardar.

A large Ethiopian angel, Chioke, accompanied Pastor Mike to the pulpit, his countenance glowing brightly. The glory of the Lord anointed the pastor as he smiled across his flock.

Christine had only agreed to come this morning to meet Gary's girlfriend, Heather. Her objectivity was her barrier against the unabashed praise going on around her, people standing with their hands raised and singing a song she didn't know. The room felt claustrophobic, as if she couldn't breathe. She wanted to run outside, but something kept her here.

"This morning," Pastor Mike began, "we are going to talk about Jesus." The congregation tittered. "That's no surprise to you, I know. We talk about Jesus every Sunday. But today, we are going to look at the miracle-making Jesus, the one who fed the 5,000. Turn to John, Chapter 6, and follow along with me."

Christine squirmed in her seat, as everyone around her ruffled well-worn pages. Her hands were empty, but John pulled out a Bible from the pew in front of her and smilingly offered it to her. She couldn't exactly refuse. The instinct to run was even stronger, but the only way now was to make a scene since John and Pat sat to the left of her, and Molly to the right. She was trapped. Swallowing hard, she fumbled through the book, looking for the page that everyone else seemed to have already found. John took it from her and found the right place for her.

"Now, we read in John how the people followed Jesus and His disciples who had gone off to be by themselves," Pastor Mike instructed. "Because of His miracles, the crowd had followed them. Not that they believed that Jesus was the Son of God, but because they wanted to see the miraculous. When Jesus saw this great crowd, He knew they had to be fed, so He took all the food they had—the five loaves and the two fishes—and then He lifted it to heaven, thanked God for His sufficiency and divided it among the people. After they were fed, they immediately wanted to make Jesus king."

Christine squirmed in her seat, but she followed along as the minister continued to teach. Maybe she could just sneak out during this part and show back up later to catch Heather. As she started to rise, Miklos sensed her intention and placed a hand on her head. Christine found herself settling back in the pew, as if she were an errant school girl who had to stay for the lesson. She tuned back in to the sermon.

"I am the bread of life," Pastor Mike read. "Are you hungry? Are you thirsty? Then come and sup with me, He said. Eat my flesh and drink my blood. He was the one true sacrifice for all. You're sitting there thinking, 'But pastor, you don't know what I've done! God could never forgive me.' Or you're sitting there thinking, 'I don't need God. I've got everything I need.' Or you're thinking, 'Where was God when I was in trouble? Where was He when my brother or sister was killed? How could God let such a thing happen?'"

Christine felt as if someone had slammed a fist into her stomach, knocking out all the air. Suddenly, she was listening intently.

"God didn't make it happen," Pastor Mike continued. "Satan did. He is a liar and a deceiver and a murderer. Don't blame God for that. It's Satan's desire to drag everyone into the pit with him on that last day. If he has to go, he wants to cause God pain by taking all His children with him."

Christine felt tears well up in her eyes. How she wanted to believe in a God who could take away all the pain. How she yearned to know the joy of these people. But she was a well-educated, sophisticated journalist. She had been taught to be objective and not get swept away with the tide. This service, she mused, while harmless, was still only another form of emotional manipulation. Pastor Mike concluded his message with an invitation to "come forward and make Jesus your Lord and Savior."

Typical, Christine snorted under her breath as she rolled her eyes toward the ceiling. Absently, she thumbed through the Bible in her lap. Beside her, Molly rose as Pastor Mike invited her to the pulpit. Christine's eyes followed her to the front.

"Most of you know that the Changes Plus abortion clinic is now performing abortions in the last trimester," Molly began. "Babies who would live outside the mother's womb are being exterminated every day. We cannot allow this to continue."

The congregation applauded enthusiastically.

"I have spoken to the pastors and pro-life representatives in every church in Sedona," Molly continued. "For the last year, we have been giving presentations to adult Sunday school groups, educating them on the subject and truths of abortion. Prayer warriors have been raised up in every church. Now, the network is complete. While there are some pastors who stubbornly cling to the belief that it's a woman's right to abort her child, most will stand with us."

Kerestel lifted his sword to call his troops to attention.

"We can no longer stand by and do nothing," Molly said fervently. "If we do not act, we will be as guilty as those who do the abortions. As you know, tomorrow is the day of our silent prayer vigil in front of Changes. Will you join us?"

All over the sanctuary, people rose to their feet—John and Pat first. Then like a wave, they all stood, until no one but Christine was seated.

✝✝✝✝✝

The angels around the room waited in anticipation. Those warring angels who were veterans of uncountable battles looked forward to the coming one with joy. Never had their prayer coverage been stronger in any place, and now with Molly's announcement, unity would begin to form in the body. A trumpet sounded as all the angels lifted their voices in praise to God.

The demons who were near enough to hear shuddered. Quench-Bersha and Zethar-Zebah, the master of abortion, must be informed!

Nod, the wandering exile, trembled with excitement as he zoomed away from Immanuel Faith Chapel toward the desert and the Legion of Commanders.

Surely, the Commander Vaizaitha will reward me for my sharp ears and quick feet, he chortled, as he flitted toward the underground headquarters.

Commander Vaizaitha sat at the stone table conferring with his generals when the squirrelly Nod poofed into their midst.

"Commander, Commander, Commander," he buzzed. Vaizaitha reached up and swatted him as if he were a fly, knocking him to the floor. As the little demon sat up and shook his head, the Chief of Decay, Rosh-Rot, oozed into the room.

"Most unholy Commanders," Rosh-Rot declared as he saluted. "I come with important information concerning the territory of Zethar-Zebah!"

Vaizaitha looked up in disgust. "Speak, weasel, and waste no more of my time."

Nod hopped up and flew in front of Rosh-Rot's face. "It's my report. I was here first!"

Rosh-Rot reached up and enclosed Nod in his fist, green slime dripping through his fingers as he annihilated the squealing imp. Slinging the remains aside, he continued "his" report.

"It appears that some of us are not doing our jobs properly," he sneered, staring directly at Quench-Bersha. "The believers who were *supposedly* rendered impotent are now united and planning a direct assault upon the territory of Zethar-Zebah, namely the household of Changes Plus."

"What!" shouted Vaizaitha, rising to full form. "Why was I not notified sooner?" he glared at Quench-Bersha. "I thought you told me they were under control."

"Obviously not, Commander," Rosh-Rot continued, "for I also regret to inform you that the Hosts of Heaven are encamped around the entire perimeter of Sedona, with a ceiling of protection so thick over the Immanuel Faith Chapel that not even one of my more innocuous imps could pass through."

All yellow eyes in the dark room fastened on Quench-Bersha, as Vaizaitha reached over and grabbed him by the scruff of his scaly neck and lifted him out of his chair. "If I have to appear before our Lord Satan again simply to explain your blunders, I will take your head with me as a sacrifice of restitution!"

Casting him to the ground, Vaizaitha pointed a shaking clawed talon at Quench-Bersha and bellowed, "Now take your worthless hide to your post and don't come back until your task is completed!"

Turning to Rosh-Rot, Vaizaitha clapped a congratulatory hand on his shoulder. "Sit with us, Chief. You have proven that you have much to offer."

After the service, Pastor Mike introduced Heather to Christine and found an empty classroom in which they could meet privately. Childish crayon pictures of Bible stories were taped to the walls, and there was the strong smell of Elmer's glue.

"I can't stay very long," the blonde teenager said in a small frightened voice. "My mom doesn't even like for me to come to church."

"Why doesn't she want you to come?" Christine inquired gently.

Heather looked down at her hands, which twisted nervously in her lap. Her nails had been bitten down to the quick.

"She doesn't like church," Heather mumbled disconcertingly. "She's not a Christian."

"I see," Christine said noncommittally. "Thanks for helping me out."

"Sure," Heather shrugged. "But I don't want you to use my name or anything."

"No, I won't," Christine promised. "I thought you could help me understand what was happening with Gary and why someone would want to kill him."

"I don't know!" Heather almost yelled, her voice breaking. She began to cry. Christine searched in her handbag and finally found a crumpled tissue. She handed it to Heather, who blew her nose. "It's so awful!"

"I know," Christine spoke soothingly. She wasn't at all sure the emotional teenager could help her.

"My mom said awful things about him," Heather cried. "She said she was glad he was dead." She looked up at Christine, tears streaming down her cheeks. "How could she say that?"

Christine's heart was moved by the distraught girl, but she let her go on.

"I can't believe he's dead," Heather sobbed. "He was the only good thing in my life!"

Christine remembered her own desolation and anger. "I know you don't think so now, but it gets easier. I lost my sister when I was about your age in somewhat similar circumstances."

"I don't think it'll ever get better," Heather cried, hiccuping as her tears subsided.

"You know what made it easier for me?" Christine asked.

"What?"

"I helped them find her killer."

Heather dried her eyes with the tissue. "I know that Jesus said we should forgive our enemies, but it's really hard."

"Tell me what you know about his last few days," Christine prompted, trying to ignore the girl's last remark.

"Gary and I were spending a lot of time together, not alone, but with friends," Heather stated. "He didn't believe that we should spend too much time without chaperons. He said it was too tempting—that we might do something we'd regret."

"He sounds like a very wise young man," Christine interjected.

"He was," Heather recalled fondly. "Gary was so good. He taught me to look at things in a new way. At home, right and wrong are relative, but Gary showed me that God has a constant standard for us."

"So you and Gary spent a lot of time with his friends," Christine steered the conversation back. "Was he being harassed by anyone?"

"No, no one except my mother," Heather grimaced. "She was always making some nasty remark to him, but he always treated her respectfully. He did hate coming to the house though."

"Because of your mother?"

"Her," Heather explained, "plus all of her New Age stuff. He said he could actually sense demons hanging from the ceiling at our place."

The teenager jumped up and began to pace nervously around the room, then she burst out:

"I hate it there! It's . . . *dark*, and I hate her friends, especially Libby."

"Who's Libby?" Christine asked.

"Dr. Brinkman," Heather spat. "She runs that abortion clinic they were talking about this morning."

"Why do you hate Dr. Brinkman?"

Heather chewed on her lower lip, a trapped look in her eyes. She looked down at her shoes and mumbled, "I just do, that's all."

"Is it because of her clinic?" Christine offered.

Abruptly, Heather snatched up her purse and edged toward the door.

"I've really got to go," she hedged. "You won't tell my mom I talked to you, will you?"

Christine tried to calm the girl's fears, hoping she would continue.

"No, of course not," she assured Heather. "Our conversation is strictly confidential. You can trust me."

"Thanks," Heather said, looking relieved. "Bye." The girl turned and practically fled.

Christine leaned back in her chair and stared at the empty doorway. This was an interesting avenue to explore. Heather looked terrified when she mentioned Dr. Brinkman. And it certainly sounded as if Gary was not a favorite with Star White, although if he had been filling Heather's head full of nonsense about demons, she could understand the mother's animosity. Christine made a mental note to drop in on Star White.

CHAPTER
6

Christine leaned back in the chaise lounge by the swimming pool in Molly's backyard, her eyes heavy as she relaxed. The morning service had left her feeling on edge. Disturbing questions burbled to the surface of her mind as she examined her views on the ultimate questions of life and afterlife, things she'd not thought about in a long time. *Could there really be a God? Could I have been wrong all this time?* The answer always seemed to be sucked away just as she reached out to grasp it, like the filter humming in the background as it skimmed along the bottom of the pool.

The distant clatter of Sunday dishes drifted out of the kitchen with the comfortable sound of familiarity. She had offered to help clean up, but Pat and Molly insisted that she should pretend she was a tourist. She'd never had anyone take care of her the way they did, always solicitous of her well-being. Exhausted with the age-old theological struggle, she finally dozed off.

When Christine awoke, she found John sitting in the chair across from her, a strangely soft look on his face as he watched her sleep.

"Hi, sleepyhead," he smiled.

"Hi, yourself," she yawned tiredly. "I can't believe I dropped off to sleep."

"Sunday afternoons are made for naps," he said, stretching and yawning.

Christine sat up and ran her fingers through her thick dark hair, a little embarrassed to be caught in such a vulnerable position.

"I hardly ever take naps," she said, rubbing her drowsy hazel eyes. "They usually make me cranky." John just grinned.

"What are you smiling about?"

"Nothing," he laughed. He reached out his hand as she struggled to her feet. "Pat's making ice cream sodas. You want one?"

"Sure," she said a little more graciously.

They walked into the kitchen together where Molly and Pat were discussing the prayer vigil at Changes Plus.

"What about Pastor Cole?" Pat asked. "Has he changed his mind?"

"No," Molly lamented. "He has too many liberals pressuring him to not take a stand. Privately, he's with us, but he has a lot of pro-abortion people at his church."

Pat set a chilled root beer float down in front of her brother. "How about you, Christine?" Pat asked. "Can you join us?"

Christine felt that old familiar gnawing in her stomach. She tried to remember where she'd left her Tums, when she realized that she hadn't taken one in days. She had felt fine until today.

"I'm afraid not," Christine declined.

"Why not?" John asked, skimming the root beer foam off the top of his soda.

"I just believe it's a woman's choice to decide what's best for her," she said defensively.

Christine braced for the condemnation from the three family members, but all she saw was disappointment mixed with compassion.

"Are you willing to consider another viewpoint?" Molly asked, slowly wiping up a spill with a blue-striped kitchen towel.

"Molly, I know you look at things differently because you're a Christian," Christine said, "but I don't believe a fetus is a human being."

John and Pat just looked at one another, allowing their mother to take the lead as they concentrated on drinking their sodas.

"You're a journalist, Christine," Molly continued. "Isn't a journalist supposed to first gather all the facts before writing a story?"

"Of course," Christine relented, "but in this case the facts are colored by your belief system which considers abortion to be wrong." Christine squirmed on her chair, wishing she'd never started this conversation.

"Have you made a study of fetal development?" Molly pushed.

Christine started guiltily. Since her own abortion, she'd never had the desire to look at any pictures.

"No," Christine answered, "but I remember enough from high school biology. A fetus is just a piece of tissue."

"Would you be willing to look at some material I have and try to keep an open mind?" Molly's gentleness was hard to attack. Her appeal to Christine's fairness as a journalist was an effective weapon, and Christine finally capitulated.

"Yes," Christine said slowly, her heart thumping uncomfortably. Molly left the kitchen, and none of them spoke. It was as if John, Pat, and Christine held their breath.

Molly brought back a color brochure and laid it down in front of Christine. Clutching the counter, Christine felt faint as she looked at the picture of a ten-week fetus. It was a baby! It had fingers and toes and a tiny little face. Her chest felt as if it would explode, and suddenly she was sobbing. Molly motioned for John and Pat to leave, and she took Christine in her arms and slowly rocked her back and forth.

"I didn't know," Christine cried. "I didn't know."

"I know you didn't, dear," Molly said soothingly. "How far along were you when you had it done?"

Christine's walls collapsed in Molly's motherly embrace. The scene of her own abortion played through her mind; she vividly remembered the pain and emptiness.

"Four months," Christine sobbed. "I didn't know it was a baby. They didn't tell me it was a baby."

"They never do," Molly said, stroking Christine's back. "They take your money and get rid of the problem, quickly and efficiently."

Christine pulled away from Molly, who handed her a tissue. She blew her nose and looked down guiltily, as in her mind, she was reliving the whole thing. It was ten years ago, but it was just as if it were yesterday.

"I was engaged during my senior year in college," Christine explained, "but when I got pregnant, Randy decided he didn't want to be tied down and split for California. A girlfriend drove me to an abortion clinic and back home that night. She was the only one who knew. There was no one I could talk to. I was so weak, I barely made it through finals."

"Did you ever tell your mother?" Molly asked gently.

"No," Christine sniffed. "I didn't want her to know. I was . . . ashamed." She reached for another tissue. "Sometimes, I still wonder if it were a boy or a girl, you know, and what it would look like." Her tears fell into her empty lap.

"Christine, you can't bring your baby back," Molly said tenderly, "but you can accept God's forgiveness and healing. That's the only thing that will give you peace. You've taken a big step in recognizing that what you did was wrong."

"How can God forgive me, when I can't forgive myself?"

Christine felt as if her heart were being torn from her chest, as the tears which she had suppressed for so long continued to pour out.

Finally, Christine allowed Molly to pray with her, but she still could not ask Jesus to come into her life. It was still too threatening. But she would attend the prayer vigil and cover the story objectively. It was the best she could do.

Inside Immanuel Faith Chapel, Kerestel raised his arm to quiet the buzzing throng of angels.

"I have just come from the throne room of heaven," Kerestel beamed addressing the crowd. "The groundwork has been laid for a full frontal assault on the territory of Zethar-Zebah." A cheer rose from the assembly. "Because of the integrity of this body of believers, we have been empowered to engage the enemy. Tomorrow, these beloved saints will take a stand assembled across the street from Changes Plus—in front of God and in front of man—as they silently pray for the women and children who are the victims of abortion. They will be a mighty fortress."

Monchi, an eager young angel, raised his hand from the center of the crowd. "Sir, what makes this time different? I mean, we were always told before not to engage the enemy."

"Good question, son," Kerestel smiled. "The saints' methods here are in line with God's command in His word. He has said, 'But the wisdom that comes from heaven is first of all pure; then peace-loving, considerate, submissive, full of mercy and good fruit, impartial and sincere. Peacemakers who sow in peace raise a harvest of righteousness.' As it says in Proverbs, 'If anyone turns a deaf ear to the law, even his prayers are detestable.' The saints here will remain within the confines of God's law and man's law."

"I do not understand, Commander," Monchi puzzled. "The others were believers also."

"Yes, but they were disobedient to man's law," Kerestel explained. "In this world now, it is within the law to commit the heinous act of abortion, and against the law to try and steal this right from another. Until such time as this law is overturned, we must work within it. Thank God for His grace and mercy. It is by His law of love that hearts will be changed. As it is written, 'The fervent prayers of a righteous man availeth much!' "

Kerestel looked at Monchi, "Does that answer your question?"

Monchi nodded affirmatively, and Kerestel continued. "Then if we have no further questions, let me apprise you of the battle plan. Guardians, guarding your charges is your first priority. Engage the enemy only in defense. Warriors, you are to remain cloaked until my signal, at which time we will surround the saints and dispense with anything that dares to cross us.

"Zethar-Zebah knows of the impending assault of the faithful and will be prepared for the onslaught. I'm sure he's not overlooked any possible weak point in our defense. Be alert! Quench-Bersha will send the Prince of Tumult, Rezin-Rohgah, into the crowd with his demons of strife, anger, judgment, scorn and division to try and break our ranks. We must render them impotent. They must not propagate their seed among the faithful."

"Another thing," Kerestel warned. "It has come to our attention that the female Yoko-Sharuhen is working her evil through Changes Plus. She owns Star White and Elizabeth Brinkman. These two women, if present, have guardian demons; stay clear of them.

"Now, let God arise, and His enemies be scattered," Kerestel enjoined. "To your posts!"

✛✛✛✛✛

Monday morning dawned clear and sunny, the air charged with new birth. *How ironic,* Christine thought, as she parked her car in the lot next to Changes Plus. *Everything outside this building is coming alive, and inside, everything is dying.* Christine shut down her emotions and shifted into her reporter's mode. Shoving her recorder and her notepad into her bag, she got out of the car and headed for the double glass front doors of the clinic. Inside the waiting room, soft New Age music played soothingly in the background, and huge pillow-back chairs welcomed the clients. One entire wall was a bookcase filled with women's magazines.

She approached the receptionist, who smiled and greeted her warmly, "Good morning, do you have an appointment?"

"No, I would like to see your director, please," Christine asserted, showing her press pass.

"One moment," the receptionist said, rising from behind her desk. "I'll check and see if she's available."

Christine sat down next to a scared looking young man.

Obviously waiting for his girlfriend, she thought. *He has a lot more guts than Randy had.*

"Miss," the receptionist's voice returned her to the present. "Dr. Brinkman will see you now. Please follow me."

Christine was led down a short hallway to an enormous office tastefully decorated in Southwestern style, with expensive Native American art throughout. A painting of Cathedral Rock hung behind her desk.

Dr. Brinkman rose to extend her hand, which Christine took in hers, noticing that it was cold. She also noticed that as Dr. Brinkman spared no expense on her office, she spared no expense on her wardrobe. The woman's rust-colored ultra-suede suit brought out the highlights in her auburn hair. The gold and turquoise necklace must have cost as much as Christine's trip to Sedona. But it was her ring that caught Christine's attention—a gold coiled rattlesnake, with emerald eyes, and a forked ruby tongue.

"What brings you to Sedona, Miss McKay?" she gestured toward a wing-backed chair.

"The sunshine," Christine quipped, breaking the ice. "It's so lovely here."

"Vacationing, then?" the doctor probed. "Sightseeing in an abortion clinic?"

"Actually, I'm doing research for a series of articles on abortion in the '90s," Christine said, taking out her recorder. "I was hoping you could answer some questions for me. You don't mind if I use this for my note taking?"

Uncomfortable, Dr. Brinkman said, "What could I possibly help you with?"

"First of all, I'm intrigued by the name of your clinic. Maybe you can start there." Christine clicked on the recorder and waited for Dr. Brinkman to either answer or ask her to leave.

Dr. Brinkman sat back in her chair. The two women stared at each other and finally Christine clicked off the recorder.

"Look, Doctor," Christine stated, hoping she sounded believable. "I'm pro-choice. You have nothing to fear from me. All I want is some information on procedure, statistics, philosophy, and how the industry has changed in the past ten years."

The doctor visibly relaxed. "Fine."

Christine turned the recorder back on and repeated her request. "May I tape our conversation, Dr. Brinkman?"

"Yes, of course, Miss McKay. Now you asked about the name of our clinic? Changes Plus is one of a national chain of exclusive clinics. We are a full-service women's clinic, which offers more than the simple solution of abortion. We offer our clients post-abortion counseling, self-esteem workshops, self-actualization classes, and we even have an aerobics class that meets three times a week. Our clients are not simply pregnant children off the street, rather we cater to public and professional women who desire a greater degree of privacy."

"But what does the name Changes Plus mean?" Christine inquired again.

"The change is not merely the removal of an unplanned pregnancy, but we attempt to enrich the total life and health of our clients," Dr. Brinkman smiled. "That's Changes . . . Plus."

"Interesting," Christine said. "So your philosophy is that abortion can actually enhance a woman's life?"

"In that a woman is able to control her own destiny," Dr. Brinkman answered evenly. "Yes, I do believe some women's lives are enriched through an abortion."

"I see," Christine continued cautiously. "So it is in your attempt to enrich a woman's life that you would do second trimester abortions?"

"And third," Dr. Brinkman answered proudly. "A woman must be able to make a choice without the emotional blackmail of a time limit set by a male-dominated society."

"Have you ever done an abortion on a viable fetus?" Christine asked pointedly.

"It all depends on what you consider to be viable," Dr. Brinkman answered. "A woman has the power to decide whether or not to end her pregnancy at any time. It's her choice."

"Then you're saying if she aborts, the fetus is not viable, and if she carries to full term, it is viable."

"That's not the question. The question is whether a woman has the right to control her own destiny." Dr. Brinkman checked her watch.

"And to control her own destiny then she must be able to control her own body at any cost?"

"Let's talk about the cost of unwanted children," Dr. Brinkman pontificated. "Not only emotionally, but financially, these children are a drain on the woman and on society. Children who are unwanted are often battered and abandoned." The doctor's voice hardened. "It's better that they were never born."

"May I sight your statistical source for that information?" Christine asked.

"I'm the source," Dr. Brinkman looked away. "I was one of those children who shouldn't have been born, and I am making sure that no other child has to go through the hell that I did."

Christine was stunned at the doctor's candor. "Then you also must see yourself as a champion for the children."

"In a way, but my main concern is for the woman who finds herself in crisis."

"May I share your personal story?" Christine asked.

"I'd prefer you not," she answered, looking at her watch again.

"Would you mind giving me a tour of the clinic?" Christine inquired.

"I have to leave for an appointment, but I'm sure my nurse, Katona Whitefeather, would be happy to show you around." Dr. Brinkman picked up the phone. "Tracy, would you send Katona into my office, please?"

The door opened, and in walked a tall, model-thin woman in her early thirties, her jet black hair plaited in one long braid down her back. She wore a crisp white lab coat, and a pink stethoscope hung around her neck.

"Yes, Libby?" Katona addressed Dr. Brinkman informally.

"Katona, this is Christine McKay from the *St. Louis Sentinel*. Could you conduct her on a tour of our facility? I have an appointment, or I would do it myself."

"I would be happy to," Katona smiled at Christine as she shook her hand. "Right this way."

The tour was perfunctory at best, but Christine had expected as much. She was shown empty examining rooms, peeked in on an aerobics class, and watched as adult women were "self-actualized." She could hardly believe her eyes. They sat on big, fluffy pillows on the floor, repeating positive slogans led by none other than the librarian she had met.

They swayed as they intoned, "I am happy, healthy, and free. I am in control of me; the master of my destiny."

"Katona," a frightened Tracy met them as they left the classroom. "There's a crowd gathering across the street. I think it's a bunch of pro-lifers. Shall I call the police?"

"Definitely." Katona raised an eyebrow as she turned to Christine. "These Christians are all alike—a bunch of hypocrites. All noble when there's a cause. They stand out front and picket us, but where do they come when their daughters are in trouble?

Changes Plus. Would you like to wait in my office while I see what's happening?"

"Of course, but first I need to use the restroom," Christine said, hoping for some time to really look around.

"Down that hall, to the left and it's the first door on your right. My office is the first one to the left of the elevator."

Katona and Tracy raced down the hall, as Christine headed for the elevator. Looking both ways to see if anyone was watching her, she pushed the up button, and the doors immediately opened. She nervously hummed to herself, hoping no one would be around when the elevator reached the second floor.

I can always tell them I thought Katona's office was the first one on the left upstairs, Christine told herself.

She cautiously peered out of the elevator into an empty hallway, then stepped quickly to the first door, shoving it open. It was an empty surgical suite, clean and spotless, just like the examining room she had already been shown. The second door was just a supply closet.

Then she noticed at the end of the corridor a set of double doors wide enough for a gurney, its glass windows curtained. A medical file hung in the plexiglass pocket on the wall next to a fire extinguisher. Quickly, she opened the folder and scanned the contents: medical tests, results, doctor's notes, and a final phrase that shook Christine. The girl was twenty-eight weeks pregnant.

As she closed the file, from beyond the doors she heard the sound of metal hitting tile as if someone had dropped a heavy surgical instrument. Then she heard a baby's cry. Her throat tightened as she placed the file back in its holder. Instantly the crying stopped. The silence was deafening. Suddenly, Christine was pushed against the wall as the door opened and a masked woman carried out a black trash bag.

Christine felt her stomach lurch, and she ran for the lighted exit of the stairway. Without stopping to explain, she dashed past

Katona and Tracy and burst through the front doors of the clinic. Tears blinding her, she fought her way through an angry crowd which shouted obscenities and blasphemies at the pro-life group across the street. Seeing Molly's familiar face, Christine charged through the traffic and collapsed into her friend's comforting embrace.

"They killed . . . they killed . . . ," Christine stuttered as she sobbed and wiped her eyes with the back of her hands. "They killed a baby."

"Sh-h-h-h," Molly rubbed her back, as Christine continued to weep inconsolably. "Honey, they kill babies every day. That's what they do."

"But I heard it cry first!" Christine stared into Molly's astonished face. "It was born alive!"

"Oh, no!" Molly sank to her knees, taking Christine with her. Suddenly, they were surrounded by concerned friends, asking questions.

Pastor Mike knelt down by Molly. "Are you all right?" Molly shook her head no. Sirens wailed in the distance, as Jabez, the demon of sorrow, launched himself toward her. Swiftly, her guardian Jeremio pinned him to the sidewalk, and Molly rose to her feet assisted by Pastor Mike. John pushed through the crowd and tenderly lifted Christine. Still weeping, she clung to him and buried her face in his chest.

The gentle pastor encircled the three of them with his arms as Molly helped Christine tell him of what had just occurred inside the clinic. Pastor Mike covered his face and wept with them. Around them, the believers began to pray, and the pastor beseeched heaven, "Father God, it says in Psalm 72 (NIV): 'For he will deliver the needy who cry out, the afflicted who have no one to help. He will take pity on the weak and the needy, and save the needy from death. He will rescue them from oppression and violence for precious is their blood in his sight.' Almighty Father, receive into your hands this your unnamed child, who was killed because of his mother's right to choose death for him.

Lord, we ask forgiveness for this woman. Forgive her sin and send your Holy Spirit to convict her so that she might choose life for herself and for her future children. We ask this in Jesus' name, Amen."

Christine could hardly believe her ears. Instead of condemning this woman to hell, this man was asking his God to forgive her and save her, as if she hadn't done anything at all. Every face she saw was lifted to heaven, lips moving in silent prayer. Arms were raised all around her, as people joyously praised God for His mercy.

Looking across the street, Christine saw clenched fists raised in anger, as loud hateful insults were hurled in her direction. A rock flew past her ear, hitting Pastor Mike on the cheek. He dropped one hand to his face and continued to pray as blood trickled through his fingers. Christine's soul cried out.

He's such a gentle man. Why do they have to shed his blood? He didn't do anything wrong.

Seeing his first opportunity, Miklos pricked her heart with the tip of his sword, but not deeply enough, for as Christine remembered another gentle man, Jesus, the hatred for the angry mob welled up and covered over the healing wound.

The demon throng merged with the heckling crowd as Zethar-Zebah commanded his forces to attack. The mob surged forward urged on by their unseen demon cohorts, who cackled and pushed them to further violence.

Impatient for the battle, the demons rose from the crowd and rushed ahead to attack the seemingly unprotected believers. Zethar-Zebah stood, eyes bulging, as his first line of assault melted in the light of a thousand angels as they uncloaked with swords drawn. Screeching to a halt, the second division of cowering devils turned tail and dove through the wall of people behind them, who then suddenly lost their urge to fight. The police arrived as the crowd dispersed, scattering down the side streets.

A uniformed police officer got out of his car and approached Pastor Mike, "What seems to be the problem here?"

"No problem, officer," he said, wiping the blood from his face. "Just a difference of opinion, that's all. My people and I only met here to pray, and a crowd across the street started throwing rocks."

"Did any of your people cross the street?" the policeman asked, removing his sunglasses.

"No, sir, we didn't even talk to them. We just stood here in silence and prayed."

"Well, we got a complaint that you were interfering with the operation of this clinic and were harassing their clients."

Pastor Mike held his tongue in check. "No sir, we weren't interested in harassing anyone or interfering in any way. We simply met here to *pray—silently.* How could we interfere when we didn't even cross the street?"

"I'm just telling you why we were called," the officer explained, replacing his sunglasses. "I think it's time you broke this up and moved on."

"I think you're right," Pastor Mike said. "We're finished here." He turned to the crowd of believers. "It's time to go home now. Thank you for coming out and supporting us today. More has happened than we could even imagine. God will prevail."

The believers parted as the policeman returned to his squad car. "Darn religious fanatics," he said, shaking his head.

✝✝✝✝✝

Christine removed the last page from her typewriter, editing as she read. *I never thought I'd ever write a story with this slant.* She rose and thumbed through the phone directory for the nearest office supply with fax services to send the pages to Jack. Quickly, she penned a note.

"I know this is not what you expected—me neither. Call you when I can. Christine."

She jotted down the fax number she needed, grabbed her keys, and raced out the motel door, with Miklos and his company in tow.

CHAPTER
7

Christine held her breath as she watched John make the final approach into San Diego, skimming low over the pink and white stucco houses. She gasped as he nearly missed the parking garage on the left before his front wheels touched the tarmac.

"I can't believe they let them build that garage on the flight path," John muttered. As he parked the plane and shut down the engine, he turned to Pat and said, "Why don't you two go and pick up the car? I'll meet you out front with the luggage."

"Sounds good to me," Pat answered, ducking beneath the wing. "Come on, Christine, before he changes his mind and makes us carry our own suitcases."

Christine chuckled. "It's a deal." She was conscious of John's strong hand on her elbow as she stepped down from the plane. Looking up to thank him, she caught him sticking out his tongue at Pat's back. He colored as he realized he'd been caught.

"Don't tell on me, okay?" he winked.

"I'm not a tattletale," Christine smiled. "But I do take bribes."

"I'll give you a surprise at the art show."

Pat turned to ask Christine if she was hungry yet, only to realize she was alone. Looking back toward the plane, her heart warmed as she spied their exchange. *If only*, she thought. *They look so cute together. Father-God, soften Christine's heart so she can hear the truth and accept your Son, Jesus, as Lord and Savior.*

"Christine!" she yelled over the noise of an incoming jet.

"I'm coming," Christine sprinted across the tarmac. "Good thing I wore my running shoes!" she declared as she reached Pat.

As they stood at the car rental counter, they discussed lunch plans.

"We could eat at the hotel, or if you can wait, there's a great place in Seaport Village," Pat suggested.

"I'm dying for fresh seafood," Christine answered dreamily. "I love shrimp scampi."

"Seaport Village it is."

After checking in at the Marriott, it was a quick drive to the village, a quaint shopping area on the San Diego Harbor. John had opted to attend the opening luncheon for the art show participants at the hotel, leaving Pat and Christine to explore on their own. As they walked off their lunch, they strolled by a large bookstore and coffee shop.

"They have the best cappuccino cheese cake," Pat gushed. "You've got to try it."

Christine patted her stomach. "I don't know if I've got room, but I'll split a piece."

"You won't regret it," Pat said, weaving her way to the counter. "Coffee?"

"Sure, why not," Christine answered. "No sugar." She decided she might as well peruse the bookshelves while Pat ordered. "I'm just going to look around."

"Fine," Pat stated. "I'll find us a table."

Christine wandered past cookbooks, paperbacks and plays and every cartoon book ever written. *This is such a neat place!* she thought. Then her eyes fell on the sign that marked the shelf directly ahead.

Zaham, a most foul spirit, hovered over the section of books boldly marked *OCCULT*. He glared at Christine with huge, golden eyes, tipping his hoary head from side to side in question.

"What could a human who has such a big contingent of angels want with any of these volumes?" he puzzled as he surveyed Miklos and the others in attendance.

Miklos eyed the nasty demon, adjusting his girth so that his sword was clearly visible. He had nothing to fear from this tempter, whose main task was to ensnare the innocent minds of the searching by drawing them to this God-forsaken shelf of deadly books.

Christine was safe, for Zaham had nothing to offer her. She had already discovered the lies of the occult long ago. *Now,* thought Miklos, *if we can just get her to seek the truth again. She is so close.*

She meandered to the next shelf which was marked *RELIGIONS.* Slowly, she ran her index finger across titles until it came to rest on a huge volume.

"Alright!" she exclaimed, reading the title aloud. "*The Great Gods of Our Father's Fathers: The Myths and Legends of Early Civilizations* by Uges Curry, Ph.D." Then she looked at the price: $59.95. And it was discounted! "Not so alright," she muttered. Undecided about whether to shell out the money, she carried the book to the table.

"What'd you find?" Pat said, reaching for the huge volume. "Yuck!" She handed it back without even opening it.

"Research," Christine said nonchalantly. "But I'd better read fast." She pointed out the price tag.

"Whoa, trash is getting expensive," Pat declared wryly.

"It's not trash. Dr. Curry is considered one of the foremost authorities in his field."

"Let him stay in his field," Pat remarked as she cut the cheesecake in half. "If you really need it, I'll buy it."

Christine thumbed through the index, looking for references to sacrificial rites. There were several.

"It would be nice to have, but they may have something better at the exhibit in the Museum of Man at Balboa Park. Surely, they have something cheaper." She took a bite of cheesecake as she read the back cover. "Hey, it says here he's in the Archaeology Department at San Diego State."

"Why don't you call and find out if the good doctor is in?"

As the women called Dr. Curry and made their plans, the four angels, Miklos, Pesach, Wardar, and Pat's guardian, Yoel, flanked the table facing outward. The territorial spirits closed in, hissing and muttering their displeasure.

"What are you doing here?" Zaham challenged boldly, backed now by his cohorts. "Out . . . out . . . get out. You're not wanted here. Out . . . out . . . out." The demons buzzed like nasty gnats.

The angels chuckled and drew their swords. The demons quickly backed up, giving them a wide berth as Pat and Christine rose to leave.

"Let me just put old Uges back on the shelf," Christine quipped. As she slipped it back into the proper place, Zaham knocked the other books over and pinched her finger. "Ouch!" she said, sucking on her injured digit, as Zaham cackled mischievously.

But the demon's cackling turned to screeching as Miklos flicked off an ear with the tip of his sword. "Cackle now, you foul spirit."

✝✝✝✝✝

As Pat circled the top floor of the covered parking lot for the third time, a van finally backed out, and quickly Pat nabbed the empty space.

"Don't forget to lock your door," Pat cautioned. Walking across the footbridge, Christine wished she'd brought a sweater to ward off the brisk ocean breezes.

As they walked across the center of the campus, they heard the sound of tinkling bells. A young man was selling rainbow makers—crystals on strings to hang in sunny windows. Pat shook her head as they passed a female student handing out New Age literature.

"Save the trees," the girl called, waving a leaflet at them.

"Yeah, right," Christine answered. "What about the trees that died for that trash?"

Pat poked her in the ribs and pulled her along. "You're terrible," she said snickering.

The angels weren't quite as amused. They surrounded the two women with swords at the ready as they climbed the steps to the building that housed Dr. Curry's office.

"Look," Christine said, pointing at a placard. "Dr. Curry is giving a lecture at 3:00. What time is it?"

"2:40," Pat answered, checking her watch. "We've barely got time to catch him."

Christine already had her notepad open as they walked down the tiled hallway. They passed the lecture room which was already filling with students and other academicians.

As they stopped in front of Dr. Curry's office door, Pat leaned forward and whispered, "If I begin to snore, just punch me. These long-winded egotistical geeks bore me to tears."

"Sh," Christine hushed her as the door opened and a handsomely tanned man of obvious Scandanavian descent greeted them.

"Can I help you?"

"Dr. Curry?" Christine stammered. "Dr. Uges Curry?"

"I am," he smiled, "and you are?"

"We just spoke on the phone. I'm Christine McKay."

"Miss McKay! Please come in," he said, gallantly stepping aside. "I'm sorry I only have about fifteen minutes to give you right now."

"That should be enough," Christine smiled. "This is my friend Pat Fisher."

"Please sit down," he indicated the two oxblood leather chairs opposite his ornately carved desk. "Just let me move those magazines for you."

Pat gasped as she noticed the carving standing on one corner of his desk. It was a stone statue covered with snakes and a skull necklace.

"Coatlicue!" Christine said, leaning over to admire it. "That's the same statue I saw in a picture at the library in Sedona."

"How could anyone worship something that looks so hideous?" Pat asked incredulously.

"Ladies," Dr. Curry intoned, "you are looking at the Aztec version of Mother Earth, Coatlicue. This is a replica of the statue that was unearthed in 1824 from beneath the Zocalo in Mexico City. It had lain under the square in front of the cathedral since the destruction of Tenochtitlan, the Aztec capital, by Cortes and his men."

"It's gross!" Pat shivered.

Dr. Curry picked up the little stone statue and lovingly caressed it as he pointed out its intricacies to them.

"See here," he said, "what appears to be her head is actually formed by the facing heads of two rattlesnakes. Notice that her skirt is also made of writhing braided rattlesnakes. Isn't it magnificent?"

"What's that around her neck?" Christine asked.

"It's a necklace," he explained. "It's made of alternating hearts and hands. The skull pendant is actually a bowl into which the sacrificial hearts were thrown after being cut from their living victim."

Pat groaned and turned away from the terrible image. Dr. Curry laughed.

"The Aztecs would not have found this sculpture to be horrifying, Miss Fisher," he said, setting it back in its place of honor. "To them, it was a powerful reminder of the forces of Mother Earth to whom they owed their sustenance."

"You said what *appears* to be her head," Christine observed.

"That's right," he went on. "Actually, she has been beheaded, symbolizing the manner in which her offerings were sacrificed." Dr. Curry sat on the edge of his desk and smiled down at them. "The virgin offering never realized that she was the sacrifice until she was lifted high overhead by one of the priests. He then flung her over his back and her head was removed from her body. They danced in a circle with the bleeding victim as blood squirted in the four directions, blessing the priests, the women, and the maize, supposedly causing fertility of both land and people."

Wide-eyed, Christine quickly scribbled notes on her pad, noting that the "head" of Coatlicue was roughly the same as the drawing she had seen on the rock wall at Gary's murder site. What all had Sheriff Anderson left out of his report?

"Were men ever sacrificed to Coatlicue?"

"Absolutely not, Miss McKay," he chuckled. "It would have been considered a complete affront to masculinity to offer a man as a sacrifice to fertility. After all, they believed that all life proceeds from Mother Earth." He paused and thought a moment. "Of course, small children of both sexes were often sacrificed to other gods and goddesses of fertility, but I've never found any record of a man being sacrificed in such a way."

Christine continued her questioning. "Were men sacrificed in any way similar to crucifixion to *any* god or goddess?"

"The closest thing to crucifixion that I can think of is when they staked their victims out on the altar," he answered, "especially the young men, sacrificed to gods of war and in the sacrifice of New Fire."

"What's the sacrifice of New Fire?" Christine pressed.

Dr. Curry rose and crossed to a glass front cabinet which he unlocked. With great reverence, he picked up a wicked looking knife and brought it over for them to inspect.

"This is an actual Aztec sacrificial knife," he said with pride. "Observe the curvature of the blade. This was so that the victim's chest could be torn open and his still beating heart could be incised and removed almost in one action. Very efficient."

Pat blanched and grabbed her throat, but Dr. Curry was so enthused about his subject, he didn't even notice.

"Its purpose may have been gruesome, but just look at the fine detailing of the elaborate handle."

Christine touched the sharp edge of the blade with her index finger.

"Careful," he cautioned, just as she nicked her fingertip.

"Ouch," she said, sucking the tip of her finger. "What's it made of anyway?"

"The blade is made of chert, which is a coarse flint and, as you've just discovered, flaked to a razor sharp edge. It's exquisite." Dr. Curry stroked the layers of turquoise and fine shells that made up the handle of the instrument of death. He almost seemed to be hypnotized by the awful thing he held lovingly in his hands. His voice became animated.

"During the festival of The Tying Up of Years, which only occurred every fifty-two years, a male prisoner was stretched out and his heart was removed with this very knife. Then a turquoise plate was inserted into his chest cavity and a fire was kindled upon it. Before the festival, all fire in the entire city had been extinguished. So when this new fire was kindled in the young man's chest, it was the beginning of light all over the land for the next fifty-two years." Dr. Curry expounded excitedly. "He was the source of all light to the Aztec people."

Pat groaned and rubbed her forehead. "This is giving me a headache. I think I'll wait outside."

Christine nodded and turned sideways so Pat could leave.

Dr. Curry checked his watch and returned the knife to its resting place.

"Just one more question, Dr. Curry," Christine said. "Are there any Aztec groups still in existence?"

"Well, I suppose there could be descendants of Montezuma's three daughters who survived the massacre by Cortes," he answered noncommittally, "but they probably would have become Catholic converts and rejected their former religious practices."

Christine closed her notepad and stood, extending her hand. "Thanks, Dr. Curry. You've been most helpful."

He took her hand in his and instead of the expected shake, he lifted it to his lips, kissing her still stinging fingertip.

"It was my pleasure," he flirted. "It isn't often I find such a lovely woman interested in such deadly matters."

Christine withdrew her hand and quickly said goodbye. She thought she heard him chuckle as she retreated down the hall. Outside, she found Pat sitting on the steps.

"Are you alright?" Christine asked, placing a concerned hand on her shoulder.

"Fine, now that I'm out of there," she answered. "How could you listen to that stuff? That guy gave me the creeps."

"He sure wasn't your average professor, was he?"

"He may have looked like a Norse god, but looks aren't everything," Pat countered.

"You've got a point. He made a pass at me before I left." Christine chuckled. "He kissed my 'boo-boo.'"

"Yuck!"

"My sentiments exactly," Christine said, slinging her purse over her shoulder. "I wonder where the bookstore is."

They found a campus map and wound their way through the buildings to the SDSU bookstore. Wandering through the packed aisles, Christine finally found a selection of Dr. Curry's books.

Pat picked up a slim volume. Handing it to Christine, she asked, "How about this one?"

"*Blood Rites: Appeasing the Hunger of the Gods.* Ooh, this looks good," Christine mused, thumbing through the color plates. As she neared the back of the book, she froze. There, in brilliant detail was a picture of a man crucified upside down, chest open. Scanning the caption, she noticed the date: February

1941, Berlin, Germany. Continuing, she found other pictures dating as late as 1972, in which people and animals had been killed in a similar fashion. Fascinated, Christine looked at the $29.95 price tag.

"That, I will *not* buy!" Pat remarked, only half serious.

"It's not like I don't have a credit card," Christine smiled, trying to ease the tension. "I live on plastic. Pat, I'm investigating a murder story. I need anything that will help me understand what happened to Gary Knox."

"I agree," Pat acquiesced as Christine took out her Visa card. "Don't spend your money. Please, let me." Pat took the volume and marched to the cash register.

Back at the hotel, Christine thumbed through her newfound treasure while Pat attempted to nap away a nagging headache. There was a light knocking, and Christine quickly paced the distance to the door. Peering through the peephole, she saw John checking his watch. Quietly, she opened the door, with her finger to her lips.

"Sh, Pat's asleep."

"I just thought you'd like to see the display downstairs," he whispered.

"Just a second. Let me put my shoes on, and I'll jot a quick note to Pat in case she wakes up."

Downstairs, they entered the ballroom that had been transformed into a western art gallery. John painstakingly described every painting and sculpture before pointing out the pieces he had contributed. He watched her reaction as she stopped and stared at the painting that was central to his exhibit.

"How do you like your surprise?" he asked, studying her face.

Christine was stunned. In front of her was a stormy desert landscape with Cathedral Rock rising in the background. A dark storm cloud seemed to descend from the sky, and in the center of the painting sat an Indian maiden with Christine's face. The hair was darker, but John had painted Christine; there was no mistake. The maiden's face and hands were lifted skyward, illuminated by a shaft of light that cut through the menacing cloud. Slowly, Christine met John's eyes.

"I call it 'In the Eye of the Storm,'" John said proudly.

"It's beautiful." Christine didn't quite know what else to say. "But, when did you have time to paint it?"

"I started it the morning after our night in the desert," he explained. "Acrylics dry fast. I had the vision for it that night, and I wanted it for this show. I hope you don't mind."

"No, I'm honored," Christine said, swallowing the lump in her throat. No one had ever done anything that made Christine feel as special as she did at this moment.

"You should be," John teased. "Three people have offered me over $15,000 for it."

Christine's eyes flew open wide. "You've got to be kidding!"

"You don't think it's worth it?"

"I don't think *I'm* worth it," she said looking down, suddenly aware of his closeness.

"I do," John said softly, placing his finger under her chin and raising her face to meet his gaze. "To me, you're both priceless."

Time seemed to stand still as Christine lost herself in the warmth of his eyes. As if remembering something that was slightly unpleasant, John abruptly removed his hand from her face and turned to straighten the canvas.

"Well, I'd planned to take you both to dinner, but my sister may sleep through it," he joked.

"I need to change anyway." Christine was puzzled, not understanding the change in his attitude. Any other man would have pressed his advantage. "I'll wake her up, and we'll meet you in the lobby."

"Great, that'll give me time to take care of some business."

"Okay, meet you at six?"

"Sure," he answered, giving her a brief smile.

Christine noticed a sadness in his eyes. Perplexed, she headed across the elegant lobby.

"I wonder if I'll ever understand men," she muttered under her breath, stepping into the elevator.

"Probably not," answered an elderly woman in a flowered hat. "I never have."

Unlocking the door to their room, she noticed Pat's bed was empty and the bathroom door was slightly ajar. Her friend was ensconced in bubbles up to her chin, reading a magazine.

"John's taking us out to dinner," Christine said through the crack in the door.

"Why don't you two go ahead," Pat yawned. "I'd rather just eat in the room tonight."

"Are you sure?"

"Yeah, I rarely get a chance to just kick back on my own without Mom or John around," Pat continued. "I think tonight will be a 'pamper Pat' night."

"Well, enjoy yourself," Christine called out, slipping into a silk blouse and changing her shoes. "Do you want me to bring you anything?"

"Get him to take you to Cafe Eleven," Pat suggested. "It's a little country French cafe in the Hillcrest area. They have the *best* chocolate toffee cheesecake in the world."

"You and your cheesecake," Christine laughed, putting on her lipstick.

"Bring me back a piece," Pat yelled as she heard the door closing behind Christine.

John accepted Pat's recommendation, and as they pulled up in front of the little storefront cafe, Christine remarked on how quaint it looked from outside. Inside, the cafe was decorated in mauve, gray, and black, giving it an elegance beyond its size. As John made arrangements with the host for their table, she noticed the artwork on the walls.

"The paintings change every month," John explained, coming up behind her as she studied a modern floral watercolor.

"I love watercolors," she commented.

"I've never been able to express my ideas as clearly with watercolors as I can with the depth and brightness of oils and acrylics," he continued. "I've never been a pastel kind of guy."

Christine laughed. "No, I can see that."

As they were seated, John was handed the wine list. He declined. Christine noted this, and decided to say nothing.

The waiter removed the two pink crystal wine goblets, as he recited the specials for the day, which included a delicious sounding red snapper grilled in caper butter that enticed them both, but they decided to look over the menu anyway.

"If you want an appetizer, I suggest we either share a Brie en Croute or the Mushrooms a la Sherri," John advised, pointing out their descriptions on the menu. Reading them, Christine decided on the mushrooms. When the waiter returned, John ordered their appetizer and the snapper with salad for both of them.

Miklos and Aaro perched on the seats behind the couple as Pesach and Wardar stood nearby.

"I have some cause for concern about your Christine," Aaro turned to his companion.

"I know," replied Miklos. "She is growing fond of John, and I fear that she is not yet ready to make the choice that would enable their joining."

As the angels conversed, John and Christine were engaged in a similar conversation.

"But I don't understand," Christine was saying. "If you loved someone, what difference would it make if they went to church or not?"

"It says in the Bible that we shouldn't be 'unequally yoked,'" John said, searching for just the right words to make her understand. The tensing of his jaw betrayed his deep frustration at their situation. "I can't marry, or even become seriously involved with someone who doesn't accept Him."

"That's ridiculous," Christine said astounded, speaking in as reasonable a tone as she could manage. "There's no freedom in that kind of relationship. 'You've got to think like I think or I can't love you.' What kind of so-called Christianity is that?" *How did we get into this conversation anyway?*

"The kind of Christianity the Lord Himself endorses," John smiled, despite the misery he felt. "Look at it this way. Suppose someone of different beliefs, like you and me for instance, were to marry. You wouldn't understand my devotion to God first and to you second. God would be sort of like 'the other woman.' It might cause you to resent God *and* me. Or, I would be torn away from God to save my relationship with you."

"Either choice is impossible in your scenario," Christine retorted, conscious of her growing anger. This evening wasn't turning out at all like she expected. "Why can't there be a third choice? Live and let live."

"Live and let live only applies in platonic relationships," John tried to explain. "Chris, when two people are made one flesh in marriage, they have to be of the same Spirit too, or it will never work."

Christine was silent. Suddenly, she wasn't hungry anymore and pushed away her half-empty plate. The waiter chose just that moment to arrive with the dessert tray. Using the distraction to change the subject, Christine informed John of Pat's desire for a piece of chocolate toffee cheesecake.

"If there's cheesecake within eating distance, my sister will sniff it out," John chuckled affectionately. Christine softened. "Are you ready for dessert?"

"Not really," she answered, turning her face away from him. "I couldn't even finish all my fish."

John nodded sadly and told the waiter to box up a piece to go and returned his attention to Christine.

"I'm sorry if I upset you," John continued as the waiter left.

"I'm not upset," Christine lied. "I just don't agree with you."

"I'm sorry about that too," John sighed, folding his napkin carefully.

"I just don't think that kind of rigidity belongs in a marriage," she said, masking her churning emotions with a deceptive calmness.

John had no answer for her. Miklos looked downcast. Aaro placed a comforting arm around his brother's shoulder.

"Take heart, Miklos," Aaro soothed. "It is not finished. For everything there is a season."

✝✝✝✝✝

The flight home the next morning was a quiet one, and not even Pat's good humor could raise Christine's spirits. John and Pat teased one another, but something was different. It was as if a door had been closed, and Christine was sad.

Once back in Sedona, Christine tried to say goodbye quickly, saying she had to find another motel room.

"There's a quaint little motel near the airport," Pat suggested. "If you don't mind being way up here. Or better yet, why don't you just come home with us."

Christine glanced at John. He looked away uncomfortably. "I don't think that's a good idea right now," she smiled stiffly at Pat. "Thanks anyway."

Christine let Pat hug her goodbye before hurrying to the car she had left in the parking lot. Her composure was a fragile shell in danger of shattering, and Christine didn't want John to know how much she hurt. Gulping hard, she felt the burning tears spill over as she drove away.

It's not fair! she thought, slapping the steering wheel. *It's just not fair!* But then, nobody ever said it was.

CHAPTER
8

A tiny bell tinkled as Christine pushed open the glass door of the Crystal Unicorn, Star White's New Age bookstore. The sound of woodwinds echoed through the store from taped music, while shafts of rainbow-colored lights spilled over the bookshelves from hundreds of crystals of all sizes hanging in the windows. The cloying scent of sandalwood incense almost made her sick.

This is going to be fun, Christine thought, *if I can hold my breath long enough*. Fingering the one feathered earring Pat had loaned her, she mused, *I hope I look "New Age" enough*.

While the atmosphere was meant to deceive and soothe the customers, Miklos, Pesach, and Wardar had no such delusions. They unsheathed their swords as Christine stepped into the abode of hissing, slithering serpent-like demons coiled in every corner of the room.

Achish, the Serpent Charmer, dashed behind a ceiling beam and panted in fear at the intruder's arrival. Quietly, he summoned one of the serpent demons called Nahash.

"Quickly," he rasped, his long tongue flicking anxiously. "To the desert. Find Yoko-Sharuhen and our great chief Mibzar. Tell them that three guardians accompanied by the woman Christine have entered my bookstore."

"At your command." Nahash coiled and disappeared through the roof. The other serpents in the room slithered behind bookshelves, warily peeking out as the angels swept a path around Christine.

"May I help you?" Star, who had been restocking a section of herbal medicines, rose lithely and smiled.

"I hope so," Christine used her most disarming voice. "I'm looking for any books you might have on goddess worship."

"Any particular one?" Star inquired, leading her through the section on feminist literature and past metaphysical titles to a large variety of books on goddesses.

"I'm not sure," Christine feigned confusion. "I'm really new at this. What do you suggest?"

"Well," Star said, running her fingers over the titles, "if you want a good introduction, Senora Stone's *A Feminist View of Our Beginnings* is excellent." She handed Christine a slick covered paperback.

"Hm, it does look good," Christine smiled, pretending interest. "You know what really interests me are the Sedona vortexes. I had a *wonderful* out-of-body experience with a goddess while meditating at Cathedral Rock."

"How exciting!" Star gushed. "It was probably the Earth Mother; Cathedral Rock is a feminine vortex. What did she look like?"

"Beautiful!" Christine lied. "Long flowing hair, with a white gown. She had a snake wrapped around her waist: a black rattlesnake. But it didn't frighten me. She said her name, but I don't quite remember. It started with a C, Cora I think."

Star froze, and her eyes brightened. "Coatlicue?"

"Yes, that's it!" Christine snapped her fingers. "You've met her too?" *Bingo!* Christine could hardly suppress her glee.

"Many times," Star said, touching Christine's arm. "It's rare for her to appear to a novice though." Star seemed puzzled.

Miklos turned to Pesach. "I have yet to see this human's guardian demon."

As if on cue, Yoko-Sharuhen glided angrily through the crystal covered window. Waltzing by the angels like they were old friends, she drew next to Star and addressed them.

"I wasn't expecting such distinguished 'guests' today," Yoko-Sharuhen oozed. "Had I known you were coming, I would have laid out refreshments for you."

"Nothing you could offer would be 'refreshing,'" said Wardar coolly.

"How can you be so sure of something you've never tried?" Yoko flirted. "There are many definitions of heaven you know."

Wardar straightened. Pesach pointed his sword in her direction. "Silence! Your wiles are wasted on us."

She turned her attention to Miklos, who warily moved to better cover Christine. "What about you? Is there nothing you crave beyond what you know? Or is this human more to your liking?" She nodded in Christine's direction.

Miklos growled in anger as Pesach and Wardar restrained him from attacking her. Yoko-Sharuhen cackled in glee that she had found a weak point.

"What are you going to do, you fine, strong angel," she crooned, "when I have her staked out on a bed of sacrifice? Of what use will your love be then?"

"Enough," Pesach snapped at the taunting demon.

"Enough, indeed," she snarled. "I demand to know your purpose! What do you want in this place?"

"Our purpose is to protect this human," Pesach answered. "Nothing more."

"If you will not tell me, then I have other ways of discovering your treachery," she hissed. Wrapping her arms around Star White's body, she began to whisper insinuations into her ear.

Christine picked up another book and pretended to thumb through. "Do you have any books about Coatlicue?"

Star ignored her question as Yoko-Sharuhen dominated her thoughts. *She's lying. How could she know about me? You are my chosen vessel—no other.*

Christine watched the transformation of Star's face as the demon took control of her body. Star reached forward and snatched the book from her hand.

"Enough of your lies," Star snapped. "What do you really want?"

"Excuse me?" Christine was caught off guard.

"You're lying."

"I beg your pardon," Christine exclaimed, taking a step backward as Miklos and the others urged her to leave.

"You're not interested in goddess worship," Star pointed her finger at Christine. "You're a reporter. Your name is Christine McKay."

More surprised than frightened, Christine stood frozen as the maniacal laughter of a satisfied Yoko-Sharuhen emanated from the mouth of Star White. The woman was insane. Abruptly, Christine turned on her heel and strode to the door, the mocking laughter following her to the car. Pulling onto Highway 89A, she left West Sedona and headed downtown.

How did she know who I was? What did I do to tip her off?

Christine was puzzled. She certainly didn't believe in special powers; Star White was no psychic. Dr. Brinkman must have told her, she decided. Christine pulled into the parking lot of the Sheriff's Department and sat there a moment composing herself. Consulting her notes from Dr. Curry's lecture in San Diego, she formulated the questions she wanted to ask Sheriff Anderson. Finally, she opened her car door and headed up the concrete steps to the front door.

Seeing no one at the front desk, she passed by and found Sheriff Anderson in his usual position, chomping red licorice and reading the *Red Rock News*.

"Sheriff?" she called, poking her head into his office.

"Why, Miss McKay, our big city reporter," he drawled. "Wondered when you'd be showing your pretty face around here again."

Christine rolled her eyes and leaned against his doorjamb. "Can I sit down?"

"Sure," he said, standing and indicating the chair across from his desk. "What can I do for you? Wait, don't tell me." He closed his eyes and muttered, "Something about the Knox kid."

"Why didn't you tell me his body had been mutilated?"

The air from the Sheriff's padded chair whooshed as he collapsed into it in surprise. "How did you know about that?"

"So he *was* mutilated?"

"No comment," the Sheriff uttered quickly, realizing he'd just made a big mistake.

"Come on, Sheriff," Christine urged.

Sheriff Anderson covered his face with his hands and thought for a moment. Grimly, he looked up at her.

"Okay, I'll make a deal with you. You tell me what you know first, then I'll tell you what I know."

"I believe he was. . . ."

"Stop right there." The Sheriff raised his right hand like a traffic cop. "I said tell me what you know, not what you believe, or what you think, or what you perceive."

Christine stopped. *You wily fox.* She decided she'd go for the bluff and hope she was convincing.

"Gary Knox was beheaded, for one thing."

"Geez, Louise," he whispered to himself. *Bingo!*

"Not only that, his heart was missing."

"How the. . . . Where'd you get that information?" the Sheriff insisted, his expression clouding in anger.

"I'm right, aren't I, Sheriff?"

"I wanna know who told you," he bellowed.

"I have my sources," she said coolly. *Bull's-eye. Right on target!*

"Miss McKay, there's only two ways you could know what you've just told me," he glowered. "Either someone in my department leaked the information to you, or," he paused for effect, "you were there when it happened."

"Wait a minute, Sheriff," Christine defied him. "You told me you'd tell me what you know, if I told first. Now give."

Sheriff Anderson leaned back in his chair, his arms locked behind his head as he studied her for a long moment. Christine felt as if she were being measured for a coffin.

"If this winds up in the papers, I'll have your tail," he growled, leaning forward.

"No papers . . . not yet anyway," Christine agreed. A powerful relief filled her.

"Okay, I'm only going to say this once," he began, pointing his finger at her. "The Knox boy was found crucified upside down. We found his head on a pole, and his heart was missing. Nobody but the hikers who found him, me, the investigating team, and the coroner knows this." The Sheriff's face was pale, remembering the grisly scene. He leaned over the desk and whispered fiercely, "We didn't even tell his mama! Now who told you?"

"You did, Sheriff, just now," Christine smiled, slapping her hand on his desk.

"Why you little. . . ."

"I've been doing a little research on my own," Christine placated him. "I think I can help if you'll let me. I'm not your enemy, you know." The red-faced Sheriff was silent as he glared at her. "I think you may have some people who are attempting to mimic Aztec ritual sacrifice. But there's only one thing."

"What's that?"

"They're sacrificing men to a goddess of fertility to whom the Aztecs only sacrificed virgins."

"What do you mean?" the Sheriff asked, his interest piqued. "We only have one victim."

"In Sedona, yeah," she said, reaching into her bag and pulling out the folder of clippings that Jack had given her. She slid it across the desk and continued. "In addition to these, I just learned of a new sacrifice at the Temple of Delphi in Greece."

The Sheriff whistled. "Great Jumpin' Jehosophat!" he exclaimed, flipping through the file. "I'll say one thing for you, sugar, you sure do your homework."

"That's what they pay me for."

"Let me get this straight now. You're sayin' that people all over the world are killing other people like the Knox kid was killed. Why? What's the motive?"

"I think it's got something to do with the vortexes," Christine explained.

"Here in Sedona?" the Sheriff asked.

"Sheriff, these supposed vortexes are located all over the world," she went on, her features animated. "I believe someone took the Harmonic Convergence to heart and believes that blood sacrifice will bring on a New World Order and the return of Quetzalcoatl, the Aztec god of peace. The odd thing is," Christine speculated, "only men are being sacrificed, not women or children, not yet anyway. It doesn't jive."

"I don't get your point," Sheriff Anderson pushed.

"Remember this?" she asked, showing him the sketch she had drawn of the rattlesnake graffiti.

"Yeah, so?"

"It's the so-called face of the Aztec goddess Coatlicue," Christine explained with an air of self-confidence. "She's also known as Mother Earth and is one of the goddesses of fertility. Only young virgin girls were sacrificed to her—they were beheaded. That's another thing," Christine thought out loud. "I haven't quite made the 'crucifixion' connection."

"Sounds like a horror movie to me," Sheriff Anderson snorted in disbelief. "Somebody's been readin' too much of that Stephen King."

"I know that it sounds a little hard to believe," Christine agreed, but she was determined not to be dismissed. "You'd have to read everything that I've read and see everything that I've seen to understand it. There's no way that I can prove it to you yet." Christine reached for the file folder. "You'll just have to trust me."

"Up 'til now, I didn't have any reason not to trust you." Sheriff Anderson stood and peered out of his office window. "You just lied to get information out of me. I hope you're not just whistlin' Dixie now."

Christine raised her hand in a mock Boy Scout salute, "No more lies, Sheriff. We may need each other before this is all over."

For the first time since meeting him, Christine felt a respect for this hard-nosed old Sheriff. At least he had listened. Standing, she extended her hand.

"Friends?"

The Sheriff smiled cautiously, taking Christine's small hand. "Let's just say we aren't enemies. Keep in touch, and stay on 'vacation' for awhile. Deal?"

"It's a deal."

Christine left his office feeling positive about the meeting. At least they were on the same side now. As she approached her car, she noticed the door was ajar. "Forgot to lock it again," she muttered, mentally upbraiding herself. Jerking open the door, she gasped. A pool of drying blood covered the driver's seat, and in the middle was a coiled snake fetish. *Somebody wanted to make a point*, she observed, slamming the door shut.

"You still here?" Sheriff Anderson asked behind her. Startled, she jumped. "Little skittish, aren't you?"

"Somebody left a message in my car," Christine remarked dryly. "Care to read it?" She opened the door.

"Good Lord," he grimaced. "Go on in the station and have Maxie get you some towels." He reached in and picked up the fetish with the tip of his pencil. "Looks like the ones they sell in every gift shop in town. We'd never trace it. I'll take a sample of this blood and have the lab run it through."

It was another hour before Christine was able to leave the station. Hastily, she drove her freshly cleaned car back up the steep Airport Mesa mountain road to the motel to call Jack. *You're not going to believe this, Jack old buddy*, she thought dialing the phone.

"Where have you been?" Jack barked into the phone. "I called your motel, but you'd checked out."

"I took a little side trip to San Diego for some research," she answered, bristling at his tone of voice.

Jack groaned. "Great, that's all I need from you. More expenses."

"It didn't cost the paper a cent!" Christine's voice rose defensively. "What's the problem?"

Jack was silent for a moment. "I'm sorry, Chris. It's just that things have been a little crazy around here. You need to catch the first plane home."

"Jack! I can't leave now. We're really close to a break-through."

"It's not my decision. It's the new owners'."

"New owners!" Christine was stunned. "What new owners?"

"While you were jetting around, there was a hostile takeover by Jarrett Publications."

Christine whistled. "They're a national chain. What about the Reeds? Their family's owned the *Sentinel* for a hundred years."

"Gone," Jack said sadly. "They forced them out of their offices the next day."

Christine asked the next obvious question. "What about us?"

"I don't know yet," Jack sighed. "There's a big meeting scheduled for the editorial staff tomorrow morning. I guess we'll find out then. The rumor is that half the staff will be cut."

"Jack, no."

"I think we both better dust off our resumes," Jack made a half-hearted attempt at humor.

"I'll catch the next flight out of here." Christine had never heard Jack so down. "Hang in there, boss."

"Yeah, you too."

Hanging up the phone, Christine reached for her bag and drew out her return ticket before calling the Sedona Airport. She only had an hour to pack and turn in her car before catching the next plane.

Then she dialed the number to Pat's gallery, but it was busy. Reluctantly, she looked up Molly's number, hoping John didn't answer. She wasn't in the mood to deal with her feelings about him right now.

"Hello," Molly's cheerful voice answered.

"Hi, Molly, it's Christine."

"Hi, hon, what can I do for you?" Christine smiled at the endearment.

"I just called to say goodbye," Christine said quickly. "There's a big meeting tomorrow morning in St. Louis. I've got to be there."

"Anything wrong?" Molly could hear the tension in her voice.

"The paper's been sold, and none of us know if we have a job or not."

"Oh, Christine," Molly sympathized. "Well, you know you've always got a home here."

Christine felt tears well up in her eyes. Her own mother wouldn't have been as sympathetic. "Thanks, Molly. You're a real friend."

"Give me a call when you know what's happening," Molly urged. "I'll pray for you."

"Please tell Pat thank you for me, and I'll be in touch with her."

And John? Molly thought. But something stopped her from mentioning him. God would work that situation out.

"I'll do that. God bless you, honey."

"You too," Christine answered. "Bye."

Christine hastily threw her clothes into her soft-sided bags and gathered her notes, stuffing them into her briefcase, then snatched up her keys. Angrily slamming her suitcase into the trunk, she cursed Jarrett Publications under her breath. She barely had enough time to check out of the motel and return her key before takeoff. Racing to the ticket counter, she checked her bags and got her seat assignment as the flight was announced.

A brisk wind was blowing as she crossed the tarmac and climbed the portable staircase. Suddenly, she thought she heard someone call her name. She turned, and there was John, standing at the fence, waving his arms to get her attention. He cupped his hands and shouted at her, but she couldn't understand what he was saying over the noise of the engines. As the lady behind her pressed forward, Christine watched as John used exaggerated motions to get his point across.

First he pointed to his eye, then he folded his hands in front of his face. Next he held up four fingers, then pointed in her direction. Mentally, she added the symbols together. *I pray 4 you.* She smiled and waved, then ducked under the low door of the plane. Taking her seat, she pressed her face against the window and watched John become smaller and smaller as they taxied down the runway.

I pray 4 you. Those words had never been a comfort to her . . . until now. A warmth filled her heart at the thought of someone spending time praying to God on her behalf. But it wasn't just someone, it was John. John talking to God. John pleading for her safety. Maybe there was hope after all.

No, she sighed. He would expect her to accept his Jesus, his way. She just couldn't do it. The warmth turned to sadness as she leaned back and closed her eyes.

Miklos, too, bade goodbye to his friend Aaro. Only God knew when they would meet again. Pesach and Wardar rode on the wings with the rest of the guardian angels, who were holding up the plane.

"Peace," Miklos soothed. "Peace. For everything there is a season," he repeated Aaro's comforting advice. Then he remembered the Scripture: "Peace, peace," they say, when there is no peace. and "There is no peace," says the Lord, "for the wicked." The prophets Jeremiah and Isaiah offered no comfort—for Miklos or Christine.

Then Miklos heard a voice from heaven as the Lord Almighty spoke: "Peace I leave with you; my peace I give you. I do not give to you as the world gives. Do not let your hearts be troubled and do not be afraid. For *everything* there is a season and a time for every purpose under heaven" (John 14:27, NIV; Eccl. 3:1).

CHAPTER
9

After the plane touched down at Lambert Field, an exhausted Christine retrieved her luggage and climbed aboard an airport shuttle for the long-term parking. She was the sole passenger on the creaking bus as it wound its way through the dark, deserted parking lot. Finally spying her yellow VW, she stepped warily down the steps and felt her heart beat faster as she looked over her shoulder, fumbling with the key to the trunk. *Man, it's spooky out here!*

She flung her bags into the car, then quickly opened her door and slammed it shut, her hands shaking as she started the motor. The time change, plus a three-hour layover in Phoenix, had sapped the last of her energy. Paying the parking fee, she drove the twenty-six miles home.

Great Warrior Drive was quiet, and the single street light cast a lonely glow into the darkness. She pulled into the garage, alighted and opened the adjoining door to the house and quickly snapped on the dining room light. Retrieving her bags from the car, she dropped them just inside the door, then went through the house, flicking on all the switches. Still scared, she flopped down on the bed and dialed Jack's number.

"I'm home, and I need a favor," Christine yawned tiredly.

"Well, hello to you too," Jack replied, laughing sleepily. "What time is it?"

Christine glanced at her clock radio. "Almost midnight."

Jack groaned. "What's up?"

"Just talk to me for awhile, okay?" She held the phone away from her ear as he cursed. "You told me to call if I ever needed you," Christine snapped. "Tonight I need you."

"Okay, talk," Jack yawned.

"Thanks for taking care of the house while I was gone," she ventured. Stuffing a pillow behind her head, she lay down flat on the bed, her back aching between her shoulder blades.

"The contractor did a pretty good job fixing up the place, didn't he?"

"I didn't look at it real close, but it looks like he even matched my wallpaper," she said tiredly, her eyes burning with weariness.

"I'd think you'd be more worried about having a sliding glass door again," Jack laughed. "The thing cost a bundle."

"That too," Christine sighed, smiling. "You're a real sweetheart, Jack."

"That's what I keep telling you," he said, his voice sensuous. "You're finally catching on."

She rolled over onto her side and closed her eyes. It was nice to talk to someone who could love her just the way she was—someone who wouldn't insist she change.

"How early do I have to get up for the meeting tomorrow morning?" she asked sleepily.

"Get up for the meeting?" Jack laughed. "Don't you plan on showing up for work?"

"Jack, it's Friday!" She yawned again. "Besides, if you're right and we are canned, it won't make any difference anyway."

"You've got a point," he agreed. "The meeting's at three. I'd like to spend about an hour with you going over some stuff."

"Good, I can sleep in," she giggled.

"You slug," he taunted. "If there was a way to hook up a machine to your brain so you could write and sleep at the same time, you'd do it."

"Good idea!" Christine was growing tired of the empty banter, but she didn't want to be alone in the house.

"Now go to bed," he ordered softly.

"I am in bed."

"Hang up the phone, Christine," Jack droned.

"Ooh, you must be serious," she teased. "You called me Christine."

"Good night," Jack said finally and hung up on her.

"Pffft," she blew a raspberry at the receiver and hung it back in its cradle. With the light on, she drifted off to sleep.

Unbeknownst to Christine, she was not alone. Miklos, Pesach, and Wardar patrolled the house. Something just didn't feel right. Searching in the closet, Miklos dispatched Mizzah, a spirit of fear, but they knew there were more. Pesach sensed the presence of a chief, but couldn't discern which one. He was nearby though. His stench filled their nostrils.

Well hidden in the slimy sewer beneath the house, Tartak held court. Those demons devoted to destruction, Hormah, Shemed, and Shiphishion, offered their suggestions for the final neutralization of the situation.

"The thing that I find most amusing," Tartak chortled, "is that the dwelling above was just repaired from our last assault."

The demons cackled in glee. "How about a lightning strike?" offered Shemed.

"No, no, no," Tartak shook his massive bull-like head. "That would be attributed to an act of 'God.' No, it must be something more creative. Something with a sinister flair."

"Perhaps a gas leak!" offered Hormah.

Tartak glared at his stupidity. "No! That could be explained away. We have been instructed to make sure that our involvement is made clear."

The group sat silently pondering the possibilities. Suddenly Shiphishion's eyes lit up. "I've got it!" Leaning forward, he quietly whispered his plan.

Tartak leaned back and laughed uproariously, "Perfect! We shall command a ritual."

✝✝✝✝✝

Shicron, the demon of drunkenness, zipped through the pack of inebriated patrons at Nick's Pub. He paused with interest as Christine raised her glass for another toast, her vision a little blurred after her third margarita. "May the fleas of a thousand camels infest the armpits of Marcus Jarrett!"

The entire company of freshly fired newspaper employees broke out in gales of laughter. Jack slapped Christine on the back, spilling her drink. Miklos warily eyed the sniggering Shicron as he took up residence behind Christine, barred from intervening by her decision to find solace in drink. How the angels despised this household of the enemy. Finding nothing out of the ordinary, Shicron thumbed his nose at Miklos, Pesach, and Wardar, and drifted on.

"Can you believe they actually had *security guards* escort us out of the building?" Christine slammed her hand on the table. "But I fooled them." She winked at Jack and leaned back in her chair. "I stole a paper clip anyway." Pesach and Wardar dismally shook their heads and turned away.

Lord, let me not end up like these, Miklos sent up a prayer, surveying the room. Lining the walls were dejected and powerless guardians, doomed to stand idly by as their charges destroyed themselves. Seeking out Jack's angel, Feodor, Miklos issued a command. "She must not drive home."

Feodor smiled. "I'll do what I can." Leaning over, he prodded Jack's calloused conscience. At that point, Jack noticed Christine's inebriation and felt compelled to offer her a ride.

"Chris, maybe I ought to take you home," Jack coaxed. "You never could hold your liquor."

"Pooty parper," Christine slurred. Then she stood, swaying slightly. She now knew what they meant when they said you don't feel drunk until you stand up. "Whoa," she exclaimed, leaning back on Jack's arm. "Let's go, buddy."

Jack steered Christine out of Nick's Pub and to the corner parking lot, where he unlocked the passenger side door and tucked her inside. The night air was chill, blowing in off the Mississippi. Those sultry hot days, when a moisture haze would hang in the air, were at least a month away.

"Thanks, Jack," Christine cooed, leaning her head back on the seat. "You're such a sweetheart." Jack rolled his eyes.

"You're going to regret this in the morning," he sing-songed, starting the car.

"I regret it now," she groaned, her face a sickly green. He quickly jumped out of the car and opened her door just as she leaned out and began to heave.

✝✝✝✝✝

Yoko-Sharuhen and Tartak hovered overhead as Star White sat cross-legged on the floor, chanting and staring at the flickering candle.

"This is almost too easy," Yoko-Sharuhen laughed in derision. Tartak took Yoko's hand, and their bodies intertwined. Together, they took possession of Star. Using her hands, they quickly gathered the essentials for the fire ritual.

Star hastily ripped the picture of a house from a magazine and grabbed a stoneware plate from the kitchen. Pushing everything off the coffee table, she assembled a makeshift altar. Retrieving her candle from the floor, she set it on the table and ran to the bathroom for a sterile needle.

Everything was ready. She knelt in front of the altar and closed her eyes. The flickering candle added to the aura of evil as the demons within her drove her onward. Taking the picture of the house, she centered it on the plate.

"I give my blood to you, O Enlightened One, to add my power to your desire. As you have willed it, so mote it be."

Quickly, she pierced her middle finger with the needle. As she smeared the blood along the roof line of the house in the picture, the demons in O'Fallon laid a blanket of hell's fire in Christine's attic.

✛✛✛✛✛

Molly Delarosa's heart began to ache. It was a familiar feeling to her, a burden to pray for a loved one. Asking the Lord who, she sensed it was Christine in trouble and dropped to her knees beside the bed.

Oh Lord, I humbly beseech you to place your hand over Christine right now. Lord, only you know what's happening and what needs to happen. I feel she's in terrible danger, Lord, and I'm asking you to intercede on her behalf. I don't quite know how else to pray, so I'm counting on your Holy Spirit to lead me.

For an hour, then two, then on into the night, Molly prayed for Christine. Finally, she felt the burden lift, knowing that God had answered her prayer.

✛✛✛✛✛

During the drive home, Christine slowly sobered. Popping a mint in her mouth to take away the nasty taste, she turned to Jack and yawned.

"Not that it matters now, but you never mentioned how you liked my story, Jack," Christine complained.

"What story?" he inquired innocently, passing a car in the slow lane.

"The abortion piece I faxed to you from Sedona."

"When?" Puzzled, Jack glanced quickly at her.

"On Monday afternoon," she said exasperated.

"I never got any story from you."

"Jack, I sent it myself," she insisted. "You must have gotten it and lost it."

"I'm telling you I never saw it," Jack declared, his mouth tightening. "If I'd seen it, I would have printed it. That's why I was so upset with you. I kept waiting for you to give me a story, but I never got anything. Maybe you sent it to the wrong fax number."

"I'm not stupid," she grumbled, running a brush through her hair. She stopped and waved it at him. "I've called that number hundreds of times. Besides, I got the confirmation it had been sent."

"Well, I don't know what to tell you," Jack shrugged it off, as they turned onto Bryan Road. "What's that?" He pointed at the red glow in the southwestern sky.

"Gee, that looks . . ." Christine began. "Hit it, Jack!"

The closer they got to her house, the more Christine tried to convince herself that it was a neighbor's. As they turned onto her street, their way was blocked by a huge ladder truck. Police were redirecting traffic around the fire scene, so Jack pulled to the side of the street and parked. Even as she left the car, Christine told herself it was somebody else's house.

"It's *your* house," Jack shouted over the noise of the crackling flames.

"Not any more," Christine said numbly, as she stood in front of the blazing inferno, hugging herself.

Jack looked at her. Her face was pale in the flickering firelight, her eyes wide. He could see the tears trickling down her cheeks. Placing a comforting arm around her shoulders, Jack tried to turn her away, but she began to sob and collapsed in his embrace.

"Oh, Jack, everything's so screwed up," she cried. "My house is gone. I don't have a job. I have no place to go."

"Come home with me," Jack suggested. "I've got an extra bedroom if you insist on being alone tonight." There was a hint of an invitation in his kind gray eyes.

Mercifully, Christine was saved by her neighbors, Tom and Julie Baxter, who chose that moment to find her and offer their condolences. Jack dropped his arms and stepped back.

"I'm so glad you're okay," Julie cried, taking her cold hand. Quickly, she removed her old white sweater and draped it around Christine.

"It was the darndest thing," Tom chattered, his hands stuffed in his front pockets. "I was bringing in the trash can when I heard this loud explosion. I looked up and your whole roof was on fire. I hollered at Julie to call 9-1-1 and ran for your hose, but the fire was too hot to get close enough by then. It was the darndest thing I ever saw. It must have been a gas leak or something."

"I've never smelled anything quite like it," Julie continued, wrinkling her nose. "It smelled just like rotten eggs burning."

"Sulphur?" Jack offered, the reporter in him taking over.

"Yeah, that's it!" Tom answered. "Like sulphur. I remember a kid in high school made a stink bomb in chemistry class with it. We had to evacuate our building until it cleared out."

Julie turned to Christine. "Do you have a place to stay tonight?"

"We were just discussing that when you walked up," Jack answered, casting a questioning glance at Christine. She avoided his eyes.

"I guess I could get a motel room tonight," Christine sighed and looked at her feet.

"I won't hear of it," Julie interjected. She spoke with a quiet firmness. "Our spare room is empty, and there's no reason you should pay out good money for a motel."

Jack sighed. "If you need me, you know how to reach me. I mean it." He shook his finger for emphasis. "If you need anything, you call me."

"The last time I did, you complained because I woke you up," Christine smiled sadly, planting a sisterly kiss on his cheek. "You're one in a million, Jack."

He gave her a quick hug and turned to weave his way through the maze of fire hoses. Christine didn't even watch him go. Her attention was consumed by the still roaring blaze. The hypnotic red and yellow flames took on a life of their own, and she imagined she could see dark figures dancing through her house. Noticing her hesitancy to leave the scene, Julie put her hand on Christine's shoulder. She turned with a start.

"There's nothing you can do here," Julie soothed. "You might as well spare yourself the heartache." Trying to swallow the lump in her throat, Christine nodded in agreement and allowed Julie to lead her up the driveway. "I'll send Tom back out to let the Fire Chief know you're here in case they need you for anything. Everything's going to be alright."

"I'm glad I haven't had time to pick George up from the kennel. All I have left is my car, my cat, and my credit cards," Christine said tearfully.

"And lots of friends," Julie reminded her. "Don't you worry about a thing."

Still in shock, Christine followed Julie inside. Smokey wagged his cocker spaniel tail at her. As Julie made up the bed in the spare room, Tom puttered in the kitchen, making coffee. Christine slumped at their kitchen table, with her head buried in her hands.

"You know what I hate the most?" she told Tom as he set a steaming mug of coffee in front of her. "The photos. I've only got one picture of Mom and my sister Laura in my billfold. The rest are gone."

Tears glistened on her pale oval face, and she began to sob. Tom felt inadequate to console her. He shifted from one foot to the other, patting her on the back, then poked his hands in his back pocket. Just then, Julie walked into the kitchen, and Tom gratefully turned Christine over to his wife.

"Your bed's made up, honey," Julie comforted her. "Why don't you try and get some sleep."

Christine turned her red-rimmed eyes toward her neighbor. "I don't think I'll ever sleep again."

"Sure you will," the sisterly Julie assured her. "I bet a nice hot shower would help. I've laid out a towel and washcloth for you."

Julie was right. The shower did help to ease the tension in her muscles, but her mind would not shut down. Over and over through the long night, she replayed the tragic events of the day: first Marcus Jarrett announcing that all senior staff was being cut, then making a fool of herself at Nick's, and last of all, her house burning. Every penny she'd earned over the last five years had gone into that place. Could it have been arson? Alternately, she wept and beat her pillow in anger.

Miklos preferred her anger. "Sadness will overwhelm her and keep her from pushing onward," he lamented. Just as quickly as he dispatched one demon of depression, another would pop up and latch itself to her.

Pesach, too, was concerned. "It was intended that she die in the fire. Praise Almighty God that His hand was upon her and delayed her from returning home sooner."

"Let us not forget that it is promised 'weeping may endure for a night, but joy comes in the morning,'" Wardar encouraged. "A season of weeping can be a cleansing thing."

✜✜✜✜✜

Finally, Christine drifted off to sleep, tossing and turning fitfully, waking every twenty minutes. Something played at the edge of her consciousness, something she was forgetting. Suddenly, she sat bolt upright in bed. *My briefcase!* All of her research was in that bag.

Frantically, she dressed. *Did I leave it in the car? Or did I take it in the house?* For the life of her, she just couldn't remember. As she replayed coming home in her mind, she saw herself drop the leather case just inside the door leading to the garage. A sick feeling welled up within her. *Oh no! It's gone. Maybe the contents were spared.*

Trying to convince herself that if she wished hard enough, it would be there, Christine slipped down the hall and out the front door. A misty morning fog obscured the view of her house. Cautiously, she crossed the street, and the closer she got, the more she realized that the wish would not come true. Her house was leveled, burned to the foundation. What had been her basement was now filled with water, ashes, and debris. Glass littered the blackened yard, and there was only an inky muck where yesterday morning her azaleas had bloomed.

Miklos, Pesach, and Wardar watched in disgust as demons of every size danced over the ashes of Christine's house. The villainous conga line circled around an object floating on a piece of wood in the basement: a coiled serpent formed from the melted aluminum frame of the new sliding glass door. Miklos drew his sword in anger, plunging it into the nearest demon before he could be restrained. Screeching, the demon shriveled and vanished.

"Caution, brother," Wardar laid a restraining hand on Miklos' sword arm. "Don't step beyond your authority."

Pesach joined Wardar in his attempt to cool Miklos' temper. "Remember, our duty is to protect, not to seek revenge."

Miklos barely heard Pesach's warning as his attention was turned to Christine who had discovered the rattlesnake. She was on her knees, hugging herself and rocking, as she stared in horror at the image. Her guardian touched her shoulder and tapped into Christine's memory: the rattlesnake on the rock wall, the rattlesnakes that made up the face of Coatlicue, the rattlesnake fetish in her car . . . the ruby and emerald rattlesnake ring on Dr. Libby Brinkman's finger. Christine blinked, shook her head, and leapt to her feet.

"That's it!" she said out loud. *Somehow, this all ties together with Gary Knox's murder. I know it.*

As the fog lifted in the bright, morning sun, a red and white Fire Marshall's car drove up.

"Morning! Miss McKay?" the Fire Marshall questioned as he strode up the driveway.

"Yes, good morning," she said, extending her hand.

"It doesn't look like a very good one for you though," the marshall said sympathetically. "I'll have a few questions for you after I sift through this mess. Is there someplace we can talk afterwards?"

"Across the street," she indicated, self-consciously running her hand through her sleep tousled hair. "I'm staying with my neighbors temporarily."

"Good enough," he said, jotting a note on his clipboard. "This will take a while."

With that, the marshall began to circle her house, sifting through the rubble. Christine trotted back across the street and found that Julie was up making coffee.

"What do you want for breakfast?" Julie enthused, humming cheerfully into the refrigerator. "I've got eggs, cereal, pancakes?"

"Don't go to any fuss," Christine pulled out a chair at the table and sat down. "Cereal's fine by me."

Julie crossed to the pantry and ran down the list. "I've got oatmeal, corn flakes, puffed wheat, shredded wheat, and granola."

"Granola," decided Christine, amused at the variety.

"Tom buys it on sale," Julie rolled her eyes. "Every time he sees a coupon for a box of cereal, he cuts it out."

After breakfast, as she and Julie drank another cup of coffee, the Fire Marshall rang the bell. Smokey barked and was hushed by Julie as she opened the door.

"Hi, Ben, come on in," Julie greeted the marshall and stepped aside as he entered. "Want a cup of coffee?"

"Sounds great," Ben said, his tall frame following her into the kitchen. "Hello again, Miss McKay. I'm not sure I introduced myself earlier."

"Ben, where are your manners?" Julie scolded. "Christine, this is Fire Marshall Ben Hinshaw. We go to the same church."

"Nice to meet you, Marshall," Christine smiled.

"Just call me Ben," he said, grinning.

Julie set a mug of coffee down in front of him, and he stirred in two heaping spoons of sugar.

"That was a mighty hot fire," Ben reflected. "You mind if I ask you a couple of questions?"

"No problem."

Ben pulled up his clipboard to make notes. "First off, did you have any chemicals stored in the attic?"

"No, there was nothing but dust up there," Christine answered, sipping her coffee.

"The fire appears to have started in the attic and progressed to the rest of the house," he offered, tapping the table with his pen.

"Was it electrical?" she asked.

"Not by appearances," the marshall shook his head. "Did you have any combustible compounds stored in the garage?"

"Just some gasoline for the mower and some old paint, but that was all on the floor," Christine said, leaning forward on her elbows.

"Okay," he jotted a note. "Were you using any kind of portable propane or electric heater?"

"No, I have central air and heat."

"Had you noticed the smell of gas, even slightly?" he continued.

"I just got home from Arizona night before last." Christine cupped her chin in her hand. "There was nothing out of the ordinary."

"Could you have left your stove on?"

"No, I used the microwave to heat up some water for coffee."

Julie, who had sat silently listening, interjected, "Ben, you seem troubled. Do you have any suspicions?"

"None that I'd like to share with my superiors," Ben hedged, running his fingers nervously through his short-cropped hair.

"What do you mean?" Christine pressed.

"Well," Ben leaned back on two legs of the chair and sighed. "This may sound weird, but I can't find any reason for your house to have caught fire. You said you don't store any chemicals, yet my firemen and several witnesses claimed to have smelled burning sulphur. There's no trace of sulphur on the property. In fact, there's nothing that you wouldn't find in a simple campfire. I really don't know what to make of it." He glanced at Christine, whose face was pale.

"Are you saying, Ben," she said, slowly and deliberately, "that my house just burst into flames by itself?"

"No, I'm not saying that, not for the record anyway," Ben answered. He paused and sipped his coffee. "My findings are inconclusive. But between you and me, I've got a notion that something outside of the natural realm had a hand in that fire."

"You mean . . . ," Julie began, and then Christine interrupted. "What *do* you mean?"

"I've only seen one other fire like this in my life," Ben said hesitantly, "and it was the result of a . . . curse."

"A curse!" Christine spat out, pushing back her chair. "Come on."

"I know it sounds farfetched," Ben held up one hand. His voice was sincere. "My parents were missionaries to Nigeria when I was a teenager. The local witch doctor took a dislike to our interference, and to prove that our God was not as strong as his, he cursed the church. He sat down in the dirt and built a little effigy out of twigs and grass, then he took out his knife and slit his palm to let the blood drip out over the likeness of our chapel. Then he stood up and crushed the whole thing with his foot and stomped off."

"So?" Christine shrugged. "What does that have to do with my house?"

"That night," Ben continued, "the church exploded into flames and burned to the ground in minutes. There was no explanation for that fire either, and there was the smell of sulphur in the air. Within a week, all missionary activity within that witch doctor's territory was crushed."

Christine and Julie looked at each other in disbelief. "So," Christine said slowly, "you're telling me somebody sat down in my yard, built a little house, bled on it, stomped on it, and my house burned down?"

"No, they wouldn't have to be anywhere near your house," Ben declared, placing his hands on the table and pushing away. "Look, Miss McKay. I don't know you from Eve. I don't know anything about your personal beliefs or what you're involved in. But if I were you, I'd take this seriously. Somebody, somewhere, is out to get you."

"So what do we do now?" Christine stood.

"Well, professionally, I'll file my report, which will state that the fire was of unknown origin," Ben said, as she followed him to the door, "and personally, I'll be praying for your protection."

"Thanks," Christine said, finding that she actually meant it.

After closing the door, she rejoined Julie in the kitchen, catching her friend praying fervently under her breath. She looked up as Christine entered. Suddenly wanting to know, but not knowing how to ask, Christine was blunt. "Are you a Christian?"

"Why, yes," Julie answered, smiling.

"It figures," Christine returned with a wry smile. "I seem to be surrounded by them these days.

"If you are, it's for a good reason," Julie answered, clearing the table. "God loves you very much, Christine."

"I wish I could be sure of that," Christine sighed.

"Well, the only way I know to be sure is to receive Him into your heart."

"Somebody else already told me that," Christine shared, thinking of Molly. Suddenly, she felt an overwhelming urge to hear her voice. "Can I use your phone?"

"Sure, use the one in the den," Julie answered, running the dishwater. "You'll have more privacy in there."

Christine dialed Molly's number, but it was John who answered, and she found she was glad. Quickly, she told him everything that had happened: losing her job, the day at the bar, the house burning down, and finally, ending with Ben's outlandish explanation of some sort of "voodoo" magic.

"Christine, I agree with the fire marshall," John told her seriously. "Why don't you come back to Sedona? You can stay here with us."

"What for?" she argued. "If the fire marshall's right, and I'm beginning to think he is, then Sedona's the last place I want to be."

"Because you have a job to finish," he pointed out. "You're the only one who's close to finding out who killed Gary Knox. They want you to quit now."

"Who wants me to quit?" She paced to the window, staring at the blackened ruin of her home.

"The enemy," John answered matter-of-factly.

Looking for another excuse, Christine hedged, "I don't have the money to fly back to Sedona."

"You're talking to a pilot," John reminded her. His voice was teasingly cheerful. "I'll fly in and pick you up."

"But what about my cat?"

John laughed, and she could just imagine him shaking his head and see his eyes sparkling, "Even your cat. Is it a deal?"

Christine paused, mentally going over the reasons she shouldn't, but her heart won out. "It's a deal."

CHAPTER
10

In the underground cavern that was their haven, Vaizaitha and the Legion of Commanders pored over a topical map of Sedona, as they laid out the plans for the coming battle. Suddenly, the walls began to rumble and the ground to shake. A pungent stench filled the room as every eye turned in terror to the doorway, for there, in all of his demonic glory, stood Lord Satan himself.

Eyeing the clique of incompetent pop-eyed devils trembling in his presence, he singled out Commander Vaizaitha for his first assault.

"A chair, idiot," he barked, "or am I expected to sit on the floor like one of your dogs?"

Vaizaitha scrambled to offer his own chair. "Forgive me, Master. I was so taken aback by your unexpected visit that my senses left me."

Satan settled down, fanning his enormous cape behind him. *Let them sweat*, he thought, as he glared at each warlord individually. Then his eyes rested upon Quench-Bersha. *You're next.*

"And how is it going among the believers?" Satan purred, watching Quench-Bersha turn a paler shade of green, his yellow eyes wide.

"As . . . as . . . as well as can be expected, your Eminence," Quench-Bersha stuttered, almost unable to form a coherent thought.

"Oh, it is, is it!" Satan hissed. "Then explain to me why the number of devils being dispatched back to me has increased. The angels are getting their power from somewhere."

Quench-Bersha squirmed in his seat, growing increasingly uncomfortable at the attention being paid to him. He gazed around the table, but no one dared to meet his eyes.

"Would you mind detailing your activities as far as the believers are concerned?" Satan demanded.

"Well, uh, we've tried . . . with some success . . . to penetrate the ceiling of angels covering the churches, but . . . but . . . but we have been turned away at almost every attack," Quench-Bersha trembled. "I don't know what's going on, but . . . even my minor demons can't slip through anywhere. And the faithful, well, we can't seem to find a foothold. Not even a toehold."

"Then you're not looking hard enough," Satan droned, flicking the scum from beneath a fingernail. "Perhaps you need assistance. No . . . replacement."

"But Lord Satan," Quench-Bersha began, as out of nowhere two massive soldier-like demons grabbed him from behind and dragged him from the room. The others ducked their heads, hoping they would not be next.

"Now, children," Satan continued, as if nothing had happened, "let me see. Mibzar, can you offer some explanation as to why more of the faithful were not lured away into your territory?"

"Well, I . . . well, I . . . no, sir," Mibzar looked down in shame at the table.

"Good answer," Satan snarled. "At least you admit your ignorance, without making excuses for yourself. Would you like me to tell you why you've been so ineffective?"

No one dared answer. Satan continued, loving the absolute terror he was able to evoke in his followers. "Because you've been too obvious. Subtlety. That's the game. You can't go charging in and say, 'Here I am. I'm evil.' Christians are equipped with a sensing device for evil. No, the way to win more souls is to cloak yourself in their jargon. Talk like them. Act like them. Look like them. Write speeches like theirs. Make confessions like theirs. No one is fooled by a blatant imitation. Most of what you say must be the truth. Use the Bible, then add a little twist. How do you think I got Eve to bite the apple?"

Mibzar sighed with relief. "For example," Satan explained, "talk about the Christ; after all, there were many anointed ones. Talk about God, the universal mind. Anything you can throw in about light, use it." He paused. "But why am I telling you this. You're supposed to be the expert. Perhaps you need more training."

Mibzar's eyes bugged as he felt the hot breath and talons of the same guards who had removed Quench-Bersha.

"We'll talk later," Satan promised as he waved goodbye.

Turning his attention back to the remaining hierarchy, Satan leered. "From seven, to five. Hmm. Let's see. Who's next on my list?"

The tension was maddening as each one waited to be the next prey.

"Tell me, Zethar," he turned to the head of abortion at Changes Plus, "how is it that a hostile element was allowed to witness a live-birth abortion?"

Zethar-Zebah's face showed surprise. "This is the first I've heard of it," he stonewalled. "When did this occur?"

"The day of the believers' victory over you and your troops," Satan glowered. "The day they made no noise, yet put a hundred thousand of your troops to rout. From my reports, the angels made mincemeat of your first rank, and your second rank turned tail and ran without even attacking! I was embarrassed to be your Lord. I could just hear all of heaven laughing at me. So," he glowered, pointing a taloned finger, "I've decided to replace you."

Zethar turned to Yoko-Sharuhen with a pleading look.

"Master," Yoko appealed, standing and facing Satan. "Surely you are not going to replace us all? My brother, Zethar, and I have come to depend upon one another. He works through the same hands as I do. We are often working as one spirit to accomplish your tasks. I ask you . . . no, I entreat you . . . spare him. Punish him if you must, but do not supplant him."

Yoko-Sharuhen moved to Satan's side and bowed low, taking his hand in hers and placing a humble kiss upon the gnarled knuckles. Satan pondered her request, enjoying her impertinence.

"Very well, Zethar, your sister's plea has saved you this time." Stroking Yoko's face, Satan smirked, "I'm sure her love for you will allow her great strength as she undergoes punishment in your stead . . ." Yoko's eyes flashed fire, but she did not flinch. She would not grovel. She knew her Master and how he hated weakness. " . . . to be determined at a later date," Satan concluded, pleased with her.

Turning to Vaizaitha, Satan grumbled, "Is there no one you can send for refreshments? I thirst."

Vaizaitha snapped his fingers at Humtah, their host, who was relieved to be dismissed. He returned with his finest hemlock tea and gooseberry tarts for the entire company. As they ate, Vaizaitha sensed the atmosphere had changed and ventured to chat with his Master.

"Sir," Vaizaitha began warily, "I'm wondering how it is that I am expected to complete my assignment without . . . I mean . . . I have so few commanders left. . . ."

"Spit it out!" Satan bellowed, licking the gooseberry jam from his fingers.

"I need more help than this," Vaizaitha complained, pointing at the remaining horde.

Satan threw back his head and laughed. "Finish your tea. There is time for talking later."

Put in his place once more, Vaizaitha seethed and sulked in his chair, mumbling under his fetid breath. Humtah busied himself, running from chair to chair, refilling teacups, as his little cohorts served more tarts. When Satan had his fill, he shooed away the tray-carrying imps and turning to Humtah, issued his first compliment of the day.

"Delicious," he grinned. "Now, I would find it most helpful if you would take your pathetic self and assume your post in the place of the lizards—above ground. You're no longer needed here."

"Yes, sir. Yes, sir," Humtah bowed and scrapped as he walked out backward, his bat-wings twitching nervously.

Satan rose to his full height, towering over the table as he addressed them. "Your comment earlier was that you need more help? I agree with you, Commander Vaizaitha. In fact, that is why I'm here." He turned his whole countenance upon the now cowering Vaizaitha. "It has seemed that from the very beginning, you have been quite full of yourself. If you were as important as you think you are, I wouldn't have a job."

Satan strutted to the front of the room and whirled to face them. "You imbeciles. Do you really believe that this whole plan depends upon you? All I've heard is 'when *we've* succeeded,' 'when *we've* brought about the final battle,' 'when *we're* in control,'" he roared, releasing all his venom.

"Control this!" Satan screamed as lightning bolts and fireballs shot from his fingertips, knocking them all scuttling for cover under the table. His hideous, maniacal laughter echoed through the underground chamber. Slowly, the cowering commanders slithered back into their seats ready to duck for cover again if need be.

"The facts are these," Satan returned to his chair and the business at hand. "You have failed." He let that thought sink in, then continued. "While you have been playing children's games here, my people all over this world have completed their objectives. Since you were not able to stop the human Christine McKay from besmirching the good name of our Changes Plus abortion clinics, I had to have my servants buy her newspaper. Even though her story never went public, there was great potential for disaster. Not only that, but the attempt to murder her did not take into account the fact that she now has *three* angels, not one, but three. Do you think three angels are going to allow your slimy carcasses anywhere near her? If God assigned three guardians to her, you can bet His eye is upon her at all times. All He has to do is summon one of His believers to pray for her, and you're impotent." He slammed his fist on the table, emphasizing each syllable. "IM-PO-TENT!" The company shuddered.

"You and your mealy-mouthed bunch of baby killers are the only holdup in the whole plan," Satan glared. "At every other vortex, innocent blood has been spilled, except for those assigned to you! Now I've had to come and baby-sit as if you were fresh out of school. You couldn't even subdue one single woman, when she was already ours. She has slipped right through your hands, time and time again."

The demons at the table hung their heads in fear and shame. "So," their Master continued, "when Mibzar and Zethar-Zebah are returned to you . . ." Everyone looked up astounded. "Yes, they will be returned to you. But with a little less hide and much less pride. And when they are returned, they will be accompanied by my private assassins. I am sending Bizjothjah, He Who Has Contempt for Yahweh, and Rezin-Rohgah, and his demons of division. The first will take command over Zethar's post; the second will teach Quench-Bersha how to disband a body of believers."

"Time is of the essence," he ordered, turning to Yoko-Sharuhen. "Possess Star White's body and stay there. Move up the date for the next sacrifice. If anyone, and I mean anyone, gives you any resistance, finish them."

Satan bowed his head to Desmodus. "To you, I give my only commendation. Your sacrifice has been exquisite."

"Thank you, Master," Desmodus prostrated himself before his Lord, relieved that he would not feel the acid tongue of Satan.

As quickly as he had arrived, the hideous Lord of the underworld swirled his cape around him and dropped through the floor in a flash of red flame and sulphurous smoke.

In the darkest moments before the dawn, Kerestel paced restlessly from window to window within the sanctuary of Immanuel Faith Chapel. The moonlight shining through the stained glass cast shadows around the empty room as the angel captain wrestled with the ominous feeling which had settled into his spirit. Something was afoot—something had changed.

A flutter of wings announced the arrival of Delta, a young messenger angel. Approaching Kerestel, he bowed and unrolled a golden scroll from which he began to read.

"Greetings in the name of the Lord Most High. Hosanna in the Highest. Your presence is desired in heaven by the Lord God Almighty. Please attend at once." Delta smiled as he rolled up the scroll. "Will you accompany or follow, sir?" he asked.

"I'll accompany you now," Kerestel answered. "Let us make haste." With that, both angels soared skyward and spiraled into the clouds.

In a flash of time, they were surrounded by brother angels, as they entered into the realm of heaven. Delta took the lead and Kerestel followed him into the very center where is the throne of God.

The two travelers found their way blocked by a crowd of celebrant angels. It was wall to wall wings in the midst of God. Delta turned to Kerestel and whispered reverently.

"I will make my way forward and announce you, sir." He bowed and disappeared into the crowd.

Kerestel nodded to a few friends while he waited to hear his name called. "This is some celebration," he said to the nearest angel. "What are we celebrating?"

"The return of a victorious warrior captain!"

At that moment, a royal trumpet sounded and the room fell silent. A loud voice rose above the throng.

"Make way for Kerestel, Captain of the Host of Heaven, Defender of Man and Keeper of the Faith."

The crowd in front of him parted as Kerestel made his way forward. In the distance, he could see the Son waiting to receive him. As he drew nearer to the King, Kerestel noticed the massive African angel standing at Jesus' side. He quickened his pace, calling out in joy to his long-absent brother.

"Issa," Kerestel cried, reaching out and drawing the other into a fond embrace. Angelic tears of love filled both pairs of eyes as the brothers renewed their acquaintance.

Suddenly, Kerestel remembered that he had forgotten something. Swiftly, he turned and fell on his face before the Lord. "Forgive me, Master. But in my joy at once more seeing my brother, I have forgotten wherewith I stand."

Jesus smiled and motioned for Kerestel to rise. "There is nothing to forgive, Captain. You did not forget me. You were simply remembering one another." He placed a loving arm around Kerestel and led him forward. "Now," the Lord continued, "Issa is here to contribute to our cause in Sedona. He has news for you."

"As you well know," Issa took the lead, "Satan has unleashed his agents with a vengeance all over the world. No place where human beings exist has been spared from the onslaught of the enemy."

"I know that what we have been experiencing in Sedona is minor compared to the battles being fought in other parts of the earth," Kerestel answered, "but it has a determination to it that I have never before encountered."

"Captains," Jesus interrupted, "please excuse me. I must attend to urgent business with the Father. Kerestel," He said, turning to face the warrior, "why don't you show Issa the battle camp in Sedona?"

"Gladly, my Lord." Kerestel bowed. "Come, Issa. To Sedona."

The two angels departed the throne room and descended to the earth.

"How much do you know about our battle, brother?" Kerestel asked.

"I know that Satan has appropriated the power of many people in Sedona," the massive African answered. "He has used the ancient evils to breed a new group of disciples, taking the profane and using it to steal the power of their words."

Kerestel fumed. "He has wrapped himself in such a pretty package this time. Peace, freedom," he spat, "even God's gift of choice is being twisted and perverted."

The two angels slowed as they approached the base encampment in Sedona. Two guards saluted and stood at attention as they walked onto the training field. Everywhere angels were engaged in mock battle. To the left of them, a large sergeant was fencing with an entire group of young cadets. To their right, pairs of cadets were being taught thrust-in-flight manuevers. They walked on, observing the training until they came to Kerestel's tent. The sentry snapped to attention as they passed through the entry. They settled themselves onto the floor mats, and a servant appeared with refreshments.

"Satan knows he is best cloaked as the great restorer of 'rights,'" Issa said, as he popped a large fig into his mouth. "He loves playing the benevolent mother, returning to man what has been stolen by the so-called wrath of God."

Kerestel poured an amber fluid into the two goblets and handed one to his brother. "So, we are agreed that Satan is a scoundrel. But our Lord spoke of news."

"Satan has been here, in Sedona, this very night." Issa's dark eyes burned with a holy rage. "We kicked his sorry hide out of Africa, and he hurried here—to this place. His troops have thuswise been ineffective in carrying out his plan here. He has replaced Zethar-Zebah and Mibzar with two of his own private assassins." Issa placed a concerned hand on the arm of his brother. "He has also sent Darkon the Scatterer into the midst of the faithful."

"I felt it," Kerestel exclaimed. "Just before I was summoned to Heaven, I felt the darkness oozing around me."

"I believe that Satan is rallying his forces to try, once more, to bring about the New Age—the end of this life and the beginning of his reign on the earth." Issa chuckled, "He is ever about trying to rewrite the Good Book."

"They will most assuredly aim for the flock, with whispering imps masquerading as the voice of God." Kerestel rubbed his chin in thought. "Already the many denominations are pulling away from one another. He's sure to strike where he senses weakness."

"I understand that the human female McKay is back in Sedona," Issa inquired. "Who is in charge of her?"

Kerestel arose and went to the entrance of his tent. Summoning the sentry, he gave instructions and returned to Issa. "I have sent Jeremio, the Guardian of the Saint Molly Delarosa. He is protector over the dwelling where McKay is housed. As for herself, she is guarded by Miklos, Pesach, and Wardar."

"Good," Issa nodded, "Jeremio will need to hear what I must say next."

"I have a lot of confidence in my warriors, but it is clear we have our work cut out for us." Kerestel looked up as Jeremio rushed in, breathless from his quick flight.

"Captain," he bowed to Kerestel. Then he saw Issa. "Captain Issa?" he asked, puzzled at the presence of so great a warrior.

"Yes, Jeremio," Kerestel answered. "Captain Issa has come to help our cause."

"I have some vital information for your troops, Jeremio," Issa addressed the Guardian. "I understand that McKay has moved into your territory."

"Yes. She arrived yesterday."

"Satan has rallied his forces in and around Sedona, assigning Bizjothjah, Rezin-Rohgah, and their entire family of spirits of division to come against the faithful here," Issa continued. "We are counting on you to assist Aaro, along with Miklos, Pesach, and Wardar, to build a hedge of protection around your territory."

"Yes, sir," Jeremio agreed.

"McKay is in more danger now than ever before," Issa warned. "The enemy will stop at nothing to annihilate her."

"The will of God be done," Jeremio promised. "As far as I am able, she will remain safe."

"Good." Kerestel clapped a proud hand on his brother's back. "Go now, the sun is almost risen."

"The Lord go with you," Issa bid as Jeremio departed.

Turning to consider Kerestel, Issa saw that his countenance appeared troubled. Issa strode over and embraced his friend. "Do not lose heart, brother. Remember, we win. The saints will prevail, for Jesus Christ is now and forevermore Lord. And at His name, every knee will bow in heaven, on the earth, *and* under the earth."

Kerestel smiled. "And *every* tongue will proclaim He is Lord, to the glory of God the Father."

"Amen," finished Issa, "and amen."

CHAPTER
11

In the first moments of the light, the mountains of Sedona appeared black against the indigo sky. As the sun rose higher, they turned from a smokey violet to a dusty rose. The beauty of the morning desert gave no clue to the evil that lay hidden within the red rocks. The angels monitored the demons' activity, cloaked in rays of sunlight, lest they provoke an attack at an inopportune moment.

Christine stirred, stretching and yawning as she awoke from a wonderful night's rest. She opened her eyes and watched the crisp white, lacy curtains billow in the fresh, dew-laden breeze. She couldn't remember the last time that she had slept so well.

"Even Molly's guest room makes me feel loved," Christine mumbled as she turned onto her side, trying to squeeze the last possible ounce of consolation out of the comforter. Sensing that she was awake, George the cat jumped up onto her pillow and began to lick her face.

"I missed you, too, pudgy-cat," she crooned as she ruffled his golden fur. "Yes, Mommy did." Christine looked up as a knock sounded at her door.

"Christine, are you awake dear?" It was Molly.

"Yes," Christine answered cheerfully, "Come on in."

Molly entered the guest room carrying a steaming cup of freshly brewed coffee. "I hope you like it with cream," she announced, setting the cup on the bedside table. "I already added some."

"I love it that way." Christine greedily reached for the cup and inhaled deeply. "It smells wonderful," she exclaimed. Taking a sip, she closed her eyes. "Mmmm . . . vanilla coffee. How did you know it's one of my favorites?" She took another sip, swallowing gratefully.

Molly just beamed at Christine's appreciation. "I'm so glad you're here, honey," Molly smiled, sitting down on the bed.

"Me, too," Christine realized. Her mood was buoyant. "This feels like home . . . no, like home ought to be. Home was never like this."

"Now's always the best time to start over," Molly replied, an expression of satisfaction in her merry eyes. "Mostly, because now is always here."

"That's very wise," Christine laughed joyfully. "I should be depressed, but I feel wonderful."

"I've got to go back downstairs and finish cooking breakfast," Molly petted the cat and rose. "You've got just enough time for a quick shower. Get up lazybones." She shook Christine's foot through the covers.

Stepping out of the shower, Christine planned what she'd wear that day: her favorite pink Izod shirt and wear-softened denim skirt. Then she remembered. *I don't have any clothes to wear!*

Seizing the opportunity, Shuham, the spirit of depression, leaped from his hiding place behind the mirror onto her shoulders. "You don't have anything, poor baby," he whined. Miklos flicked him off with an outstretched hand, not even bothering to draw his sword. Not discouraged, Shuham launched himself at her head once more, tangling his long scaly black claws in her hair. "Everything you've ever had has been taken away from you," he crooned. "This won't last either."

Pesach and Wardar each reached down and took an arm, pulling Shuham from his nest and holding him stretched aloft as Miklos pierced his tough hide, dispatching him back to his Master.

"That one won't be back," he grinned.

Christine shook her head and refused to listen to her thoughts this morning. *No, darn it. For the first time in ages, I slept well and woke up cheerful. I plan on staying that way. Things will work out.*

Wrapping a towel around her body, she left her bathroom and walked into the adjoining bedroom, where she found that Pat had already laid out a blue chambray print sundress and a pair of sandals. Not surprisingly, everything fit. *I guess I'm going shopping today. Good thing the credit cards didn't burn.*

Christine opened the bedroom door and slammed right into John. "Whoa, sister," he said, taking her shoulders and steadying her. "Oh, you're not my sister. The dress confused me."

"If I'd come to breakfast in what I had to wear, your mother would have thrown me out of the house," she giggled.

John blushed, and Christine could hardly believe it! *He really is a reformed man*, she realized.

Over breakfast, they discussed Christine's situation. "So as it stands now, all you have is your cat and the clothes you wore here," Pat summarized.

"That's about it," Christine said. "No home, no job, no future."

"Now wait a minute," Molly interrupted scolding. "You've got a home with us, a job to do and I've never met anybody without a future. Now, all you need is a plan."

"But Molly, I can't sponge off of you forever," Christine lamented.

"You are not sponging off of me," Molly informed her. "I consider it a privilege to be able to bless you with what God has blessed me with."

"But there must be something I can do to repay your kindness," Christine offered, helping herself to another piece of toast.

Molly and Pat exchanged a sly look. "Well," Molly began, "there is something I was going to talk to you about. I guess now's as good a time as any." She paused, searching for the right words. "Tonight, the Joshua Intercessors group is meeting here for some fellowship and a program on abortion. I thought, maybe, you might be able to share with them some of your own story, or . . ." she quickly continued despite Christine's grimace, "maybe you could just tell them what happened at the prayer vigil and the live-birth abortion. It would sort of be like reading your article out loud."

"Molly, I don't know," Christine backpedaled. "I really don't feel that I have any place attending a prayer meeting."

"It's more of an informational meeting," Molly assured her. "Some of the people who are part of our group know that abortion is wrong, but they're not really clear on the specifics of why. We've had some new people join our group. We're going to show a clinical film about abortion procedures."

"I'm not sure I could watch," Christine frowned. "Some reporter I am, huh?"

"Please try," Pat interjected, leaning forward. "The strongest voice for anti-abortion is someone who's been through that experience, because they know the lie that's been perpetuated in the name of choice."

"You were looking for a future," Molly added. "This is your chance to make a difference."

"I just can't see myself as a militant pro-lifer," Christine hedged, dusting the crumbs off her hands.

"Why not?" Pat zeroed in. "You were militantly pro-choice before you knew the truth."

"Ouch," Christine flinched. "A wise man once said truth's arrow bears the sharpest point." She paused thoughtfully. Seeing no way out, she said, "Okay, I give. I'll do my best to help."

"Good," Molly said rising to get the coffeepot. "Now, we have some shopping to plan."

✛✛✛✛✛

Christine nervously paced the kitchen, as Pat laid out the cream and sugar beside the big, steaming coffee urn.

"Hand me that tray of cups, would you?" Pat turned and asked, arranging the spoons.

"Huh?" Christine realized she had not been paying much attention.

"Will you sit down and relax?" Pat scolded.

"I'd rather help if I could," Christine offered. "How about if I set these cups over there?"

Christine was puzzled as Pat chuckled. "Sure, go ahead. That'd be great."

Members of the Joshua Intercessors were greeted at the door by Molly, and they began to file into the living room. Pat introduced Christine as they wandered into the kitchen for a cup of coffee before beginning the meeting. Finally, they were all settled, and Molly stood up to open with prayer.

"Father God, we thank you for the fellowship of believers who have gathered here this evening. We ask that your Holy Spirit will guide us and teach us in what you would have us to learn. Thank you for giving your Son Jesus so that we might have the choice of life. Amen."

"Cathi, would you read the Scripture?" Molly asked.

Christine watched as a spunky brunette stood, opened her Bible, and began reading.

"The Word of the Lord from Joshua, Chapter 1, verses 3 through 9 (NIV): 'I will give you every place where you set your foot, as I promised Moses. Your territory will extend from the desert to Lebanon, and from the great river, The Euphrates—all the Hittite country—to the Great Sea on the west. No one will be able to stand up against you all the days of your life. As I was with Moses, so I will be with you; I will never leave you nor forsake you. Be strong and courageous, because you will lead these people to inherit the land I swore to their forefathers to give them. Be strong and very courageous. Be careful to obey all the law my servant Moses gave you; do not turn from it to the right or to the left, that you may be successful wherever you go. Do not let this Book of the Law depart from your mouth; meditate on it day and night, so that you may be careful to do everything written in it. Then you will be prosperous and successful. Have I not commanded you? Be strong and courageous. Do not be terrified; do not be discouraged, for the Lord your God will be with you wherever you go.'"

Murmurs of "thank you, Jesus," and "amen" drifted through the crowd, as Christine let the words from the Scripture sink into her consciousness: "do not be discouraged, for the Lord *your* God will be with you wherever you go." She squirmed uncomfortably in her chair, not quite sure why she had agreed to do this. *If these dedicated Christians only knew the "real" Christine* . . . she thought. Suddenly, she was aware that Molly was introducing her.

"Christine?"

The group applauded politely, as Christine stood and walked to the front of the room.

"I'm not very good at this," Christine started, "so I'll ask you to bear with me." She cleared her throat. "The same day as your last prayer vigil at Changes Plus, I discovered something that has changed my life," she said, realizing for the first time what a change it *had* made. "I interviewed Dr. Elizabeth Brinkman, the director of the clinic, before you arrived. Then I was given a tour of the facility by her nurse, Katona Whitefeather. What I saw was a crisp, clean, medical environment—nothing that spoke of the reality of abortion. I witnessed classes in self-actualization, aerobics, and other seemingly harmless activities to support women in a time of need."

She paused to gather her thoughts. "It was only after you arrived and provided a distraction, that I was able to slip away and find the reality behind the closed doors." Suddenly, Christine felt tears well up in her eyes at the strength of the memory. She was surprisingly unashamed as the tears trickled down her face. "I heard a baby born alive. I heard its cry. Then I heard its death." Christine looked over at Molly and saw that though she, too, was weeping at the memory, the older woman was able to give her an encouraging smile.

"Nobody will ever be able to tell me again that abortion isn't murder," Christine went on, feeling a surge of strength. "When abortions were only legal in the first trimester, you would have been hard pressed to convince me that it was wrong." She hesitated, then decided to tell the whole story.

"I am I guess what you would call an 'abortion survivor,'" Christine continued, her voice wavering. "When I was four months pregnant, I had an abortion. It wasn't until I came here that anybody ever bothered to show me the truth. What I . . ." She stopped, wiping her tears with a handkerchief John handed her. "What I carelessly did away with was a baby. It had fingers and toes and little eyes, and I never knew. I believe if there were someone to tell women and girls who were considering abortion the truth, the real truth, the whole truth, that they would choose life. Somebody out there is lying. Why, I'm not really sure, but you can bet that they've either never had an abortion, or they have and are doing their best to convince themselves it was just a piece of tissue."

Christine looked around the crowded room. Everywhere, eyes glistened with empathetic tears, even John's. She drew her speech to a close.

"Your battle isn't with abortion," she concluded. "You're not even fighting the women who seek them, or the doctors who perform them. Your enemy, the thing you must fight, is the lie! And even I know," she said, locking eyes with John, "that the only way to conquer a lie is with the truth." She sat down and heaved a sigh of relief. The room rose as one to applaud her courage.

"Let's refill our coffee before we watch the video," Molly announced, as Pat led the way into the kitchen.

"You did great," John said warmly, squeezing Christine's hand affectionately. "I'm proud of you."

"It wasn't easy," she replied. "But I feel really good about what I said. It helped to talk about it."

"The next time will be even easier," he assured her.

"Next time!" Before she could continue, they were interrupted by others in the group, who thanked her for her candor. She and John were separated by the crowd of well-wishers, and soon it was time to regroup in the living room. Christine found her first opportunity to slip into the kitchen for coffee and a couple of cookies. When she reentered the room, it was darkened, and the film had already started so she sat down beside Pat, who had saved her a chair in the back.

The doctor on the screen was giving a warning: "This is not a pretty sight. If there are small children in the room, I suggest they be removed before continuing. What you are about to hear and see is graphic." The music came up and the titles ran, as they sat waiting for the film to continue.

The voice-over narrated the scene of a doctor's waiting room. Several women and girls sat reading magazines. "If you didn't know any better, you'd think this was a dentist's office. Perhaps even a minister's waiting room. But this is the lounge of a typical abortion clinic in the United States today."

The scene shifted to a nurse doing an intake interview, where she asked the girl several basic questions, such as: When was your last menstrual period? Are you allergic to any medications? Everyone was pleasant and polite.

Once more the scene changed, and a man in a prisoner's uniform was being led down a long hallway toward a waiting electric chair. A priest was on one side of him, and a guard on the other. The scene flashed to a young girl being led down a long corridor, and then back to the prisoner. The impact of the comparison was startling.

The narration continued: "The only difference between these two prisoners of circumstance is that one has already been a party to the taking of an innocent life, and the other . . . well, she's about to."

The video progressed through the stages of prepping for the abortion, and then the doctor's voice-over described the procedure precisely. Christine was on the edge of her chair, sickened by what she saw as the abortionist removed parts of a fetus.

Christine felt a pain in her chest as a deeper reality dawned on her. *My baby died that way!* It was like asking a mother of a drowned child to watch a film of a child drowning. She began to sob, and Pat placed a reassuring arm around her shoulders.

"Before this young woman will be able to get up," the voice-over continued, "the nurse must take the remains to the baby disposal room, where as we see here, the body parts must be reassembled like a puzzle to assure that nothing remains in the uterus."

Christine looked at the little body on the towel. She had to get out of there! Rising quickly, she slipped back into the kitchen and was leaning against the sink, staring out the window into the night as Pat came up behind her.

"Are you okay?" Pat asked concerned.

"I don't know if I'll ever be okay," Christine wept. "It was awful." She paused and turned to Pat. "You amaze me! You can sit and watch horrible pictures like that, but you couldn't sit and listen to simple descriptions of an ancient sacrifice."

"I can't explain it either," Pat admitted. "But if I'm to fight this evil, then I need to know the truth."

"How's this for some truth?" Christine said angrily. "The baby isn't the only victim, but that seems to be the only one you people care about. What about the woman who discovers after her abortion that she was wrong? And she can't change it? She can't ever have her baby back. What about her?" Christine sobbed, scalding tears of years of pent-up frustration streaming down her face. "According to you, the baby has 'gone to be with Jesus.' What about me?" she screamed. "I'm still here, and I have to live with it every day of my life!"

Pat took a step back and stared, hardly able to believe that this angry, weeping woman was the composed reporter she knew and cared for as a friend. Unbeknownst to both of them, their voices carried to the living room, and Molly had come to see what the shouting was about. She stood at the doorway, mouth open in surprise as she heard Christine's tirade against the entire group. The words rang too true to be ignored. Molly quickly crossed the distance between them and swooped Christine into her motherly arms.

"You're right," Molly cried. "Oh, God forgive us, you're right."

Pat placed a hand on her mother's back. "Seems to me I heard earlier today that a wise man once said, 'truth's arrow bears the sharpest point.' Jesus says that the truth will set you free. Don't you think it's about time you accepted the truth," she said, placing her other hand on Christine's back. "That's the only way you can be free—free from the anger and pain you've kept bottled up inside you all these years."

Christine didn't answer. She pulled out of Molly's embrace and fled to her bedroom. Pat started to follow, but Molly stopped her.

"Leave her be," she cautioned. "The Lord's doing a good work there, and we don't want to interfere."

John stuck his head into the kitchen. "Everything alright in here?" he asked, peering around the room. "The film is over and the troops are getting restless."

Molly nodded, indicating that everything was fine, and led the way back to the living room. The group had already begun to pray when they entered, so all three—Molly, Pat, and John—knelt in the back. As each individual listed their personal prayer concerns, Molly sensed an evil presence. Opening her eyes, she was aware that she was not the only one. Pastor Mike, too, was gazing about as if looking for a foreigner. Soon others were also turning their heads, peering about the room.

Standing, Pastor Mike shouted, "Satan, in the name of Jesus, get out of this house. We'll not have you interfering with our prayers any longer."

Jeremio wished that for once these humans could see into the supernatural as he could. Surprised demons spun and were jettisoned through the walls as Pastor Mike took authority over them.

Upstairs, however, Miklos, Pesach, and Wardar had their hands full as the demons came from every direction. The air was filled with their stench. Ozem, a demon of anger, and Kinah, the master of lamentation, each had a firm grip on Christine and refused to be dislodged.

Christine felt as if she were slipping down a dark hole, and there was no bottom. Wave after wave of sorrow washed over her as Ishma-Ithmah poured his desolate bereavement into the room. She was drowning in a pit of despair.

Miklos shot across the room, his sword singing with fire, as he sliced off the head of anger. Then he gripped the tail of lamentation, who sunk his teeth even deeper into Christine's neck. *I can't go on like this*, she sobbed. *Help me! God, if you're there, help me!*

Instantly, the room was filled with every spare angel from downstairs, who swiftly disbanded the demonic horde which was attacking Christine. With wide eyes, Ishma-Ithmah retreated into the darkness, followed by Kinah.

The angelic warriors saluted one another and departed, leaving the three guardians maintaining their posts. Kerestel's report was accurate. The demonic activity had been stepped up.

Christine's sobs slowly subsided, and she drifted into an uneasy slumber. Miklos, Pesach, and Wardar bowed a greeting to the two dream-giver angels, who appeared in the doorway.

"The Lord has said that it is time," Lenis, the younger of the two, addressed Miklos. "Her heart has softened enough to allow the Holy Spirit to move her toward a choice."

"Thanks be to God!" Miklos exclaimed. "I've waited long for this day."

"Please stand aside," directed Icon-El, who shone like the image of God.

"She will think this is another nightmare, won't she Icon-El?" Lenis spoke to the kind, furrow-browed angel now standing at the foot of the bed.

"An interpreter is being called to cross her path," Icon-El answered. "Do not fret, gentle one." He smiled at the younger dream-giver. A tender heart was sometimes a great burden for an angel, he thought, but said nothing.

On an unspoken cue, Lenis raised an angelic hand and placed it at the top of Christine's head as Icon-El reached down and placed one at her feet. Miklos stood with sword ready, watchful as the special angels went about their task. Soon, Christine began to dream.

The white corridor before Christine seemed endless, with rows of doors flanking both sides. Yet, it was the doors at the far end which called her onward. Christine walked toward them, hands outstretched. As she stood in front of the doors and pressed down on the handles, she heard the steady beating of her own heart.

The doors swung wide, revealing a surgical suite. There was a woman lying on the table surrounded by masked medical personnel. At first, she couldn't see who it was, and then she was suddenly lifted up. She saw herself! She was looking down into her own face.

The abortionist entered the room. It was Dr. Brinkman, wearing an ancient Aztec priest's costume complete with full feathered headdress and face paint. In her hand, she held the curved sacrificial knife, the one Christine had seen in Dr. Curry's office.

Christine floated helplessly above the scene, unable to speak. Stop! *she tried to scream, but nothing would come out of her mouth.* There's got to be a way to stop her!

Dr. Brinkman raised a pair of massive forceps and spoke a foreign incantation before placing them under the sheet between the bent knees of the victim. Christine heard the baby's cry, but it seemed to be coming from Dr. Brinkman's mouth as from underneath the sheet emerged the demon Shashak. Christine knew that face! The demon cackled, and Dr. Brinkman dropped the forceps. The sound of metal striking tile echoed in Christine's memory. She was sucked through the roof, and the hospital faded.

Suddenly, there was no building, no doors, and she stood in a sandy valley. To the right and left were dark, craggy trees and stones that took on ominous shapes in the dusk. She could see that a fire burned on the nearest hill, and chanting voices seemed to be coming from the same direction.

I'm not afraid, *she thought.* I should be afraid. *"But perfect love casts out all fear" ran through her mind. It was almost audible. She began to climb the hill. She was aware that there were rattlesnakes in the brambles, but she felt no concern. A force was driving her upward, up the hillside, and closer to the fire and the strange shadows it cast in the dark.*

Then she heard it, a wail, unearthly and evil. It sounded like a baby: no, a million babies. Cats. She recalled that Siamese cats cry like babies. But something told her that this noise was not feline in nature.

No, *she thought,* there's nothing natural about that sound.

As Christine approached the crest of the hill, she dropped into a crouch and moved into the shadows of a giant boulder.

I want to see who they are before they see me.

There were six figures dancing around a bonfire. As they twirled around, she noticed that they were all women, each wearing a colorful feathered cape. Tucked into the sashes of their costumes were what appeared to be daggers. No, not daggers, but spikes. Great, steel spikes.

Then, from a cleft somewhere behind the fire appeared two massive demons and a woman, all dressed in Aztec feathered costumes. Behind them came a congregation of twelve women dressed in white feathered capes. The dancing stopped, and Dr. Brinkman, dressed as the high priest, faced the crowd. She raised her hands in the air and all fell silent.

Speaking to the sky, she called out, "Where is the sacrifice?"

Just then, the crowd parted and a young man, blindfolded and bound, was ushered into the front of the assembly. He was flanked by the two Aztec demons, and they roughly forced him to his knees before the priest.

What in God's name is this? *Christine thought, sucking in her breath. But she already knew. They were going to crucify him. Who was he? She had to get closer. Before she could move forward, two rough hands grabbed her arms from behind. A craggy-voiced Shashak called out to the crowd as he dragged her into the firelight and threw her in front of a stone throne at the feet of none other than Star White.*

"Goddess, look what I've got here."

Star glared at her. Around her neck she wore a massive necklace of still bleeding human hearts and hands. Looking up at her face, Christine saw that Star had become Coatlicue, the Earth Goddess.

Coatlicue purred at Christine, "Come, see what has been done."

She led the way to a stone altar hidden on the other side of the fire. Everyone followed, and the two Aztec demons dragged the young man between them.

"Who are you people?" Christine tried to say, but her tongue was paralyzed. Not only that, she could not move her body. She stood like a statue beside the altar and watched as the ceremony continued, unable to intervene.

From behind the altar, Dr. Brinkman as the priest, lifted up a hollow stone bowl filled with a dark liquid and set it in the center of the altar.

"Speak to us, oh blood of the innocents," Dr. Brinkman intoned as she lifted her hands. A loud crying filled the air—the wailing sound that Christine had heard as she crept up the hill. "The ancients cry out for a sacrifice," Star/Coatlicue exclaimed.

From the shadows, the two demons raised up from the ground a crude, wooden cross.

No! Christine tried to scream, but no sound would come. She tried to move, but was as petrified as the stone altar.

"There is power in the blood," Coatlicue chanted, circling Christine, and the worshippers repeated, "There is power in the blood."

The young man was again brought forward and pushed to his knees. His blindfold was removed and he stared up into the face of his killers.

"God forgive you for what you're doing," he sobbed. Then he saw Christine. "Help me, please," he cried as he was jerked to his feet. "Please!!"

The demons laid the cross down and forced the young man upon it, binding his feet together and spreading his arms onto the crossbeam. Four of the dancers untied their sashes and kneeling, offered forth their steel spikes. Dr. Brinkman held aloft a ceremonial stone mallet and then offered it to one of the demons.

Christine could hear the young man scream as they prepared to nail his wrists to the cross.

"The name," he screamed, "use the name!" His voice rose to a shrill wail as they pounded in the first spike. But he continued to cry out to her. "Use the name . . . use the name . . . use the name." Wham-ting, steel striking steel sang out. Wham-ting. "Use the name!" Wham-ting. "Use the name!" Wham-ting. Wham-ting. Wham . . . wham . . . wham . . . wham . . . wham . . . whamwhamwham.

"USE ... THE ... NAME ... THE ... NAME ... NAME."

"The name," Christine cried out as she sat up in bed, her sweat-soaked clothes clinging to her body. Quickly, she snapped on the bedside lamp and scanned the room. She lowered her face into her hands and shuddered. "The name," she panted. "What name?"

Just then, Molly rapped gently on Christine's door. "Are you okay in there, honey?" Without waiting for an answer, she went on in. The glory of God filled the room and almost felled Molly with its power. "Glory be!" she exclaimed, sitting down on the bed beside Christine.

"What time is it?" Christine asked, rubbing her eyes against the bright light.

"About 10:30, hon," Molly answered. "Did you have a nightmare? We heard you screaming clear downstairs."

"I don't know," Christine answered foggily. "It started out kind of scary, but I don't know, I wasn't afraid. It was like I was just a spectator."

"Why don't you tell me about it?" The gift of interpretation was given to Molly as Christine explained the dream. She listened intently until Christine was finished.

"What does it all mean?" Christine asked. "I know it's not just some nightmare. Something tells me it has a meaning."

"You're right, Christine," Molly mused. "I believe you've been given the key to the whole mystery surrounding Gary's death and more. Why don't you get a good night's sleep, and we'll discuss it in the morning," Molly said, rising from the bed. "I need to do some praying."

After Christine got ready for bed, for the first time in years, she said a little prayer. *God, if you're up there, thank you for bringing me to this family. Molly keeps saying you have a special purpose for me. If that's true, I sure would like to know what it is, and I'd sure like to know you a lot better. I guess the next move's up to you.*

Lenis looked at Icon-El and smiled. "May I?" he asked the older angel. At Icon-El's nod, Lenis placed one hand upon her forehead and whispered, "Peace."

She smiled and drifted off into a deep sleep, safe and at peace the rest of the night as Miklos and the others stood guard.

CHAPTER
12

John squinted at the bright sunlight streaming through his studio window. If he could just capture the quality of that pure light, his painting would be complete. The face of an angel, void of life, stared back at him from the canvas.

It just isn't fair, John thought, tossing his paintbrush onto the bench. *When I belonged to the devil, I could paint spirit beings that oozed life.*

"Why can't I paint them now?" he yelled at the ceiling.

"Excuse me?" Christine's small voice spoke from behind him.

Whirling, John blushed and pulled a cover over the canvas. "I didn't know anybody was around."

"Your mom sent me up to get you for breakfast," Christine answered, frowning at the covered easel. "Why did you hide it?"

"It's not finished," John explained, wiping off his brush. "I make it a habit never to allow anyone to see my work before it's completed."

"Oh," Christine said, turning to leave.

"It's nothing personal," he grumbled, dismissing her.

"I'm sure there's *nothing* personal where I'm concerned," Christine snapped, flouncing back down the stairs. He was so infuriating!

John wiped his hands fiercely on a rag and slapped it down on the bench. "God! Why did you put her in my life if I can't have her?"

Exasperated, he loped down the stairs into the dining room, where everyone was already seated for breakfast. Christine was in the process of telling her dream to Pat as Molly sat making notes on a small legal pad. Pouring himself a cup of coffee, he listened intently as Christine related the message-filled vision.

"Wow," exclaimed Pat, helping herself to more bacon. "That was a holy dream if I've ever heard one."

"What do you mean, a holy dream?" Christine questioned. "It was full of blood and sacrifice and murder. . . ."

"So's the Bible," John quipped in a better humor. "Did you ever read about the prophets of Baal? Nasty guys."

"Not now, John," Molly shushed him. "Are you ready for me to tell you what I'm sensing your dream means?" At Christine's nod, Molly continued, "Well, we're going to pray first, because if you're to hear from God from my mouth, I want to make sure they're His words."

They all bowed their heads. "Father God, you alone are our wisdom. I come to you today, leaning not on my own understanding, but trusting that you will give me the words to say. Open Christine's heart to your message. Thank you, Lord. In Jesus' name, Amen."

Molly consulted her notepad, then began, "I believe God is trying to communicate several things to you with this dream. Typical signs and symbols aside, the one thing that rings throughout is His omnipresence. He was showing you events through His eyes."

"The white corridor," she explained, "is life's walk, full of choices, which were represented by all the doors. You chose the most obvious and elected to have an abortion. Then God showed you the reality of abortion. His children are His children, no matter what stage of development they're in."

Molly paused, and Christine uttered, "I can't believe you got all of that out of one short part of the dream."

"I'm not finished yet," Molly continued, underlining a thought on her tablet. "There's some of this stuff I don't understand, so I'll try to do the best I can. God wanted to make a connection clear in your mind between Dr. Brinkman, abortion, and the Aztec rituals you've been researching. I don't know why."

"I think I know why," Christine interjected. "But go on."

"Do you remember the way you felt as you tried to stop the abortion you were watching from above?" Molly asked, leaning forward. "Do you remember what you were thinking?"

"Yes," Christine answered, recalling. "I was thinking there's got to be a way to stop her . . . if I could only make her hear me. I felt so frustrated trying to communicate."

"God made it very clear in my spirit," Molly went on, "that He wanted you to know He was there during your abortion. He wanted you to know what He felt as He watched your pain. He said, 'There's got to be a way to stop her,' but you couldn't hear Him.

"Now for the demon that was delivered," Molly glanced at her notes. "Well, that has a dual meaning. First, it was to let you know that your abortion opened you up to a special kind of attack, and second, it was God's way of letting you know that He's in the business of delivering you from evil."

Pat softly began to pray as she sensed the Holy Spirit was beckoning Christine. "The fact that you weren't afraid," Molly went on, "was a sign that you had accepted God's protection and His perfect love. You witnessed, I'm sure, an actual sacrifice up to a point. Again, God made the tie between Star White, Dr. Brinkman, and this whole mess. I believe that they're involved in this somehow. God's trying to show us that."

"I believe that too," Christine agreed.

"Wouldn't surprise me," John mumbled. "But sacrifice is even a little far out for Star."

"I'm glad you didn't marry her," Pat sighed with relief. "I love Heather, but her mother is a real air-head."

"She's not as dumb as she acts," John groused.

Molly glared at them both. "Can we get back to the subject at hand?" she scolded, noticing Christine's wide-eyed stare at John.

"Christine, even Satan knows that there's power in blood sacrifice," Molly explained. "It's an act of covenant. That's why Jesus had to die the way He did, and why we don't have to die at all. The man cried out to you for help, but you were powerless—just as all of us are powerless without Jesus. What was he screaming out to you at the end of the dream?"

"The name," Christine recalled. "Over and over again, he kept screaming, 'use the name.'"

Molly picked up her Bible and opened it to Philippians, Chapter 2, verses 6–11 (NIV), and read: "'Who, being in very nature God, did not consider equality with God something to be grasped, but made himself nothing, taking the very nature of a servant, being made in human likeness. And being found in appearance as a man, he humbled himself and became obedient to death—even death on a cross! Therefore God exalted him to the highest place and gave him the name that is above every name, that at the name of Jesus every knee should bow, in heaven and on earth and under the earth, and every tongue confess that Jesus Christ is Lord, to the glory of God the Father.'

"He was talking about the name of Jesus as Lord," Molly explained. "Not just the name Jesus, but Lord Jesus, the Christ, the Son of God."

Christine's eyes snapped open wide. Suddenly, it all made sense. A roomful of angels held their breath, leaning forward to catch the words.

"Are you telling me that God was asking me to call His Son my Lord?"

"Exactly," Molly smiled. "God sent you a dream to tell you that He loves you and He's calling you and has been for as long as you've been alive. It's just now that you're ready to listen."

"I am ready to listen!" Christine said excitedly. "Last night, I prayed for the first time since I was a little girl. I prayed and told God that if He has a special purpose for me that I sure would like to know what it is, and I said I wanted to know Him a lot better. I told Him the next move was up to Him."

"Well, the dream was the knocking," Molly explained. "Your prayer was like saying, 'Who is it?' God's interpretation of this dream is Him saying, 'It's me.' Are you going to invite Him in?"

The silence was heavy, as heaven and earth stood still to hear her answer. John quickly closed his eyes and began to pray. After what seemed an eternity, he heard her soft whisper.

"Yes," Christine responded. "Now what do I do?"

"Would you pray with me?" Molly asked. "You can just repeat the words after me. You can choose to say or not to say anything that I pray. It's up to you."

"I understand," Christine nodded, tears glistening in her eyes.

Molly reached out her hand, and Christine grasped it with her own. "Lord Jesus, come into my life," Molly prayed, as Christine repeated each line. "I accept your sacrifice on my behalf. I receive your forgiveness for my sins. Wash me in your precious blood so that I may be born anew. I declare now before heaven and earth that I am a new creature in Christ Jesus, and He is my Lord and my Redeemer. Amen."

"Amen," Christine finished.

"Thank you, Jesus," wept Pat.

"Praise you, Lord God," John exalted.

"Hallelujah," Miklos spiraled to the ceiling and through the roof.

"Glory to God in the Highest," the angels sang throughout creation.

The skies over Sedona opened as heaven rejoiced. Jesus turned to His Father and smiled, "Another child has come home," He exclaimed as He reached out His finger and with His blood wrote the name of Christine Diana McKay in the Lamb's Book of Life.

Pesach and Wardar turned to the exultant Miklos.

"Brother," laughed Wardar. "It seems my assignment is over."

"As is mine," Pesach added.

With tears of joy, Miklos embraced his long-suffering companions. "We have fought the good fight together," he rejoiced. "I will miss you, but the battle is won."

"Indeed," Pesach said, turning a thoughtful look at the glowing Christine. "Guard her well."

"I will," answered Miklos, waving farewell as they ascended. Stepping up beside Christine, he declared proudly, "Satan's not going to know what hit him!"

+ + + + +

"What!" roared Satan from his hellish kingdom, shaking the very walls of Hades. "Send for Vaizaitha, now!"

Demons scattered for cover, as Satan paced, cursing under his foul breath. "I'll hang that worthless son of a snake by his tail and skin him alive!" Dropping onto his throne, he glowered venomously at the doorway to his chambers, waiting for the doomed Commander Vaizaitha to enter.

A gong sounded as a young scampering demon announced Vaizaitha's arrival.

"Your Eminence," Vaizaitha crooned, bowing low. "You sent for me." He flashed Satan his toothiest grin.

"I have a matter of great confidence to discuss with you," Satan the Deceiver played with his prey. "I need your advice."

Vaizaitha puffed up with pride and strutted closer to the throne.

"Be seated here beside me," Satan invited, indicating the step at his feet.

Vaizaitha hunkered down and inquired, "How may I be of service, O Great Master?"

"I'm having a little trouble with the help," Satan grinned. "It seems I have this general. No matter what I tell him to do, he fouls it up. The simplest task seems to be beyond his ability."

Vaizaitha shook his head in disbelief, "Um, I know just what you mean. Those imbeciles you put under me are all but worthless. I have to keep my eye on them every second."

"I'm glad you understand," Satan purred, "but it gets worse. I had a very important plan that I entrusted to this general, and the one key to its success, was one soul. One tiny, small soul. And you know what he did?" Satan asked, leaning forward and leering at his commander. "Just today, he lost her to the enemy."

"No!" Vaizaitha exclaimed, hoping that he would be given the assignment. He could fairly smell a promotion coming.

"Yes," Satan spat. "Now here's my dilemma. Do I destroy him? Do I punish him? It's beyond me." He turned thoughtfully for Vaizaitha's advice. "Well, what do you think I should do?"

"If you just punish him," Vaizaitha pontificated, "he's likely to resent it and then fail you again. Sadly, my advice is, throw him into the pit."

"Are you sure?" Satan asked innocently. "Shouldn't I give him another chance?"

"Sounds to me like it would just be a waste of time," Vaizaitha said, feeling secure in his promotion now.

"Okay, I agree," Satan continued. "Would you like to know who he is?"

"Yes, I might like to apply for his post," Vaizaitha groveled.

"No, not his name," Satan said, standing and drawing himself up to his full height. "I will tell you the name of the soul he lost. Today, at precisely 10:03 Sedona time, the Lord Jesus wrote the name of *Christine Diana McKay* in the Lamb's Book of Life."

All the blood drained from Vaizaitha's face as he staggered, realizing he had just ended his own existence. Falling flat on his face, he cried out, "Mercy, Master, mercy."

The two massive guardian demons appeared at each side of Satan's throne.

"Get him out of my sight," he snarled. "To the pit with him."

Each demon grabbed one of Vaizaitha's boots and dragged him on his face toward the blackness of inner hell. He beat at the rocks with his talons like a cat scrambling for dry land. But there would be no salvation. He was doomed.

Satan's ears strained for the cry of his former commander. He grinned in satisfaction as the air was filled with the bloodcurdling scream of Vaizaitha, tumbling into the endless chasm of eternal damnation. He sat back on his throne and pondered Vaizaitha's successor. Suddenly, it hit him. The obvious choice, of course.

"My Chief of Decay," Satan decided, turning to a messenger. "Bring me Rosh-Rot."

CHAPTER
13

Christine's newfound joy was marred by the image of the crucifixion in her dream. Noticing her frown, Molly questioned, "What's wrong?"

"I just can't shake the feeling that the crucifixion in my dream was a warning of some kind," Christine shared.

"What do you mean?" John asked, sitting down beside her, his joy lighting up his face.

"It was too real," she continued disturbed. "That place really exists. I know it. Maybe God's trying to tell us something."

"Tell me what the scene looked like again," John said, listening as she repeated the description of the desert sacrificial site. After she had recounted every detail she could remember, John shook his head. "That could be any one of a million places around here."

Christine looked crestfallen. "Then it's hopeless."

"Nothing is impossible with God," Molly interjected, gathering up the breakfast dishes.

Pat snapped her fingers. "Those books!" She jumped up and ran upstairs.

Christine and John exchanged a puzzled look. Pat bounded back into the room with a stack of paperbacks. "I almost forgot these," she said, handing them to Christine. "I got these the last time you were here, but you left so quickly I didn't have a chance to give them to you."

Taking the top book off the stack, Pat opened it. "Look, there's a map here of the desert floor. Maybe it'll help."

John took the book from Pat, glanced at the cover, then snorted.

"What?" Christine said, leaning over.

"*Sedona's Vortexes: Healing Mother Earth* by Trista Elkhart," he read. "What a bunch of garbage." John tossed the book aside and grabbed the next one. "Now here's a Pulitzer winner. *The Eye of the Vortex: Sedona's Bell Rock*." It was only twelve pages long, with mostly pictures.

"John, let me see," Christine laughed, leaning over his shoulder. "That's it!" she cried, pointing at a picture of the bell-shaped butte, rising from the desert. "I know it."

"I thought you said it was dark in your dream," John reminded her.

"It was, but remember I told you I was floating in the air when I left the scene of the hospital? Well, I saw that place from up above; I'd swear that's it."

"Why don't you two drive out there?" Molly suggested, sitting down across from her son. "If for no other reason than to assure you it was only a dream."

"Yeah," Pat agreed.

"What do you say, John?" Christine looked at him in anticipation.

"I'm game, if you are," John shrugged.

Christine changed into a t-shirt and a pair of jeans, then slipped into Pat's hiking boots. *Good thing we wear the same size*, she thought. On her way out the door, she glanced at her shoulder bag. *I won't need that, will I? No*, she decided. But even as she was thinking it, she pulled out her wallet and stuffed it into her front pocket.

Soon, they were packed up in the Jeep and pulling out of the circular driveway. Driving through West Sedona, Christine wondered if it was safe to explore John's relationship with Star White. Taking a small leap of faith, she crossed her fingers.

"What did Pat mean when she said she was glad you didn't marry Star White?"

John looked disgusted. "I was hoping you wouldn't remember that."

"Well, I did," she grinned slyly. "So you and Star were an item."

"Ancient history," he smiled at her. His blue eyes shone like sapphires this morning, and she felt her heart quicken.

"I'm a history buff," she pressed.

"You're just not going to let this go, are you?"

"Nope," she said, her smile broadening.

"Alright," John sighed and gave in. "It was back in my pre-Jesus days. I met her in my senior year of high school. Only she wasn't Star White then. She was Marcia Blanchard. We ended up at UC-Berkeley together."

He turned as he stopped at a red light, "And I do mean together."

"You lived together," Christine clarified, feeling a twinge of jealousy. "Are you Heather's father?"

"No!" he exclaimed. "I wasn't that dumb. Actually, Heather belongs to Star's former 'spiritual director.' "

"Is that how you got mixed up in the New Age stuff?" Christine asked.

"Yeah," he answered, shifting into a higher gear. "One of our friends in college invited us to a psychic fair and introduced us to Sri Baba and his brand of Indian mysticism. Actually, he was just Jeff White from Salem, Oregon, but we were impressed anyway."

Christine chuckled, "Sri Baba? I can't believe you were involved in that stuff."

"Oh, you should have heard our chant to Sri Baba," John chuckled, remembering. "It was supposedly ancient Sanskrit. I can't even recall exactly what it was now. Something like Sri Baba ram a lam a ding dong. Get this, I was being groomed to take over the flock."

They both cracked up.

"So Star married old Sri Baba," Christine said, smiling. "I wonder if Heather called him old Papa Baba."

John sobered. "No, Heather wouldn't remember her father. Jeff White gave Star his last name, but they were only married for two months. Even after Heather was born, they lived with me."

"I don't get it," Christine pursued. "You mean, she dumped you for the guru, but you let her come back?"

"No," John continued. "She never left. We lived in a commune. You see, it was a great honor that my woman was carrying the child of the guru Sri Baba."

"Oh, no," Christine said, becoming quiet.

John glanced out the side window at the traffic. He went on nostalgically. "She was a beautiful baby, but we were all three babies. When Sri Baba moved his commune back to Oregon, Marcia, who was now Star Lam Baba White, followed him, along with the rest of his women, taking six-month-old Heather Rose with her. She left when Heather was about a year old. In the meantime, I drifted into transcendental meditation for awhile. Then I got involved with Eckankar."

"Eckankar?"

"You don't want to know," John grimaced, rolling his eyes heavenward. "The 'ancient science of soul travel.'"

"So, when did you move back to Sedona?" she asked, delighting in his willingness to share his past with her.

"After art school in the early eighties," he continued. "Sedona was 'hot' by that time. Eckankar had a ranch here, and remember I told you about Page Bryant, the psychic who came up with the theory of the vortexes? People from all over the world began to make pilgrimages here. I was heavy into American Indian mysticism, so I went to a shaman in San Francisco who told me that my future lay in the land of my birth. So I came back home and met Star White again. She was just getting into goddess worship and was practicing Wicca."

"Star is a witch?" Christine shivered. The more she knew about this lady, the less she liked her.

"She's a witch alright," he laughed. His voice was heavy with sarcasm.

"No, I mean is she still practicing Wicca?"

"I wouldn't know," he stared at the road ahead. "The last time Star and I had any sort of contact was just before my conversion to Christianity. We bumped into each other at Bell Rock during the Harmonic Convergence. She was really heavy into worshipping Mother Earth by that time and had hooked up with a bunch of radical feminists, including Libby Brinkman," John snorted in disgust. "The four of them live together in Brinkman's geodesic dome house overlooking Oak Creek."

"Four?" Christine asked puzzled.

"All four," he counted off. "Star, Brinkman and their 'spiritual counselor,' Katona Whitefeather, and unfortunately, Heather."

"Why didn't you tell me this before?" she exclaimed. "I met her at the clinic!"

"I didn't think it was important for you to know before," he smiled, reaching over and taking her hand. Suddenly, she wanted to know everything about him. She wanted to be a part of his life.

"Tell me what you did when you meditated on Bell Rock," Christine asked, liking the way John's hand enveloped hers.

"You really want to hear this?" He glanced sideways at her, then back at the highway.

"It might be important."

"Okay, first I'd prepare myself with some deep-breathing exercises, then begin to 'tune in' to the energy of the Earth,"

John intoned, pretending to sound like some guru. "I'd say something really deep," he laughed, "like 'I am connected to Mother Earth. Our energies are one.'" Christine snickered.

"Then I would attempt to visualize the energy flowing in and out of the base of my spine as I connected. I would meld my aura with the energy of the vortex and ask that it clear away any blockages and awaken my psychic abilities."

"It doesn't sound much different than any other meditative technique I've researched," she commented, cocking her head to one side.

"I'm sure that's true," he agreed, downshifting the Jeep. "Satan has no new ideas. He just keeps recycling the same old lies." He went on. "It was at that point in the meditation that my 'inner voice' advised me on what to do next. For instance, I might be directed to experience a past life, or told to fast. . . ."

"Or to offer a sacrifice?" Christine asked, her voice taking on a serious tone.

"Not me," he remarked distastefully, "but it's conceivable. You do hear of mass murderers all the time talking about how they heard a voice tell them to kill."

"So somebody *could* have received a message from their 'inner voice' . . ."

"To sacrifice Gary?" John completed her thought. "Probably not. But it's not unthinkable. Look at Charlie Manson. He heard voices and then his followers killed for him."

"True, but he thought he was the son of God," she mused, "which come to think of it isn't far from my original hypothesis about Gary's murder."

"Maybe, but maybe there's another possibility," John theorized. He paused to reflect a moment. "What if somebody out there is channeling an entity who directs them to sacrifice at these vortexes?"

"That could be it," Christine exclaimed, recalling her dream and how Star White had suddenly become Coatlicue. She posed the question to John. "Did Star ever do any channeling?"

"I don't know, but it's possible," John answered. "At one time, we were messing around with psychics and channelers and anything else that went bump in the night."

John glimpsed Bell Rock and pointed to it through the windshield. "There it is."

Christine hadn't been paying much attention to their surroundings until now. There rising from the red floor of the desert, surrounded by chaparral and junipers, was the site she had seen in her dream.

"That's it, John!" Christine exclaimed excitedly.

"Let me show it to you from the other side," he said, passing the parking area on the right for Bell Rock Vista and driving on down toward Jack's Canyon Road.

"Pull over!" Christine shouted. As John pulled quickly to the shoulder, he also spotted the ambulance and emergency vehicles on the old Jeep trail.

"Wonder what's going on?" he wondered aloud, turning off the engine. He was out of the Jeep and headed across the highway before Christine could even unbuckle her seat belt.

"Hey, wait for me," Christine declared. "John, I'm coming too." The hot sand gritted under her boots as she jumped from the Jeep and stood, waiting for the traffic to clear. Darting across the road, she ran to catch up with him.

"Excuse me, folks, this road is closed to any traffic," a deputy said, sauntering up to them. "You'll have to turn back."

"What's the problem, officer?" Jack inquired.

"Just an accident," he said, noncommittally.

Looking beyond them, Christine spied Sheriff Anderson talking with an ambulance driver. Thinking quickly, she reached into her pocket, shooting up a quick thank-you to God. Now she knew why she had brought her wallet. Pulling out her press pass, she approached the deputy.

"I'm here to see Sheriff Anderson," she said briskly, and without waiting for the deputy's reply, she marched past him, shouting, "Sheriff! Sheriff Anderson!"

John shrugged at the deputy and said, "I'm with her." As he approached Christine, she was already pumping Sheriff Anderson for information.

"Oh, come on, Sheriff," she was saying. "All this stuff isn't out here because some hiker broke a leg." They both looked up as John joined them.

"Mr. Delarosa, what brings you out here?" The Sheriff tipped his hat. "Where's your paints?"

"I'm playing tour guide today, Sheriff," John shook hands. "Thought I'd show Miss McKay Bell Rock."

"Well, maybe you'd better come back another day," the Sheriff stonewalled. "This trail will be closed awhile."

Christine looked down at the ground, hunting for the right question. She looked back up and stared him straight in the eye.

"Sheriff, I have the strangest feeling you're trying to hide something from me," Christine began. "I thought we agreed not to lie to each other any more. Remember?" She held up a Boy Scout salute. The Sheriff glanced at John, and Christine answered his unasked question. "He knows everything I know."

"Well now, Miss McKay, let's take us a walk," he said, nodding in John's direction. "You too, Mr. Delarosa."

As they hiked up the dusty red trail, the Sheriff filled them in.

"This one was worse than the last time," the Sheriff scowled, as if he'd smelled a skunk.

"Decapitated?"

"Yep," the Sheriff continued. He panted at the unaccustomed exercise.

John coughed, and Christine turned to catch his sick expression as he swallowed hard.

"You don't have to come up here if you don't want to," she offered, laying a hand on his arm. "I've seen worse, I'm sure."

"No, that's okay," John forced a smile. "Wherever you go, I go."

"It's okay, Mr. Delarosa," the Sheriff assured him. "The body's already covered."

As they climbed through the scrub brush up a slope, Christine noticed a forked path, one side of which was blocked by a large deputy and draped with yellow tape.

"Hey, boss," the deputy touched his cap. "They sure are taking their sweet time up there."

"It was a surefire mess and that's a fact," the Sheriff commented as he lifted the tape for the others to pass underneath.

"Now brace yourself," he said, as they rounded a clump of trees.

There in a hollow clearing was the giant bloodstained upside cross that Christine had seen in her dream. Stepping away from the Sheriff, she walked past it and down to the right where she had seen the altar in her dream. It wasn't there. Puzzled, she turned and looked behind her and motioned for John to join her.

"The altar's missing," she whispered. "It should be right here."

"There sure was a big bonfire here though," he said as he pointed out the blackened circle of burnt wood and potash. Stooping down, he rubbed his hand over the smooth red rock, a puzzled look on his face. "This shouldn't be this clean. It's almost as if it's been swept."

Standing up, he called to the Sheriff, "Did your men dust this area for clues?"

"No," the Sheriff said, lumbering over. "There wasn't anything to sweep. Looks like it was done before we got here. What's this?"

The Sheriff leaned down and picked up a small chip of rock. "This is polished marble," he exclaimed. "There's no marble in this area."

"That's strange," said John, reaching for it and turning it over in his hand before handing it to Christine.

"I've seen black marble like this before," she said, peering at the rock she held.

"Where?" questioned the Sheriff, but she only shook her head and handed it back to him. "It was a long time ago at another murder site," she remembered. "It was a shining, black stone altar."

Suddenly, the huge cross crashed to the ground, its sound reverberating against the rock walls. They all jumped.

"Jeez-all-pete," the Sheriff shouted, turning and lambasting his men with a few salty words. He turned back to Christine, who tried to hide her grin. "Excuse me, Miss McKay. Now, what were you saying? Are you telling me that piece of stone came off some kind of altar? If it did, where is it? You just don't go hauling a big slab of marble up and down a hiking trail."

"It wouldn't have to be very big," Christine mused. "About three feet long, by maybe a foot wide, by two-inches thick or so. Just big enough for a couple of candlesticks and long enough to stand behind. Some portable altars are made of wood, with just a six-by-six-inch square of marble inlaid in the center."

"Boy, you sure are a walking encyclopedia," the Sheriff tipped back his hat. "How do you know all that?"

"With all the research I've done on rituals, I've absorbed a lot of information—some of which I'd rather forget."

John stood with crossed arms, watching them lift the body bag on a stretcher, which was carried by two hefty deputies.

"Sheriff, are you going to ride down with the body?" A third deputy remained by the trail, waiting for an answer.

"No, you go on ahead, Clarence," the Sheriff drawled. "Tell the coroner I'll call him as soon as I get back to the office."

The Sheriff wandered over to a knee-high boulder and sat down, taking off his hat and wiping the sweat from his face with a wrinkled, yellowed handkerchief. Hocking and spitting, he turned to Christine.

"Now, Miss McKay, I sure would like to hear more about that theory of yours."

"What theory?" John asked before she could answer.

"I was telling the Sheriff what I'd learned about the Aztec sacrificial rites," Christine explained. "In fact, I bet if we look around here, we'll find another rattlesnake symbol."

"We already did," the Sheriff reported. "It was similar to that fetish we found in your car, only bigger."

"Speaking of which," Christine snapped her fingers. "What did you find out from the lab report on the blood in my car?"

"Blood in your car!" cried John. "You never told me about that."

"We were incommunicado when I left, remember?" Christine retorted, raising her eyebrows at him.

"So what about this blood?" John asked again, ignoring the jibe.

"That's what I'd like to know," the Sheriff responded. "The lab report was inconclusive. It seemed to be a mixture of several types of blood."

"Animal?"

"Nope, human," the Sheriff shook his head. "It was the darndest thing I've ever heard. It was a mixture of several types of human blood."

"That doesn't make any sense," Christine puzzled. Then she remembered the bowl of dark liquid from her dream, but she didn't dare say anything for fear the Sheriff would write her off as just another nut. "Was there any tissue in the blood?"

"Nothing traceable," the Sheriff shrugged. "Now about this theory of some Aztec sacrifice."

"It's still not adding up," she ran her hand through her hair, lifting it off her neck. It was scorching hot. As quickly as she could, Christine related all that she had found out about the rituals and their possible connection to the Sedona vortexes.

"I think I'd better have my deputies keep a watch on Airport Mesa and in Boynton Canyon," the Sheriff said, standing and dusting off the seat of his pants. "If what you say is true, we may be able to catch these nuts in the act."

Shaking John's hand and tipping his hat at Christine, the Sheriff lumbered back down the trail, leaving them to follow at their leisure.

Miklos and Aaro wept bitter tears as they watched the demons dance around the fallen cross. Not one of the foul spirits dared approach either John or Christine, and there were no commanders in sight. A steady stream of demons spewed from the newly created supernatural fissure in the earth. Suddenly, a familiar voice greeted Miklos.

"Friend," it grated, and Miklos whirled to face the cunning devil, Rosh-Rot. "How nice of you to drop by. Would you like a little taste of blood?" He ran his finger along the cross and offered it to his archenemy.

"The Lord rebukes you," Aaro spat disgustedly, laying a restraining hand on Miklos' sword arm.

"Every single day, and it still hasn't made any difference," Rosh-Rot sneered and strutted up to the two angelic beings. "It doesn't matter that she's redeemed, you know. In fact, it makes it better for us," he boasted. "Just think of the *power* that courses through her veins. What a fitting sacrifice she'll make for Lord Satan."

Miklos strained to keep his temper in check. They were outnumbered here, and it would not be wise to provoke a confrontation. They would have their day.

"Such a big threat coming from such a powerless imp," Miklos retorted. Then turning to Aaro, he said, "Come, brother. I refuse to play the childish game of 'my father's bigger than your father' with this demon any longer. We know who the victor is."

Crossing to John and Christine, the angels urged the couple to leave this place. This time, Christine was the first to feel anxious about their surroundings.

"Let's get out of here," Christine said uneasily, goosebumps suddenly breaking out over her whole body.

John surveyed the seemingly deserted clearing as a hawk screeched overhead. He could almost sniff the evil in the air.

"Yes, let's," he agreed, taking her elbow and steering her toward the path which would lead back to the Jeep.

There are times when God in His infinite wisdom chooses to intervene when we have not thought to ask—as He did this day. Splitting the heavens, He sent down a beam of light just wide enough for Christine to see a sparkle in the chaparral directly beneath her feet.

"What's this?" she mused, leaning down to pick up the sparkling object. A chime sounded through heaven and God smiled.

"John!"

He stopped and turned around, "What?"

Trembling, Christine extended her hand. In her palm lay the first tangible link between her theory and reality. It was Dr. Libby Brinkman's ring: a gold coiled rattlesnake with emerald eyes and a forked ruby tongue.

"A ring!" John exclaimed. "A very unusual ring."

"It belongs to Dr. Brinkman," she said excitedly. "She was wearing it the day I interviewed her at the clinic. This proves it, John. Dr. Brinkman is involved in these murders, I know it!"

"Now wait a minute," John cautioned, lifting the ring from her palm and turning it over in his hand. "This doesn't prove anything."

"What do you mean?"

"Lots of people hike up through here," he pointed out. "This is one of the vortexes. What if Star and Libby just came up here to meditate? She could have dropped it while they were hiking."

"You and I both know that's not what happened," Christine asserted, taking the ring back.

"The trouble is," John argued, "we don't know. We can speculate, but it won't stand up in court."

"Who cares about court!" she retorted, her eyes flashing angrily. "I'm talking about what's right."

"So am I, and you can't accuse somebody of murder, just because you found their ring somewhere near the murder site," he explained. "It's only circumstantial evidence."

Christine knew he was right, but she hated it. There had to be a way to use this ring to find out the truth.

"I understand what you're saying, John," she agreed. "But what do you really believe?"

He stared at her, folding his arms across his chest. "Honestly? I think Libby and Star are up to their eyeballs in this—Whitefeather too."

"I'm glad to know you're on my side," she smiled, her determination strengthened by his agreement. "Now we just have to decide what to do with this." She slipped the ring into her pocket and took John's hand. It made her feel safe and protected.

"I always have been on your side, and I always will be." There was a faint tremor in his voice, as if some emotion had touched him. Christine heard it, but John felt it—God was leading him into love.

CHAPTER
14

Libby Brinkman breezed through the front door, calling into the empty foyer, "I'm home!"

"In here," Star's voice answered from the direction of their private chapel.

Setting down her briefcase and keys on the hall table, she strode purposefully into the dimly lighted meditation room. She stopped in the doorway stunned.

"What's *that* doing here," Libby barked, pointing at the painting Star had just hung over the altar. "I thought I told you to get rid of it."

Star turned to face the angry woman, and Libby noticed a change in her countenance. It startled her.

"So you did," Star replied imperiously, "but since that time, I've decided that I want it here." She straightened the frame and took a step back and admired the surreal painting of the Kachina Woman.

Libby also studied the portrait. It was pretty, really. The statue of the Kachina Woman stood in the center of a medicine wheel, flanked by breathtaking huge red rocks and blooming wildflowers: orange Indian Paint Brush, red Penstemons and Sacred Datura. Issuing from the head of the massive stone statue were three forms of the Earth Mother: Isis, Gaia, and Seydna, each uniquely divine—Isis with her Egyptian features and royal cat-like eyes which spoke of the secrets of the ancient pharaohs, Gaia the Greek with flowers plaited in her shining hair, and the antediluvian Seydna of the lost continent of Lemuria in flowing silk sari.

Libby wouldn't have minded it at all, even hanging in her own bedroom, had it not been painted by *him*. It was silly, she knew, but when she thought of that self-righteous Christian prig, her blood pressure rose.

"I wonder what John Delarosa would say if he could see where his painting hung now," Star's voice broke into Libby's reflections. Star's unearthly laughter filled the little chapel.

Libby shuddered. *That's not Star! That's Coatlicue!* Immediately, she dropped to her knees.

"To what do I owe the honor of your presence, O Most Enlightened One?" Libby offered obeisance.

"If you intend to stay on your knees as long as I am here, you will never walk again," the demon Yoko-Sharuhen spoke through the mouth of Star, for it was she who masqueraded as the Earth Mother Coatlicue.

"I don't understand, Mother," Libby questioned.

"My channel and I have become one," Yoko crooned, the evil in her voice disguised with a velvet glove. "I will inhabit this body until its death. Star White no longer exists in this dimension. She has translated into the kingdom of light."

Wide-eyed, Libby stood and gasped in disbelief, "Are you telling me Star is dead?"

"There is no death, my child," Yoko stroked the cheek of the now weeping Libby. "Death is but an illusion, a passage into a higher plane of existence. Star will always be a part of us, as we are a part of her. We are all one."

"But what will we tell Heather?" Libby said, suddenly remembering Star's daughter. "She wouldn't understand that her mother is dead while her mother's body is still here."

"Then we will not tell her anything," Yoko soothed, brushing away Libby's tears. "I am the all-loving Mother. She will never know the difference, for inside of me, I possess all of Star's love *plus* all of *my* love for Heather. And you, my daughter," Yoko said, liltingly, "you also are well loved."

A discreet cough interrupted their exchange as Katona Whitefeather stood in the doorway.

"Excuse me," she apologized. "I was just coming in to do my evening meditation. I can come back later."

"No, no," Libby laughed excitedly. "Come in. You've got to hear this. Coatlicue has come to live with us forever."

"What?" Katona asked, her brow furrowing.

"Star has transcended space and time and gone to live in the home of the goddess, and she has come to live with us," Libby explained, taking the Earth Mother's hand.

"Star, what's going on?" Katona turned to the slight, blonde woman.

"Star is no longer in this body," the demon answered. "But I, the Mother of the Earth, Mother of all the universe, have come to dwell with you so that our tasks might be completed."

Katona shook her head in disbelief, but yet she knew that voice and that countenance. This was Coatlicue.

Striding up to the altar, the "goddess" roughly swept it clear, sending candles and bowls flying through the air clattering to the tile floor.

"Since I am now here, you will no longer have to perform these silly rituals to appease me," Coatlicue said imperiously, locking piercing eyes with the startled Libby. Smiling, she turned to Katona. "You still doubt me, little one. Do not put me to the test."

Katona was taken aback by the threatening authority in the voice that before had spoken only loving words. It reminded her of Sister Mary Francis from the Mission School. Katona could still hear the scathing words as the nun pointed to the crucifix on the wall and told the kneeling row of eight-year-old girls that it was their fault that Jesus had to die because they were so sinful—the Jesus she had loved and adored. But never before had she felt the fear that now rose up within her.

"Mother, forgive me," she cried, not knowing what else to say.

"From now on," Coatlicue continued, "there will be no room for doubt. So, speak now if you wish to be released from your vows."

"No," they both cried, horrified at the thought of being without a guiding presence.

"Fine then," Coatlicue sat down regally behind the altar in what used to be Star's channeling chair. "Now sit with me, my daughters, and I will tell you of my desires. The time is short for healing my planet. That is why I have come and why I have disciplined you. The sacrifices have been successful, and the land is even now becoming fertile with the power of the blood. The blood is an atonement for the millennia of sins against my body, the Earth. The time for the final cleansing is near."

"How may we help, Earth Mother?" Libby sought to please, kissing the bare feet of the "goddess."

"All around the globe, I have directed my daughters to sacrifice at the sacred sites," Coatlicue intoned. "Now there is only one left—Boynton Canyon. A special sacrifice is deemed necessary."

Libby hesitated, and the "goddess" sensed it. Closing her fist around Libby's neck, Coatlicue pulled the breath from Libby's lungs, and she fell to the floor, gasping.

"I will not be opposed," the demon in Star White's body warned. Suddenly, Libby was released, and she grasped her throat, sucking in great breaths of air. Katona didn't dare move or protest.

"Forgive me, Earth Mother," Libby rasped. "I was only thinking, what could be more special than what we have already done? First, we offered the baby at Airport Mesa, then you requested the blood of the young Christian boy at Cathedral

Rock, and most recently, we have given you the sacrifice of the priest at Bell Rock."

"Yes, and I am pleased," Coatlicue purred, "but Boynton Canyon is both a male and a female vortex. It calls for the sacrifice of a man," she gestured, holding up her right hand, "*and* a woman." She held up her left hand, then clasped the two together, her fingers intertwined in front of her. "The two shall be as one. Neither male nor female. Both slave and both free. Of one spirit with the Earth."

"Have you selected the subjects for sacrifice, Blessed Mother?" Katona asked, fearfully bowing low lest the demon sense the growing doubt in her heart.

"Yes, the male—John Delarosa—and the female—Christine McKay," Coatlicue ordained. "John because of the wealth in his spirit, and Christine because she is his chosen Earth mate."

"But how will we lure them into our trap?" Libby questioned, willing to do anything. "The others were easy to fool."

"You will not have to go to them," the demon masked as Coatlicue promised. "They will come to you, for I have taken that which would have brought peril to us and turned it into our advantage. The ring which you so carelessly lost at Bell Rock will bring them to us."

✛✛✛✛✛

Pat waved at John, Christine, and Molly from her corner table at Rene's, an elegant restaurant located near her art gallery in Tlaquepaque. Although the cuisine was French Provincial, the decor was Spanish, with exquisite crystal and china table settings. One of John's paintings of Oak Creek Canyon hung across the room.

John pulled out a delicately carved chair to seat his mother on his right, then seated Christine on his left.

"I thought you were never going to get here," Pat scolded.

"It's my fault," Christine admitted, unfolding her napkin. "I insisted on stopping in at that little jewelry shop next to The Phoenix. They had some unusual pieces displayed in the window."

"Their prices are outrageous," Pat smiled. "But they do have some stunning gold designs, don't they. Did you buy anything?"

"No," John interjected. "We had something appraised."

At Pat's puzzled look, Molly explained, "Christine found a ring up at Bell Rock and she thinks it is Dr. Brinkman's. There was another sacrifice."

"I know," Pat said angrily. "I heard it on the radio at the gallery. It's an abomination before God! Everybody was talking about it this afternoon."

Christine took a sip of water after the waiter filled her glass. They all ordered iced tea, and he left them menus to peruse at their leisure.

"I know," Molly interjected. "Elaine called me this afternoon as upset as she was the day she found out about Gary. It's like living through the nightmare all over again."

Dejected, Christine added, "Why did God give me that dream if I wasn't able to stop it from happening again?"

"Now, don't start blaming yourself," John chided, taking her hand. "We can't second guess God's intentions."

"Absolutely," Molly agreed.

"I still think I should just confront Libby Brinkman with her ring and get her reaction," Christine went over the same territory she and John had argued about the whole afternoon.

"Let's just turn it over to the Sheriff and let him follow up the lead," John reiterated for the umpteenth time.

"I agree with John," Pat interjected, speaking with a quiet firmness. "I know the last thing *I* would want to do is come face to face with the people who would be capable of that kind of carnage."

"Good point," Molly agreed, thanking the waiter as he served her drink.

"So you're telling me," Christine argued, gesturing at John with her right hand, "that we should just give Sheriff Anderson the ring and say we found it on the way down the hill? Then *he* can go over and confront Libby, who will just tell him she lost it while she was hiking?"

"Why would she tell you anything different?" John probed, scanning his menu.

"For several reasons, the first of which is, I'm a woman." She lifted her chin, meeting his objections head on.

"I'd noticed," he smiled, never looking up. "By the way, the seafood crepes are wonderful."

"Second," Christine was undaunted, "I could get a cat to cough up a canary. I'm good at what I do. Finally," she concluded, "and most importantly, God wants me to do this. I just know it."

First John looked at Christine, who was looking at Molly, who was grinning at Pat, who was kicking John under the table.

"Uh, oh," Pat chuckled, "She's got us there."

"Okay," John gave in, "but I'm going with you. Even if I have to wait in the Jeep."

"It's a deal," Christine said, shaking his hand. Both Molly and Pat noticed he held it a little longer than was necessary.

+++++

As they drove back into the Delarosa driveway, a Sheriff's vehicle followed right behind them. It was Sheriff Anderson, who struggled out of his front seat. Seeing Molly, he removed his hat.

"Evening, Miss Molly," he greeted her, nodding politely in the direction of the others.

"Good evening, Dwayne," Molly said warmly. "What can we do for you?"

"I was hoping to speak to Miss McKay and Mr. Delarosa, if I could," the Sheriff turned his attention to Christine. "Would that be okay?"

"Sure," Christine said, turning to John, who nodded.

"Why don't you come on into the house?" offered Molly, linking her arm with his. "I've got some fresh lemonade, or I could make you some coffee."

"A tall cold glass of lemonade sure would hit the spot right about now," the Sheriff grinned.

After pouring the lemonade, Molly and Pat excused themselves, leaving the Sheriff with John and Christine in the dining room.

The Sheriff took a long draught and smacked his lips.

"Ahh, that's good," he said, wiping his upper lip with the back of his hand.

"What's on your mind, Sheriff?" John asked. He and Christine waited as the Sheriff cleared his throat and pulled his notebook from his breast pocket.

"I found another glitch in your theory," Sheriff Anderson began, flipping through his notes. "Well two, actually. Remember when you first came to my office and told me that things weren't addin' up because this group was only sacrificing young men?"

"Yes, I remember," Christine said, leaning her elbows on the table.

"Well, I sent two of my men to comb the area around the vortex at Airport Mesa and they came up with a little surprise," the Sheriff told them. Consulting the notebook again, he continued. "They found the badly decomposed body of an infant, female, approximately twenty-nine weeks gestation. There were similarities between it and the other victims."

John pushed back from the table and stared sadly at the ceiling.

"Are you telling us that this was a sacrificed *aborted* baby?" Christine grimaced and felt the righteous anger well up in her spirit.

"That's right," the Sheriff confirmed.

"What's the second glitch?" Christine prodded.

"Well, we got us a woman too," he disclosed. He reached into his shirt pocket and unrolled a cherry Lifesaver, popping it into his mouth. "This morning at Bell Rock—that was a," he looked down at his notebook, "forty-two-year-old, female Episcopal priest. She had been decapitated, and just like the others, her heart had been removed. There was only one difference." He paused for effect. "In the chest cavity, where her heart had been, we found a rattlesnake-skin medicine bag filled with crystals."

"This is just too much," John muttered, sickened by the revelations. "What do you plan to do, Sheriff?"

"Talk to Miss McKay," he said, nodding toward Christine. "She seems to have all the answers."

"I wish I did," Christine remarked, more puzzled than ever. "At this point, I'm not even sure I've got the right questions. There's so much information floating around in my head, I need to organize it somehow. Get it down on paper."

"I'll get some paper," John suggested, already striding to a corner desk.

"Good idea, John," the Sheriff agreed, slapping his hands together. "Let's work together on this. Maybe we can figure this out tonight."

"We can sure try," Christine concurred.

John brought back a yellow legal pad and handed it to Christine, who shoved it back at him.

"You take notes, okay?" Christine smiled disarmingly, batting her eyes obviously. "I've always wanted a male secretary."

Despite his inner turmoil, John chuckled. She sure knew how to make the best of a bad situation.

"Okay." Christine stood and began to pace. "Here's what we know. There are four major vortexes. There have been three sacrifices. Have your men found anything at Boynton Canyon?"

"No," the Sheriff answered. "Not yet."

"John, didn't you say that the vortexes each were supposedly either male or female?" she asked, starting to put the pieces together.

"That's right," he answered, proud of her analytical abilities.

"Which were which?" she pursued.

"Gary was crucified at Cathedral Rock, which is female," John explained, making notes as he answered. "The baby girl was found at Airport Mesa, which is a male vortex, as is Bell Rock. . . ."

"Where we found the priest, a female," the Sheriff finished the thought.

"So it appears the sacrifice must be the opposite sex of the vortex," Christine drew a conclusion. "If we follow this line of thinking, then there would have to be two sacrifices at Boynton Canyon."

"So far, haven't all the victims been Christians?" John asked.

"All except for that wee baby," Sheriff Anderson offered. "It never had a choice of what it wanted to be, but I bet it's in heaven now."

Christine felt a hollowness inside her, remembering her own baby. She pushed it aside and focused on the matter at hand.

"It's safe to assume that the priest was a Christian, and we know Gary was," she continued, looking at John. "Could that be the crucifixion connection?"

"Not necessarily," John answered. "The New Age religions teach that the cross symbolizes the union of cosmic energies and it marks places of the spirit."

"Yeah," Christine said, snapping her fingers. "I remember reading that the Aztecs used crosses in some of their rites too. They believed that the cross symbolized the actual world: heaven to earth and man to man. So it could be any one or a combination of all three ideologies: somebody who has a vendetta for Christ, is involved in the New Age and in Aztec-type ritual worship."

"Sounds like Satan," John ventured. "He certainly has a vendetta against Christ. He's the driving force behind the New Age religions, and he was certainly involved in Aztec sacrifice."

"So we've got the what and the how," Sheriff Anderson stated, ticking off on his fingers, "but what about the why and the who?"

"Well, I've already ruled out Satanism as a possibility," Christine told them. "This is too public, and it doesn't fit the normal pattern. Let's look at what we've got," she said, resuming her pacing. "The symbol for the Aztec goddess Coatlicue was found at Gary's murder site. So that leads me to believe that there is goddess worship involved. Now goddess worshippers are primarily women because of the ecofeminist belief that they are being exploited and dominated by men through a stern, overbearing sky god." She stopped and looked at Sheriff Anderson. "So they turn instead to worshipping obscure female deities, centering around the earth, fertility, and healing."

"Hey," the Sheriff interjected, impressed with her knowledge. "Didn't you say that Coatlicue was the Earth Mother?"

"That's right," she answered, continuing to pace. "Typically, these women will worship the Great Mother Earth in one form or another because they feel one with the earth. The earth is female, with womb-like caves and caverns. They relate the moon-rhythm to the monthly menses."

"So now we have the what, the how, and maybe the why," the Sheriff ticked off on his fingers again. "Now all we need is the who—who did it." He scratched his chin and leaned forward. "Missy, sounds to me like you might have a suspicion of who did it that you're not sharing with me."

Christine sat down and shared at length everything she had been thinking about the possible connection between Dr. Brinkman,

Star White, and the murders. Everything, that is, except for the ring. When she finished, the Sheriff leaned back in his chair and whistled.

"Girl," he said, shaking his head. "I only wish you had some proof to back up that hypothesis. Just seein' a snake ring on Dr. Brinkman's finger just won't cut it. That doesn't put her behind an altar all dressed up in feathers."

"What kind of proof would you need, Sheriff?" John asked, his penetrating gaze convicting Christine. She looked away.

"Something that would place one or both of those women at the scene of the crime would be a good start," the Sheriff slammed his palm down on the table. "Heck, they're both supposedly fine, upstanding citizens of Sedona. A confession wouldn't hurt either."

"Can't you go and at least talk to them?" Christine pleaded, ignoring John's unspoken censure. "After all, you found an aborted baby that had been sacrificed."

"Shoot," the Sheriff snorted. "That baby could have been aborted in Phoenix or Flagstaff for all we know. Nope," he said, standing up and putting on his hat. "It's a good theory, but my hands are tied. If I tried to walk in there and question one of those women, they'd have their lawyers camped on my doorstep. No ma'am. Now if you come up with any evidence that we could take to the bank, then we'll talk.

"Understand now," he said continuing as they walked him to the door. "I'm not writin' you off totally. Fact is, I wish I had detectives as good as you, Miss McKay." He shook their hands and walked out to his car. As he opened the door, he turned and said, "I'll keep in touch."

CHAPTER
15

The three women relaxed back in their patio chairs, sipping herbal tea from delicate tea-rose china cups. The demon Yoko-Sharuhen, inhabiting Star White's body, stretched luxuriously and sighed deeply.

"How marvelous it is to be in a body after so many centuries," she said as Coatlicue, "to breathe, to feel, to enjoy the things of the Earth as one of my children."

Libby and Katona, chastened and now fully cooperative, basked in the presence of their goddess. Libby refilled Coatlicue's cup with the steaming brew.

"Earth Mother," Libby inquired, "when will they come?"

"Soon, my daughter," Coatlicue crooned. "Soon. Then they will be ours." The demon goddess smiled cat-like in anticipation. "How long I have waited for this moment! I have lived under the Earth for an eternity, and now I will emerge like a phoenix from the burnt ashes of the sacrifice. The deserts of the world will burst forth with luxuriant growth. There will be no more hunger—no more thirst. My children will turn away from their sky god and worship only me, the one who gave birth to them and nurtures them."

"What will happen to us after you have ascended to your rightful throne?" Katona asked. "What purpose will we serve then?"

"Don't fret, dear child," Coatlicue answered sweetly. "I have reserved a place for you. When I come into my kingdom, one of you will sit at my right hand and the other at my left. Both will be equal for all is one."

"What do you mean we'll be equal?" Libby asked stunned. "You promised me before we even began that I would have a place of power in your kingdom. Now you tell me I will be equal to my former spiritual director?" Her eyes shot daggers at Katona.

"Elizabeth," Coatlicue purred. "Do you even now not understand? Everything that I have is yours. Since all is one, you will have all of my power. As will Katona," she said, indicating Whitefeather with an open palm. "There will be no favorites, no separate special ones. All will live in harmony in the same glorious light, drops in the same ocean. Is one drop of seawater greater than any other that beats the shore and carves the canyons?

"No," Coatlicue answered herself. "Likewise, you cannot be any greater than Katona, nor she than you. Because of this, I perceive we need to make some changes as far as this household is concerned." Her two subjects looked warily at one another across the glass patio table.

"I have decided after much thought," Coatlicue continued, enjoying her complete authority over these humans, "that it is unfair for you, Libby, to exercise all the control in this house. You must learn to be a servant. Both of you must obey me without question, no matter what I ask of you, no matter how trivial the task. I want you to move into the smaller bedroom downstairs."

"But this is *my* home," Libby protested.

"No longer, child," Coatlicue's voice hardened. "This is *my* home while I choose to live here among you. I want you to move your things out of the master suite today."

Libby pouted like a petulant child. "Yes, Earth Mother."

"And you, Katona, consider your flesh to be holy, so tonight you will humble yourself before your goddess," Coatlique's eyes took on the glint of the sacrificial blade. "You will learn that *no one's* child is exempt from the knife."

"Yes . . . Earth Mother," Katona answered, her brow furrowed in puzzlement.

Coatlique rose regally. "Good, let me not be disappointed in you children. Our success depends upon your obedience." She turned, leaving Katona and Libby to glare at one another.

✝✝✝✝✝

Being a baby Christian, Christine vehemently defended her position to John.

"But you don't understand," she argued. "I have to be the one to confront Dr. Brinkman with the ring."

"Why?" John asked, slamming the refrigerator door. He took a swig of milk and sat down at the kitchen table. "Didn't you hear what the Sheriff said? *Any* piece of evidence, linking one or both of those women to the scene of the crime, would be helpful."

"John, I've worked with a lot of police departments, and believe me, that ring would not be considered a valid piece of evidence," Christine said condescendingly. "*You* even said it could have been lost while hiking."

"That was before we talked to the Sheriff," he exclaimed angrily. "And don't use my own words against me!"

"I'm sorry," Christine calmed down. "But this is really important to me. This could be a great story! Besides that, I feel compelled to do it. I can't explain it."

"Well, just make sure it's God compelling you," John said, downing the rest of his milk and slamming the glass on the table. "I think you're playing with fire."

With that, he stormed out of the kitchen and up to his studio. Christine winced as she heard the door slam. She felt hot tears spilling from her eyes, and her heart ached.

God, Christine ventured to pray, *if this is you, please let me know. If not, stop me before I screw everything up. Thank you. Amen.*

Tiredly, she climbed the stairs to her bedroom. She frumped down on the bed, eyeing the Bible lying on her nightstand. Finally, she picked it up and opened it at random. Her eyes fell on Proverbs 20:24–25 (NIV): "A man's steps are directed by the Lord. How then can anyone understand his own way? It is a trap for a man to dedicate something rashly and only later to consider his vows."

What does it mean? she pondered. *Does it mean I'm doing what the Lord wants? Or that I'm being rash?*

Because she sought an answer, the Holy Spirit began to teach her. Thoughts sprang to her mind that she knew she didn't generate.

Did you or did you not give your life to me? If so, did you make the decision rashly? If you have given your life to me, everything you choose to do must be weighed against that decision. Only then can I direct your steps. You must ask yourself this: Am I choosing to do this thing because I feel led of the Lord, or because it is something I see needs to be done?

Christine understood. The Lord was directing her steps, and she believed that He was leading her to confront Libby Brinkman. Something good would come out of this somehow. John would just have to understand. *Lord God, please help him understand.*

✝✝✝✝✝

Miklos stood guard as Christine slept. The house was quiet and peaceful. Suddenly, a light glowed in the room and he felt a joy as Kerestel, Sandor, Goyo, Pesach, and Wardar appeared. Clasping hands with each of them, he greeted them in the name of the Lord.

"To what do I owe the honor of your visit, Captain?" Miklos asked.

"I have come to prepare you for the final steps in our victory," Kerestel answered seriously. "I brought your brothers so that they might be of comfort to you, for the news I bring is disquieting."

They sat, Pesach and Wardar flanking Miklos. "Tell me, Captain, is she to die?"

"That is for the Lord to know," Kerestel reminded Miklos. "We only know that there is great danger."

Sandor and Goyo returned to the room with Aaro in tow.

"Good fellows," Aaro greeted the group, sitting on Christine's bedroom floor. "What news?"

"You need to hear this too," Kerestel addressed him. "Both of your charges will shortly be given over to the hands of the enemy."

"No!" Miklos shouted. "Can we not prevent it?"

"No more than we could prevent the crucifixion of our Lord," Kerestel commented sternly.

Miklos was chastened, remembering that dreadful day. Aaro, too, dropped his head in sorrow.

"But surely there is some way we can protect them from this great danger?" Miklos offered.

"She belongs to the Lord, as does John, Miklos," Kerestel reminded him. "This is the purpose for her coming to Sedona in the first place. She was chosen to reveal the work of the enemy. Her mortal life is forfeit, if necessary. She knows that," Kerestel said, glancing at the peacefully sleeping Christine. "And you know that too."

Miklos nodded sadly, "Yes, Captain." Pesach placed a comforting hand on his friend's shoulder.

"Remember, brother, how the Lord in His great mercy allowed His hand to cover her," Pesach recalled. "I was to make sure that death passed over her *until* she was born again into the kingdom of our Lord. After that, she has eternal life. What can man do to her? We do know that God's will for her life is good and not evil, for Satan comes only to steal, kill, and destroy, but Jesus came that she should have abundant life."

"We will do our best to protect both John and Christine," Sandor promised. "The battle will be hot and furious, but sometimes the safest place is in the eye of the storm. All is not lost," he encouraged. "Remember, Satan is weakest when he thinks he has won."

"We came to warn you so that you would know not to fight," Kerestel warned. "You must not let your temper control you, nor your love for this human blind you. The Lord's good purpose will win out."

"Our Lord can take Satan's most wretched refuse and turn it into gold," Goyo added.

Kerestel stood. "It is not for us to understand. We are but to obey and trust that the Lord in His wisdom will cause all things to work for good for those who love Him." He grasped Miklos in a fatherly embrace. "We will not see you again until the battle, but do not despair, we will be near." Turning to Aaro, he clasped his hand. "Farewell, friend. Be encouraged. The hearts of the faithful are already being burdened to intercede in their behalf."

On the far side of the rock formation known as the Kachina Woman in Boynton Canyon, a horde of demons assembled. They were engaged in revelry and celebration, for all through hell, the word was out. Soon, all that was below would be above as the final rift was torn in the veil between earth and hell. Once more, Satan would reign on the earth. He would take his rightful place as god over all of this world, and *all* mankind would bow the knee to him.

The revelers fell silent as their Commander Rosh-Rot passed among them. Stopping here or there to shake a hand or receive some small token of homage, he strutted through the throng. His Legion of Commanders followed him to the foot of the Kachina Woman where he turned to address the crowd.

"Tomorrow night, this land will belong to us," Rosh-Rot pledged. "No longer will we be relegated to the underworld. No longer will we have to do our Master's bidding in secret. For all will be one with the Master. All hail, Lord Satan, King of the Universe!"

A roar rose from the demonic company. He leered triumphantly over the masses, then lifted his scaly arms in the air and continued.

"This place is hallowed ground," Rosh-Rot intoned. "Not because of myths and legends, but because it is here that the blood of the Christ will be proven to be powerless. When the final rift is opened, we will drive the enemy from this land, and from here, Satan's kingdom will be established. When he is once more in this realm, man will no longer be able to resist his power, and the New Age will come. Now go! You have your assignments. As our Master has willed it, so mote it be!"

Molly Delarosa pulled into the parking lot of Immanuel Faith Chapel and checked her hair in the rearview mirror before opening her door.

Pastor Mike sounded really down when he called me, she thought. *I hope things are okay at home.*

Greeting his secretary, Molly offered a silent prayer for guidance. "Is he in, Gladys?"

"He's waiting for you, Molly," Gladys smiled. "Just go on in."

Molly tapped at the partially opened door before sticking her head around.

"Anybody home?"

"Molly, come on in," Pastor Mike got up from behind his cluttered desk and gave her a hug. Shutting the door, he said, "Have a seat."

"What's up, Pastor?" Molly asked, with motherly concern. "You didn't sound too happy on the phone."

"I'm not sure what's up," he answered, rocking back in his chair. "I was hoping you could help me discern that very thing."

"I'll try."

"I was at the weekly breakfast meeting of the ministerial association this morning," he sighed. "Pastor Don Haney from the First Church of the Nazarene informed me that his flock was beginning to complain that they had to consort with the Methodists and Episcopalians," he shook his head regretfully, "so he pulled his support from any further interdenominational activities. That includes any pro-life projects."

"Why, he was one of our most ardent supporters," Molly's voice rose in surprise. "What's gotten into him?"

"That's not all," Pastor Mike continued wearily. "Father Shongus confided that he's getting flack from his vestry because his church has so many pro-choice activists. They told him that he would either have to cease meetings with us, or form a pro-choice group also." The pastor folded his arms in disappointment. "So out of good conscience, he withdrew his support."

"No," Molly exclaimed in irritation as she jumped to her feet. "I don't believe this!" She paced to the window. "Where are the believers?"

"I just don't know anymore," he agreed, his misery like a lead weight. "I haven't told you the worst part."

She sat back down again. "There's more?"

"The new minister at the First Presbyterian Church, Dr. Blaine Kent, was the speaker," Pastor Mike explained. "He stood up and lambasted the fundamentalist, sexist doctrine that denied the feminine side of God. He read to us from a new translation of the Bible that used what he called inclusive language." His voice betrayed his raw anger. "What it did was call God 'she' and 'father/mother.' They've removed every reference to the gender of God, Jesus, and the Holy Spirit. Wherever it says brother, it also has to be sister, and wherever the word *man* appeared, it was changed to *humanity* or *humankind*." He let out a long audible breath.

"That's rewriting the Bible!" she answered in a rush of words. "How could they do that? Didn't they read the book of the Revelation?"

"What it did was divide the entire Body!" Pastor Mike exclaimed. "Brother Jasper interrupted Dr. Kent right in the middle of the Psalms and told him he was going straight to Hell, to which Dr. Kent replied, there was no such place. Man created his own Hell."

Pastor Mike snorted his disgust. "Pastor Cole spit his mouthful of water onto Brother Clemons' suit coat, which caused Brother Clemons to say a few words not often heard from a minister." He sighed. "Everybody was either red-faced angry, or embarrassed, and nobody could get a word in edgewise. It was like all hell broke loose."

"Didn't anybody stand up for the Word of God?" Molly asked incredulously.

"I tried, but by that time, it was practically to the stage of a food fight," Pastor Mike replied wearily. "Frankly, I don't think it would have done any good. I've never seen anything like it in my life. The final outcome of it all was that the ministerial association has been disbanded until further notice."

Molly's annoyance increased, and she found her hands were shaking. Then it hit her. All hell *had* broken loose. Suddenly, her face was full of strength, shining with a steadfast and serene peace. She spoke with quiet firmness.

"Pastor, I think it's time we got to the heart of the matter," she declared. "There are some things that have been going on you need to know about."

Slowly, she cleared her throat and then she told him about Christine's suspicions, filling in every detail she could remember, including the tie to Changes Plus and Libby Brinkman. As she finished, an inner torment began to gnaw at her and a deep unaccustomed pain filled her breast. It was a suffocating sensation that tightened in her throat. She reached out a hand and fell forward to the floor.

Pastor Mike leaped out of his chair and flew to her side, his booming voice full of authority: "You loose her now, in the Name of Jesus. Spirit of Death I rebuke you! Take your hands off this child of God."

Molly gasped and then relaxed. She began to softly pray in the spirit, thanking God for the deliverance from the sudden attack. Still shaken, she allowed Pastor Mike to help her back into her chair.

"I'm going to go get you some water," he said with concern. "I'll be right back."

Molly was left alone in the pastor's office. She leaned her head against the wing-back chair and closed her eyes. Suddenly, it was as if someone had turned on a bright overhead light. Her eyes blinked open and she saw that the room was filled with the glorious light of the presence of God. Her pulse began to beat rapidly and despite her awe, she felt an intense and burning joy.

"Do not be afraid," she heard in her spirit as she was given a vision from the Lord. As if watching a movie, Molly saw a rattlesnake crawling into a hole in the ground. A hand, like the hand of God, covered the hole and closed the earth. Next, she witnessed a bowl of dark, red blood being poured onto that same ground. To her amazement, the earth split open and thousands of snakes began to escape from the rift.

The picture changed, and she gasped as she watched John and Christine tied to a tree with writhing, hissing snakes. Swiftly, the image was replaced by one of promise as Molly, herself, sat rocking a small baby. She was humming an old hymn, "Oh, precious is the flow, that makes me white as snow, no other fount I know, nothing but the blood of Jesus." The shock of discovery hit her full force as she realized the promise of a grandchild.

As swiftly as it had begun, the vision ended. She sat there blank, amazed and trembling. Pastor Mike returned with a glass of water, but stopped when he saw the glow on her face.

"Pastor," she whispered, "too bad you didn't come back sooner. You could have seen the Lord."

"What?" he said in shock. "I was only gone a minute. Just long enough to walk to the water fountain outside my door and back."

"It seemed like an eternity," she smiled. "I've seen a vision." He was too surprised to do more than nod, so Molly continued. "The Lord showed me three pictures," she began and described in detail the entire vision.

Pastor Mike stood, leaning against his desk. He was speechless. Finally finding his voice, he declared, "Molly, you've heard directly from God. Do you have any idea what it meant?"

"I do now," she answered. "As I was telling it to you, I received the interpretation. The first picture, well that was evil being hidden. The hand like the hand of God represented the appearance of godliness that covered the evil. The blood was directly related to these sacrificial murders that have been occurring, according to Christine, all over the world."

She paused, with a sense of conviction that was a part of her character. "The snakes coming out of the hole explained what the results of those sacrifices were; supernatural rifts have been torn between earth and hell allowing all manner of demons access to this earthly realm."

"Well, that helps explain what's going on with the churches," he sighed.

"The third picture is more alarming for me," Molly admitted. "My John and Christine are marked by the enemy to help them fulfill their evil intentions."

"God forbid!" Pastor Mike exclaimed.

"God already has forbidden it," Molly answered, smiling. "He showed me rocking my grandchild as a promise that John and Christine will live and not die."

"I think we'd better call a meeting of the Joshua Intercessors at your house tonight," he suggested. "We need to pray for their protection."

Pastor Mike pushed the intercom button on his telephone and asked Gladys to begin calling the list of prayer warriors to meet at Molly's house at 7:00 that night.

CHAPTER
16

Christine stood outside of John's studio door, trying to decide whether or not to knock. Finally, taking a leap of faith, she tapped lightly.

"Coming," he called. Her stomach tightened as she heard John's heavy footsteps approaching.

"Hi," she said softly as he opened the door, "Can I come in for a minute?"

"Sure, come on in," John answered self-consciously, running his fingers through his disheveled hair. "I think we need to discuss a few things." He stepped aside, allowing her to enter.

She glanced around at the disarray that made it clear John had spent the night in his studio. The white shirt he wore last night was thrown over a chair back, and there was paint on the sleeve.

"Your cleaning bill must be astronomical," she said, picking it up and folding it carefully.

A smile played at the corner of his lips as he took it from her and tossed it back on the chair. Taking her arm, he led her to the small conversation area and sat her down on the love seat. The afternoon sunlight streamed through the skylight, adding a burnished halo to her chestnut hair. He dropped into the chair across from her, picking a piece of lint off his trousers.

"So," she said, heaving a sigh.

"So," he echoed, smiling sheepishly. "I guess I need to apologize for being such a bear last night. It's just that . . ." He leaned forward and peered deeply into her hazel eyes, which were more green this morning. "I've come to care for you deeply, and it worries me that you don't seem to have any sense of danger."

Christine felt a warm glow as she realized that there were no barriers now between them.

"You have to understand that I wouldn't even consider confronting Brinkman with her ring if I didn't really think it was the right thing to do," Christine assured him. "I thought a lot about what you said last night, that I should make sure it was God compelling me and not my reporter, 'go-for-the-story' instincts."

"And what did you decide?" he inquired, reaching out and taking her hand.

"I prayed about it," she said, swallowing the lump in her throat, "and then I picked up the Bible and it fell open to a proverb, which told me that I couldn't go my own way because God was ordering my steps. I'm more sure now than ever before that I'm supposed to do this."

He turned her palm upward and lifted it to his lips, placing a tender kiss in its center.

"Then I'll stand behind you," he vowed. "I'll take you to the clinic as soon as I clean up a little."

"Have you eaten anything today?" she asked, bouncing up off the love seat.

"No," he admitted. "I've been working on something all night."

"Well, how about I fix a sandwich while you take a shower," she said, striding to the door.

"I'll be down in about fifteen minutes."

As they exchanged jibes about Christine's burnt grilled cheese sandwich, Molly breezed excitedly into the kitchen.

"Praise God, you're still here!" she exclaimed.

"Not for long," said John, wiping the milk mustache from his mouth. "We've got some things to do downtown."

"Please be home early for dinner," Molly implored. "We have an emergency meeting of the Intercessors tonight, and I'd like for the three of us to be able to talk before they get here."

John bussed her on the cheek, as he and Christine stacked their plates in the sink. "What are you fixing?" he asked, giving her a playful hug.

"Well," Molly answered, "I thought I'd throw together some spaghetti and a tossed salad and have Pat pick up garlic bread from the bakery on the way home from the gallery."

"Yummy," John shouted boyishly. "We'll be here for sure. See ya later."

"Got the ring, Christine?" he asked on the way out the door.

"You bet, right here in my pocket," she replied patting her jeans pocket.

Hopping into the Jeep, they headed toward town.

Miklos and Aaro sat dejected in the backseat.

"God grant us the strength to be true to your will," Miklos lifted his hands to heaven.

Aaro, too, raised his hands and began to sing a mournful sounding song:

> "The Lord is their strength,
> for he is the saving strength
> of his anointed ones.
>
> O, Lord save thy people
> and bless thine inheritance.
> Save them and lift them up forever."

+++++

Heather pushed open the bathroom door and stood motionless, staring in astonishment at the bruised and battered face of Katona in the bathroom mirror. Seeing Heather's reflection, the young Indian woman ducked her head, hiding her face behind the melting Blue Ice pack. Heather grabbed Katona's arm and pulled the pack away from her face.

"What happened to you?"

"Go away, Heather," Katona earnestly whispered to the stunned teenager, jerking away. "You must get away from here as fast as you can." Katona then closed the bathroom door in her face.

Heather stared in horror. Fear rose and wrapped its deadly talons around her throat. She turned and ran headlong into her mother—at least she thought it was her mother. "Star" slammed the girl against the wall and held her there by the shoulder.

"You little sneak," she hissed.

"Get your hands off me, Mother," Heather yelled. "What happened to Katona?"

"None of your business," Star shouted. Shoving the teenager aside, she stomped into her bedroom and slammed the door.

Heather ran down the hallway and beat on the door with her fists, "Mom! Mom! What's wrong with you?" she cried, rattling the knob. "Mother, open this door!"

Startled, Heather almost fell to the floor as the door whipped open.

"I'm not your mother, you little brat."

The craggy voice sent a shiver up Heather's spine. The eyes of the demon Yoko-Sharuhen, staring out of her mother's face, snapped with an indignant fire at the teenager's challenging demeanor.

"Who did that to her, Mother?" Heather demanded, standing her ground in spite of her growing terror.

"I told you to mind your own business," Star spat, waltzing back into her bedroom and raising the bamboo blinds.

"It *is* my business!" Heather could hardly believe her ears. "I live in this house, too, you know." Her mother had to be on drugs, drunk, or out of her mind. This was *not* the mother she knew. She'd never seen her like this.

Star crossed the room and sat down at her vanity table, brushing her long hair. "What happens to the body is immaterial," she intoned. "It's the soul that matters. Katona is soul-sick. She had a bad past-life regression; it was a violent episode. She was throwing herself all over the room. I could barely restrain her."

"That's a crock," Heather spat disgustedly. "*You* did that to her, didn't you?" Heather began to shake violently, as she could no longer contain her disgust for her mother's wicked lifestyle and her unholy rituals.

"I put up with you and Libby and your friends doing God knows what in that 'chapel' downstairs," Heather yelled, "and I . . . tried to pretend that it was okay . . . because it was your life and you said we should all live and let live. But this . . . this . . . this is sick! It's violent and evil. Who's next?" Heather shouted. "Me?" She was even more enraged by the fact that Star sat calmly brushing her hair as if they were discussing the weather.

"If you don't like the way we live, then you're free to go," the demon spat. "In fact, I insist you leave." Coatlicue slowly rose and turned to face the angry teenager. "Get out of my sight, you sniveling brat, or I'll turn you inside out!"

The look on her face told Heather that she was capable of doing exactly what she said. Her eyes were somebody else's. Her voice was somebody else's, and Heather knew that what Gary told her was true. There was a devil inside of her mother.

She turned and fled down the stairs, her tears blinding her as she stumbled out the front door and ran down the driveway to her Honda. Revving the motor, she spit gravel from under the tires as she headed to . . . *to where?* she thought. But it didn't matter. *Anywhere that's not here.*

Watching from the upstairs bedroom balcony, Yoko-Sharuhen cackled a malevolent, maniacal laugh.

Go, Heather, go. You're the bait to bring them to me!

From the bathroom window, Katona also watched and wished that she, too, could escape. But there was no escape for her. She had vowed her obedience to the goddess Coatlicue.

The spiritual director dropped to her knees and began to rock back and forth, crying softly. *I don't care what I promised, I can't kill Heather!* Now there was only one choice. Katona rose tiredly to her feet, humming an ancient Indian mourning song.

✛✛✛✛✛

The doorbell was ringing furiously, as Molly raced to answer it. *Who in heaven's name?* she thought, a bit agitated. Pulling open the door, she was speechless, for there stood a sobbing Heather White.

"Darlin', what's wrong?" Molly asked, gathering the distraught girl into her arms and rocking her back and forth. "Come on in, sweetie. It's okay. You can tell Granmolly all about it."

She let Heather lean on her shoulder as she led her down the hall and into the family room. Sitting down in the big, overstuffed rocker, Molly pulled the young girl onto her lap and continued to hold her.

"I used to rock you like this when you were just a wee little girl," Molly crooned. "You remember?"

Heather nodded, her weeping slowly subsiding. "And I used to call you Granmolly, didn't I?"

"Mm, hm," Molly agreed, brushing Heather's wet, stringy hair away from her flushed cheeks.

"Is Papa John home?" Heather asked, suddenly feeling self-conscious about being rocked. She slid down on the floor and laid her head in Molly's lap. "I really need to talk to him."

"He'll be home for supper, honey," Molly soothed, stroking the blonde head in her lap. "Why don't you stay and eat with us?"

"Can I?" Heather asked, looking up longingly.

"Well, of course you can," Molly smiled. "You're always welcome in my home. You're the closest thing I have to a granddaughter."

Suddenly, Molly sat up straight, remembering her vision, but she pushed it aside for the more pressing matter at hand. Rather than questioning her, Molly allowed Heather the dignity of offering an explanation for her untimely arrival. It didn't take long.

"There's something wrong with my mom," Heather sniffed and gazed up into Molly's accepting face. "Something terrible."

"Is she sick?" Molly grew concerned.

"In the head," Heather declared.

"Honey," Molly scolded.

"No, I'm serious, Granmolly," Heather sat back on her haunches. "You should have seen her . . . and what she did to Katona. You know, Katona Whitefeather, who lives with us."

"Well, what did she do that was so awful?" Molly asked, not sure she really wanted to know.

"Mom's totally flipped out," Heather grimaced. "Katona's face was black and blue. And that's not the worst part. I've got a sinking feeling that Gary was right about my mom. She's been messin' around with the devil so long, he finally moved in." Heather started crying again, and Molly gave her a tissue to wipe her runny nose. "She told me to get out or she was going to turn me inside out."

"Oh, honey," Molly said, "she didn't mean it."

"Yes, she did," Heather snuffed. "You . . . didn't see her face. She was a monster. It wasn't my mom."

Heather buried her face back in Molly's lap and shook convulsively. Molly knew something was very wrong. She could feel it.

"Granmolly?" Heather ventured of her own volition. "Can I stay with you? I won't be any trouble. I promise. Just until Mom sobers up, or whatever?"

Molly's heart nearly broke. "Sure, sweetie. We've got plenty of room." *Dear God*, Molly prayed silently, *tell me what to do*.

CHAPTER
17

John parked the Jeep across the street from Changes Plus and glanced at his watch.

"Okay, it's 3:30 now," he said. "If you're not out by four, I'm coming in."

"That should be plenty of time to get a confession out of her," Christine said grimly. "If I'm not out by then, send in the troops."

John reached over and gently brushed a stray lock of hair away from her face. "Don't take any chances, okay?"

"I don't intend to," she promised. As a second thought, she leaned over and gave him a quick peck on the cheek. "Pray for me, okay?"

"I've never stopped," he said.

Christine climbed down from the Jeep, and waited at the curb for the traffic to clear. Pushing open the front door into the waiting room, Christine spoke to the receptionist.

"Hello, Tracy?" she smiled sweetly. "Is Libby in?"

Tracy knew Christine looked familiar, but couldn't place her. Obviously, she knew Dr. Brinkman to call her by her first name.

"No, I'm sorry, you just missed her," Tracy apologized. "She took off early today for a meeting. She won't be back in until tomorrow afternoon."

"Oh darn," Christine snapped her fingers in mock disappointment. "I guess I'll just come back then." She turned to walk hurriedly from the clinic.

"May I give her a message?"

"No, thanks, I'll just give her a call later," Christine smiled and opened the door.

Running back across the street, she gave John the thumbs down sign.

"What happened?" he said impatiently, as she climbed into the Jeep and fastened her seat belt.

"The doctor wasn't in," Christine offered disappointed.

"Maybe they were lying," John started the engine. "We'll circle the parking lot in back just to make sure. Libby drives a blood-red Porsche."

"Kind of fitting, isn't it?" Christine quipped, as he made a quick U-turn and drove up the alley behind the clinic. "No Porsche."

"Well, where do we go from here?" John asked, waiting for directions.

Christine looked at her watch. "Probably back to your house. The receptionist said she went to a meeting, so no telling where she is. Besides, Molly said to be home early."

John turned the Jeep around and headed back for West Sedona.

✛✛✛✛✛

Katona Whitefeather anointed herself with oil and removed her sacred medicine bag from around her neck, dumping its contents into the stone bowl on the altar. As she sang an ancient Native American song, she lighted a twig of sage and laid it on top of the bowl to drive out the bad spirits. Pulling a leather case from under her white buckskin shirt, she laid it reverently upon the altar and opened the lid.

The shining flint edge of the curved Aztec ceremonial knife glistened in the candlelight. The turquoise stones, worn smooth by the many hands that had caressed it across the centuries, glittered with a life of their own.

I am already dead inside, she thought. *Why do I hesitate?*

"Oh Great Spirit, I invoke your light to cleanse me and purify my heart. Give to me your blessings and grant me your protection. Oh Great Spirit, remove from me my external shell of emotions and beliefs which have slowly removed me from your teachings. Guide me as I walk the rainbow bridge to the land of my Grandfathers."

Lifting the knife in her trembling right hand, she cut through the artery of her left wrist to the bone. Changing hands, she did the same to her right wrist. With blood coursing down her arms, she raised the knife and slit her own jugular vein and gracefully sat back in the stone throne behind the altar.

Katona watched the blood stream down her white ceremonial skirt. Blood was everywhere. She was putting the babies back together. Look at all the blood . . . and the man was crying, "Please don't kill me" . . . and blood was running out of his chest . . . and blood was running down the altar . . . and tears dripped from the face of the Jesus hanging on the cross at the Mission School . . . and the priest was screaming, "Please don't kill me" . . . and the crucifix was stained with blood . . . and Jesus was standing with arms outstretched, saying, "Come unto me, all ye that labour and are heavy laden, and I will give you rest" . . . and blood was dripping from His hands . . . no, not His hands, my hands . . . forgive me, Jesus . . . Do you remember me? . . . Please forgive me . . . I'm sorry for what I did . . . I didn't mean to make you cry . . . I love you, Jesus . . . forgive. . . .

Jesus stood holding the broken body of Katona Whitefeather before the throne of His Father in heaven. "Forgive her," He asked. "She really didn't know what she was doing. She was so hungry for the truth and so confused. She tried to find the balance between her people and my Word, and got caught in the middle.

But she knew my name, and she called on me. Her last words were, 'Forgive me.'"

From behind him, Satan roared, "She is mine! I have been tutoring her since she was a small toddler at her grandfather's knee. I am her Great Spirit. I am her Earth Mother. Her soul belongs to me. Give her to me!"

The face of God turned and looked away, and Jesus laid the broken body at His feet and faced Satan. "It is written, 'And everyone who calls on the name of the Lord will be saved.'" Turning back to His Father, He pointed at the lifeless, spiritless body and demanded, "She . . . called . . . on . . . my . . . name!"

God, the Father, met His Son's fiery gaze. "Are you certain that she meant You?"

"Yes," Satan retorted. "There are many ones called Jesus. Are you sure she meant you?"

"It is written, 'I am the Good Shepherd. I know my sheep, and my sheep know me,'" Jesus pleaded, placing His hand on the knee of God. "Just as the Father knows me, and I know the Father."

"Unfair!" Satan yelled. "Unfair! She killed herself!"

God lifted an angry head and pointed a threatening finger at Satan. "Be gone. It is decided."

Jesus reached down and lifted the spirit of Katona Whitefeather from her broken and bruised body, saying, "Arise my love, my fair one, and come away with me."

God smiled in satisfaction, thinking back on the day that the Mission School was first built. "Good seed in good soil," He said. "Good seed."

✝✝✝✝✝

Libby strode purposefully into the house. Checking the clock, she knew it would be time for evening meditation, so she laid her purse and keys on the dining table and headed toward the private chapel. Humming, she threw open the doors, mentally running over what had to be done to prepare the altar for the goddess. Looking up, she screamed, "Katona!"

There, in a pool of drying blood, was the lifeless body of Katona Whitefeather. Libby checked her pulse. There was none. It was then that she noticed the bruises around her neck and face. Curiously, she had died with a smile on her lips. Libby gently moved her down to the floor and closed her fixated eyes.

Enraged, Libby turned and stormed out of the chapel. Not finding Star/Coatlicue anywhere downstairs, she climbed the staircase and headed for the master suite. Standing outside the door, she heard voices coming from the other side. She knocked. It grew silent.

Suddenly the door flew open, and she was face to face with a rabid looking Star White.

"What do you want?" the demon screeched at her.

"I thought you might be interested to know, I just found Katona dead in the chapel," Libby said, watching her reaction.

"That whining little whelp deserved to die," she spat. "I offered her a piece of Godhood, and she held on to a childish myth."

"But she was my friend," Libby began to cry. It was the first time in a long while that she had cried for someone else.

"Grow up," Coatlicue snapped. "Surely, a little blood hasn't rattled you. It's almost time for evening meditation. So, get down there and clean up that mess."

"But Earth Mother, shouldn't we call somebody?" Libby looked stunned. "She did have a family, you know."

"Katona is a part of the all-encompassing family now," Coatlicue said sternly. "She offered herself as an appeasement for my dissatisfaction with her. You need not grieve, nor fear. She did as I expected her to do."

"Did you beat her?" Libby asked fearfully through a veil of tears.

"Of course not," Coatlicue crooned. "Why would I wish to harm one of my children?" Softening, she patted Libby's cheek. "All is well, my sweet lamb. Be at peace."

"What am I supposed to do with the body?"

"Katona would want to return to the earth, so prepare her for burial," Coatlicue said. "Do not fret, my daughter. Even now, I am preparing a place for her in my kingdom."

Remembering the voices, Libby asked, "Who were you talking to when I knocked?"

"What do you mean?" Coatlicue blinked innocently. "Perhaps it was the radio."

"No," Libby insisted, "it sounded like you were talking with two men."

Coatlicue glared. "What business do you have eavesdropping outside of my door?" Flinging the door open and stepping aside, she gestured. "Here. Look. There's no one in here but me. Quiet yourself, daughter. You are overwrought. Now go to Katona," she ordered, preparing to shut the door, "and clean up that mess."

Libby stood staring at the closed door for what seemed like an eternity. There were no more voices. No sound at all. She shook her head. This wasn't turning out like she'd planned. Not at all. When she first talked Katona into convincing Star that she was the perfect channeler, Libby had such high hopes for them all. Star had been so gullible in the beginning. Now it had gotten out of hand. Their Earth Goddess was a demanding, self-serving tyrant. But there was no turning back. *Katona was weak*, she convinced herself, and turned to prepare her dead spiritual director for burial.

✝✝✝✝✝

In Star's bedroom, Yoko-Sharuhen faced the new Commander Rosh-Rot, who was standing, mocking her, with a talon clapped over his mouth.

"Is she gone?" he taunted her, whispering. "I thought indeed we would be discovered!" He chortled, rolling on the floor. "My, my, my, but she is a tasty morsel."

"Behave yourself, Rosh-Rot," Yoko snapped. "And keep your claws off of her."

"The Master is pleased that you have so far advanced his cause," Rosh-Rot recovered himself. "But you let Whitefeather slip through your fingers."

"How was I supposed to stop a deathbed conversion?" she raged. "I know, I know," Rosh-Rot sympathized. "But you know our Master. He doesn't like to lose. So he sent me to let you know that he had his eye on you and to remind you that you still had Zethar's punishment to take."

Yoko's eyes flashed fire. "You tell the Master that I said I would be glad to take anything that he chooses to give me. Likewise, he should be appeased by whatever I choose to give him."

"I would prefer not to take back that particular message, if you don't mind," Rosh-Rot asserted, his yellow eyes narrowing. "The Master may put up with that kind of talk from you, but he'd fry my hide if I spoke to him in your manner."

"Tell him what you will," she said, dismissing the Commander. "I have a sacrifice to plan."

✝✝✝✝✝

Stunned, Christine stood open-mouthed in Molly's kitchen as sixteen-year-old Heather bounded across the floor and threw herself into John's arms.

"Papa John," she cried, as he picked her up and swung her in a circle.

"Heather Rose," he smiled, giving her a big kiss on the forehead.

"I'm so glad to see you! I'm staying for dinner," Heather enthused. "And—I'm coming back to live with you."

Papa John? Christine blinked her eyes and closed her mouth. *Granmolly? I'm coming back to live with you? Buddy, you've got some explaining to do.*

"Hi, Heather," Christine extended her hand. "Remember me?"

"Oh, hi," Heather said, ignoring her, and turning back to Papa John. "There's something wrong with Mom. I think maybe she's possessed."

"Whoa, honey," John chuckled. "She's always been a little strange. But," he shook his head, "possessed?"

Heather's eyes filled with tears, but she refused to let them fall. "You'll have to ask Granmolly," Heather hugged him around the waist. "I can't talk about it anymore. It makes me soul-sick."

"Soul-sick? Heather," John corrected. "We don't talk like winkies around here."

"Sorry," she said, bouncing out of his arms. "Aunt Pat said we could go swimming before supper. She's even loaning me a suit. See ya later." Dashing upstairs with the energy only a teenager exudes, she disappeared into Pat's bedroom.

"Now I wonder what's going on," he turned to say to Christine, then noticed her stone face. "I guess this must be a surprise, huh?"

"Sort of," Christine slammed her purse on the kitchen table. "Did you forget to tell me everything, or did I miss something? I thought the last time you lived with Star was when Heather was a *baby*."

"I didn't say that," John protested. "I said the last time I had any real contact with Star was at the Harmonic Convergence."

"Is there anything else I need to know?" she ranted.

"What are you so upset about?" John shrugged.

"What am I so upset about?" Christine mocked. "The man I love just had a sixteen-year-old girl wrapped around him calling him Papa, and I'm supposed to just blow it off?"

"Oh, for pete's sake, Christine," John said exasperated. "What do you want to know? I'm not trying to hide anything." He sat down and propped his feet in the chair next to him. "Go ahead. Ask me anything."

Christine felt rather than saw Molly enter the room. Flushed, she turned and apologized to Molly.

"I'm sorry you had to hear any of this," Christine excused.

"That's okay," Molly said, smiling. "I didn't hear much after you said, 'the man I love.' "

"I didn't say that!" Christine protested, blushing.

"Oh, yes you did," John chuckled.

"I did not!"

"You did too!" hollered down the voices of Pat and Heather. "We heard you all the way up here."

Blushing, Christine was beside herself, sensing the absurdity of trying to hide anything from this wonderful family.

"Maybe I did," she admitted, flustered. "But that doesn't let you off the hook." She shook her finger at John.

As Heather and Pat passed through giggling on their way to the pool, Pat shouted back over her shoulder, "Well, 'man that she loves,' are you going to tell her, or am I going to have to?"

"You stay out of it," John threatened good-naturedly. Removing his feet from the chair, he patted it, indicating Christine should sit. Reluctantly, she sat down.

"I'll just be out by the pool with the kids," Molly excused herself. "Keep an eye on the sauce for me."

"Okay, Mom," John waited until the sliding glass door closed behind his mother. "Now, where were we?"

"You were explaining to me how you suddenly acquired a sixteen-year-old." Christine folded her arms and stared at him, eyebrows cocked.

"When I moved back to Sedona," he began, "my mother refused to allow me to practice my pagan religions under her roof. I ran into Star downtown, and she offered to let me stay at her house. So I moved in with her and Heather."

"Oh, great," Christine commented self-righteously.

"Hey," John said matter-of-factly. "You've got to remember that I've been redeemed since then. That was the 'old man.' Anyway, Star and I picked up right where we left off. Heather was starved for male attention, so she started calling me Papa John. I didn't mind. I've always loved the kid." He shrugged. "Then Star started staying out overnight. She'd come home in the morning all hyped up."

John got up to lift the steaming lid off the gurgling spaghetti sauce. Stirring it with a wooden spoon, he continued.

"It wasn't long until I found out she was into witchcraft," he snorted. "Star began to blame all her problems on men, especially me."

"So, when did Heather start to call your mother Granmolly?" Christine was no longer angry. She felt sorry for the little girl who had to grow up in such a strange and horrible home.

"Oh, that came when I stole her," he stated, replacing the lid.

"You what?"

"I stole her," John explained, leaning against the kitchen counter. "Libby moved in with us while she was waiting for escrow to close on her new house. One day, when Heather was about eight or so, she wandered into Libby's room and started playing with her crystals. She cracked a very expensive one with a hammer to see what was inside. Libby went berserk and slapped Heather so hard, she knocked out one of her teeth."

"Oh no, John," Christine exclaimed.

"Let's just say I lost my temper and leave it at that," he went on. "I packed what few clothes Heather had and brought her home to my mother. We went to court to try to prove that Star was an unfit mother, but she lied through her teeth and claimed I had been the abusive one. Libby's name never came up."

"So," he concluded, "that's why she calls me Papa John and considers my mother her Granmolly. Any more questions?"

"No," Christine answered quietly, standing up. "I'm really sorry I flew off the handle. I had no right."

"Yes, you did," he said, taking her into a friendly embrace. "Remember, I'm the 'man you love.' "

CHAPTER
18

Libby replaced the mud-caked shovel in the gardener's shed. Pulling the gloves from her sore, burning hands, she slapped them down on the workbench. Closing and locking the shed, she wandered back down the hillside to the freshly covered mound.

It doesn't seem right that she won't even have flowers on her grave. Libby wiped a silent tear from her cheek. Suddenly the thought that Katona had joined Star in the all-embracing universe wasn't so comforting. She remembered the words of the goddess: *I will not be opposed.* A chill ran down her spine as she recalled the crushing pain of the air being sucked from her lungs. No, she would not oppose the goddess. She would see it through to the end and claim her final reward.

Walking back toward the house in the lengthening shadows, Libby could hear cars pulling into the driveway and she could see silhouettes through the cathedral window moving around the living room. *What is going on?* Entering through the back of the house, she tried to slip up the back stairs but the demon goddess called out her name.

"Elizabeth? Is that you?"

Oh, great, she thought looking down at the filth that covered her from head to toe.

"In here," she answered, hoping the Earth Mother would come to her. But it was not to be.

"Join us, my sweet," the grating voice beckoned.

Libby dusted off her jeans as best she could and made her way into the living room. She was shocked to find the entire inner circle gathered there.

"Why Libby, you look like something the cat dragged in," the goddess smiled innocently. "Gardening at this hour?"

On the spot, Libby stood dumbfounded. *Why is she doing this?*

Stuttering, she replied, "Just planting a little flower bed in back. I'll go clean up and be right down."

When Libby returned from washing, she saw the group sitting at the feet of their goddess, hanging on every word, as she regaled them with tales of their past lives and future glories.

"Where's Katona?" the librarian asked.

"On a dream-walk," the goddess explained. "She felt the call to seek out her destiny among her own people."

"She moved out?"

"You could say that," Coatlicue smiled. "But enough. Our priest is here." She reached out a tender hand to Libby. "Come sit at my right hand."

Pleased at her deference, Libby sat on the sofa next to the goddess.

"I love that scent," Coatlicue whispered. "What is it?"

"Tea Rose," Libby basked in the attention.

Libby held out her wrist for Coatlicue to sniff, and the goddess bit her hand, drawing blood. Libby squealed in pain and pulled away.

"Why did you do that?" Libby asked astonished, as she looked at her bloody palm.

"Isn't it amazing how we cringe at the sight of our own blood?" Coatlicue's guttural laughter filled the room. "My daughters, you must all be prepared to shed your own blood for my purpose. Tonight, we will make a pact." She paused and stared into every pair of eyes in the room. "A blood covenant. For the time is come to prepare the final sacrifice, and I must have your total allegiance."

Drawing the flint knife from its case, Coatlicue explained the procedure. "Each of you must kneel before Libby and extend your left palm toward her," she instructed. "I will ask you a question, and your answer must be 'I will die for you.' Libby will then cut your palm, and the blood will flow into the bowl. Do you understand?"

Entranced, each of the ten women nodded their assent. The first one, Joan the librarian, knelt before the coffee table and timidly extended her palm. Looking up at Libby, she saw hesitation in her eyes, so Joan smiled and whispered, "It's okay." She then looked at the goddess and awaited the question.

"Do you love me?" the goddess asked.

"I will die for you," the librarian answered fervently. She winced as Libby drew the razor sharp blade over her palm and watched in fascination as the blood trickled into the bowl. Libby handed her a tissue, and she got up, making room for the next initiate. Finally, there was only Libby who had yet to make the vow.

"Kneel in front of me," the goddess ordered. Libby knelt in front of her mistress. Sneering, Coatlicue asked, "Do you love me?"

Libby hesitated. "Do . . . you . . . love . . . me?" the demon asked again.

There was no other choice. "I will die for you," Libby intoned and sliced her own palm.

The stone bowl now contained the blood of everyone in the room, except for Star White's. Taking the knife from Libby, the goddess sliced her own palm and intoned, "I will die for you." Grinning, she lifted the bowl skyward and said, "May this blood be between me and thee until we are parted by death." Then she lowered it and greedily drank its contents. Licking her lips, she laughed at the startled faces. "So mote it be!"

✛✛✛✛✛

Heather sopped up the spaghetti sauce in her plate with her last piece of garlic bread. She still wore Pat's bathing suit and a pink terry cloth coverup.

"Wish I'd thought to grab some clothes when I left," Heather groused. "You think you could take me to get some, Papa John?"

In the middle of his second helping of spaghetti, he looked up and frowned, "Right now?"

"She's sixteen, John," Pat reminded him. "With teenagers, it's always *right now*." Everybody laughed.

"I sure can't wear Aunt Pat's clothes to the prayer meeting," Heather complained. "All she has are old lady clothes."

"Now just a minute," Pat pretended to be indignant, "who are you calling an old lady?"

"Okay, I'll run you home after I finish my dinner," John acquiesced. "Maybe I should give your mom a call first though."

"No!" Heather exclaimed. "She'll tell you not to come, or she'll just insist I come back home. If we just go, she won't give me any flak."

Christine leaned back in her chair and folded her arms. "Well, from Papa John to bodyguard, all in the same afternoon," she teased. "This will take some getting used to."

Molly sat warily observing the interchange. Her spirit was troubled at the thought of John going over to that woman's house. She didn't even want Heather to go back. Then it occurred to her.

"Sugar, why don't we just run over to your house right now," Molly pushed back from the table. "I'm already finished and I'm sure Pat and Christine will clean up and make the coffee for the meeting." Not waiting for their objections, Molly picked up her purse and nodded at Heather. "Come on, you're driving."

"I don't think that's a good idea, Mom," John said, raising his hand to protest.

"Nonsense," Molly answered, trying to hide her uneasiness. "I never did have any trouble getting along with Star when it came to Heather. I'll just explain that Heather needs a little breathing room and wants to stay with me for awhile." She kissed her son on the forehead. "Don't worry about me. Everything will be alright."

Heather bounced out of her chair and grabbed her oversized purse, digging around for her keys.

"Let's go," Heather grinned.

Pat started to say something, then changed her mind. Something wasn't right, but she didn't know what. Molly and Heather were already out the door before she could protest.

As Heather drove, Molly held on to the dashboard and prayed under her breath. It wasn't Heather's driving that led to the fervency of her prayer, but rather the growing disquiet within her. The vision of John and Christine played through her mind, but she hung on to the promise.

It was almost dark now as Heather wheeled into the driveway.

"Oh great," Heather exclaimed, slapping the steering wheel. "Mom and Libby's weirdo friends are here."

"Maybe we should come back tomorrow," Molly hesitated, fear rising in her throat.

"Oh, it's okay," Heather assured her, getting out of the car. "They're probably in the chapel chanting their little brains out. They won't even know we're there."

Against her better judgment, Molly followed Heather up the flagstone walkway. The teenager let herself in and held the door for Molly to enter. Stepping into the hallway, she peered cautiously around her. Such opulence. Such beauty. *All bought with blood money*, the thought passed through her mind.

"You can wait in the living room," Heather whispered. "I'll run up and grab a few things."

Heather bounded through the doorway which led into the living room, and Molly followed.

"Mom!" the girl gasped.

Molly looked up, her eyes adjusting to the dim light. There before her stood a crazed, wide-eyed Star White, with blood running out the corners of her mouth.

"Lord, have mercy!" Molly cried, grabbing for Heather's arm to pull her back. "Go to the car."

Heather turned to run, but her way was blocked by her "mother."

"You're not going anywhere, Missy." Star backhanded Heather and knocked her to the floor.

"Star!" Molly shouted. "What are you doing?"

The teenager was kicked in the stomach before Molly could react by launching herself at the demon-possessed Star White.

"Stop it! In the name of Jesus, stop it!"

Molly grabbed Star's shoulders and shook her. It was only then that Molly realized there were more women in the room, as they encircled her. She was grabbed from behind and pulled off of Star. Heather, too, was lifted from the floor by a stunned Libby.

"You stupid little imbecile," Libby hissed in her ear. "Why didn't you just stay away?" She dragged Heather kicking and screaming, forcefully shoving her down onto the sofa. "If you know what's good for you, you'll sit very quietly." Libby growled at the cowering girl. "*Do-not-move!*"

Molly was wrestled down beside Heather by two of the others as Libby stood discussing their predicament with "Star."

"What do we do now," Libby paused weighing her words, "O Enlightened One?" She didn't care if her anger showed. "Do we kill two more people just to cover your tracks?"

Libby gasped as a steel cold hand grabbed her by the throat, lifting her off the ground.

"Watch your mouth, you rebellious child," the demon goddess snarled, dropping Libby to the floor. "I could crush you like a bug. Don't question me again."

Libby stroked her throat and whimpered, "Forgive me, Mother."

"Very well," Star turned to Joan. "Watch them." She then pointed a threatening finger at Libby. "Follow me." The two women disappeared into the chapel. Libby avoided looking at the still blood-stained tile around the throne. The demon paced. "What to do? What to do? O Master, I call on you for help." Chuckling, she turned to a chastened Libby. "We have been blessed. Truly blessed!"

"What do you mean?" Libby asked.

"We have been given the means by which to complete our sacrifice this very night!" the demon Yoko-Sharuhen shared gleefully. "It is so simple."

Dashing out of the chapel, a startled Libby followed at the heels of her goddess. Standing in front of a pale, but defiant Molly, Star ordered, "Get up! You have a little phone call to make." The demon leered at the strong-willed woman. "I'm going to tell you what to say, and if I hear one ounce of hesitation, you can kiss your little friend here goodbye." Picking up the sacrificial knife, "Star" handed it to Joan. "If I give the word, slit her throat."

Joan swallowed and mumbled, "As you will, Earth Mother."

Molly followed Star without protest to the phone on the bar.

✛✛✛✛✛

Christine answered the ringing phone, "Delarosa residence. Oh, hi, Molly. What's up?" She frowned. "Teenagers. Where are you?" She wrote quickly on the pad by the phone. "Okay, we'll be right there." Walking to the foot of the stairs, she hollered up, "John . . . John?"

He stuck his wet head out of his bedroom door. "What!"

"Your mom just called," she explained. "Heather ran out of gas about two miles from home. They need us to come and pick them up."

"Okay!" John exclaimed, shaking his head. "Let me get a shirt on, and I'll be right down."

After telling Pat where they were going, they hopped into the Jeep and peeled out of the driveway. Pat stood in the doorway, watching them go. *Something's just not right. I feel it.* She glanced at her watch. Everybody would be arriving soon. She rushed back in to make the coffee, shooting up a quick prayer.

"Lord, I don't know what's happening, but I place it all in your hands. I roll the care of it over onto you. Thank you for keeping my family safe."

✛✛✛✛✛

John turned his beams on high. "Where did she say they were?"

Consulting the piece of paper, Christine said, "Just north of Indian Gardens in a picnic area."

"I can't believe that kid was stupid enough not to check her gas tank," John complained.

"Well, according to what your mother said, she was pretty shaken up when she got to your house," Christine excused the teenager. "It probably never entered her mind. There," she said pointing, "isn't that Heather's Honda?"

John steered the Jeep into the deserted area, his headlights striking the car. A distressed Heather sat behind the wheel.

"Poor kid," Christine said. "She probably feels terrible."

"Wait here," John said, jumping down from the Jeep. "I'll be right back." Christine shivered involuntarily as the wind rustled through the trees. Suddenly, she was aware of how isolated they were out here.

As John approached the car, the driver's side window rolled down, and a crying Heather stuck her head out.

"Papa John," she wailed. John leaned down and found himself nose to nose with a pistol. He stared down its barrel into the determined eyes of Star White.

"I'm sorry," Heather sobbed.

"Shut up, brat," Star commanded. "Nice to see you again, Johnny. How about you and your girlfriend follow us back up to the house? If you're thinking of running, don't. I've already got your mother, and I'll hold this loaded .38 against your precious Heather's head."

"What do you want, Star?" John asked, trying to reason with the demon. "Let Heather drive the Jeep. I'll ride with you."

"No way," Star snarled. "I know all about you Christians." She mimicked, 'Greater love hath no man than this, that a man lay down his life for his friends.' If I let you drive, you'd sacrifice yourself, and me, for both of them." She pulled back the hammer of the gun and placed it against Heather's temple. "Now get in the Jeep and don't try anything stupid."

John backed up, hands in the air, anger gnawing at his stomach."Alright," he agreed. "Just don't hurt her." He turned and loped back to the Jeep.

"What's up?" Christine ventured. Then Heather's car started and pulled away. "What is going on?"

"Star's gone nuts," he said through clenched teeth. "She has Mom up at the house, and a gun to Heather's head demanding that we follow her."

Christine paled. "They know! John, we can't go up there. Turn around and we'll get the Sheriff."

"Didn't you hear me?" he shouted impatiently. "She has a loaded .38 pointed at Heather's head! I'm following her."

"But, John, it's her own daughter!"

"I don't think it matters," he ground out. "I think she'd kill them both—Mom and Heather."

"Are you telling me you're going to blindly follow that insane woman up to her house so she can kill us all?" Christine was becoming hysterical.

"I haven't got a choice," he sighed.

Heather's Honda pulled off the road and turned into the gated driveway of Libby's dome house. The red Porsche was parked at the side, along with two other cars. The front door of the house swung open and Libby appeared on the porch. John turned off the Jeep and glared at her. Walking around the front of his vehicle, he opened Christine's door. He took her hand and helped her down, whispering in her ear.

"Don't worry," John soothed. "I'll think of something. Just stay calm."

Christine nodded her head, fighting the tears that threatened. Now was no time to show weakness. She watched in horror as Star dragged Heather from the car by her hair and shoved her toward the house.

Pointing the gun in their direction, Star ordered, "You two, keep your hands where I can see them."

John put one arm around Christine and the other around the sobbing Heather.

"See my arms?" he shouted defiantly. Guiding them past a smirking Libby, he was shoved in the back down the hallway into the living room. A pale, but obviously praying Molly, sat subdued on the sofa, while a slender woman held a knife pointed at her.

"Granmolly," Heather cried, falling in a heap at her feet.

"Don't cry, honey," Molly comforted, stroking her hair and looking up at John. "I'm sorry, John."

"You had no way of knowing, Mom," John shook his head. "I don't think any of us did."

"But I did know," Molly insisted, remembering her vision in Pastor Mike's study. "I guess I was trying to interfere with somebody's plans. Now, I've endangered Heather, along with you and Christine."

"Molly, you can't blame yourself," Christine began. She felt a sharp prick in her hip and turned, seeing Libby holding an empty hypodermic needle.

"Night, night," Libby whispered through an evil smile.

Christine felt herself drifting away, and she slumped against John. As he caught her in his arms, Libby stabbed a needle into his bicep. Roaring with anger, he let Christine slide to the floor and reached for the slowly retreating Libby. As he took a step, his mind began to fog, and he heard the demon's triumphant laughter as he slumped against the bar and to the floor. Heather and Molly sobbed, holding each other, totally helpless.

"Tie them up," Star ordered Joan and another woman, indicating the teenager and Molly. "Then blindfold them and put them in your car. The site should be ready by now." Turning to Libby, she barked, "Help me with him, will you?"

Soon, with John and Christine in the trunk of Joan's Lincoln, and Molly and Heather secured in the backseat, they caravanned back down the canyon road toward downtown and on to Boynton Canyon.

Floating above the car, Miklos, Aaro, Jeremio, and Heather's angel, Bendek, fumed under the taunts of the horde of demons who accompanied the caravan.

"He who is like the Lord, indeed!" they spat at Miklos. "How are you going to save her now?"

"Enlightened, are you?" they hissed at Aaro. "Shining? You look a little dull to me!" The demons cackled in glee.

Jeremio kept his head down as a slimy gorgon circled his head, chirping. "I'd like to see how your God is going to exalt you when He sees how you have failed! You're a failure. You're a failure."

The older angel drew a protective arm around Bendek as two demons tried to pierce him with their filth covered swords.

"Oh, you're blessed," a demon taunted. "Wouldn't you say he looks blessed? Oh my, yes."

Miklos felt the talons piercing his back as Kinah, the lamenter, attached himself and whispered in the angel's ear: "Let's see you brandish your sword and banish me now, oh mighty warrior of God. Ha!" Miklos sank to the trunk of the car in pain.

Jeremio shook his head, "No! I will not let this continue." Drawing his sword, he knocked the hellish creature from his brother's back and lay down on top of him, admitting his defeat.

"Leave us! We are bound to remain, but we will cause you no grief. We know that we're outnumbered this night."

"Then into the trunk with your charges," shouted Kinah, recovering his dignity. "And you two, into the backseat." Jeremio and Bendek dropped through the roof into the car. "Defeated angels are not allowed to show their faces."

Goyo and Sandor, cloaked in the headlights, wept. One nod from their Captain, Kerestel, and they would gladly lead their troops to free the saints of God. But they had their orders; it was not yet time.

CHAPTER
19

Pat checked her watch for the fifth time. It was five minutes to eight and still no sign of her family. Pastor Mike, in Molly's absence, was relating everything that had happened in his office to the astonished intercessors.

"So," he concluded, "it looks as if the enemy has laid a fine foundation for the Second Coming. I believe that if Molly and Christine are correct in their assumptions, we are in for a mighty battle."

Pat raised her hand and interrupted. "Mike?"

"Yes, Pat?" the Pastor acknowledged her warmly.

"I'm really beginning to worry," Pat remarked. "Mom and Heather left about six, and John and Christine went after them about 6:30 or so. I haven't heard anything from them. They should be back by now."

"Maybe your mother is leading that pack of heathens to the Lord," interjected Harold. His wife, Dorothy, gigged him in the ribs.

"From the sound of that bunch, I don't think they'd be ready for that yet," declared Ralph with a snort. His wife, Joanne, looked troubled.

"I get the feeling we need to pray for them," she proposed.

"Me too," agreed Alice. "I don't feel good about this whole situation."

Barb, too, felt a burden in her spirit.

"Then let's pray," Trish asserted, slapping her knee. "If we're all feeling this uneasy in our spirits, the Lord is trying to tell us something."

Dianne, a young and earnest prayer warrior, began: "Father God, we know it says in your Word that you've given your angels charge over us so that we won't even dash our foot against a stone. Father, we believe that your angels are guarding Molly, John, Christine, and Heather. We ask you right now to bring them home safely. Lord, we just ask you to show us how to pray for them."

"Father, we ask that you send your warring angels to break the grip of Satan on our friends," Trish picked up the prayer. "We place a thorny hedge of protection around them so that no evil can come against them. In the name of Jesus, we bind the enemy and command him to take his hands off of our brothers and sisters in Christ."

"Oh God!" Pat cried out to Him and slumped face first under the power of the Holy Spirit. The praying stopped. Pastor Mike knelt beside her and checked her pulse.

"She's okay," he whispered. "Let's just continue to pray as He leads us." He motioned for Harold to come over, and together, they adjusted Pat more comfortably on the floor. Harold knelt down on the carpet beside her, patting her hand and praying.

But Pat neither felt nor heard anything going on around her for she had entered the throne room of God, standing before the Mercy Seat and face to face with her Lord Jesus.

"Patricia, I have something I want to show you," the Lord said, taking her hand. He stood her before what appeared to be a huge hole in the heavens, and she stared in amazement at her own body in her living room as people prayed around her.

"Have you brought me home?" she asked, feeling the joy of His Presence.

Jesus smiled gently, "No, not yet. But there is much I need to tell you." He pointed once again at the portal. She watched as cars pulled into a small dirt parking area at what she recognized to be Boynton Canyon. It was pitch dark, yet she could see it clearly. Furtive figures scurried quietly, removing a black marble slab from the bed of a pickup. Two women carried it like a small coffin. Behind them on the trail were two women, who toted a black bag and two unlit bamboo torches each. On the other side of the Kachina Woman, two more women were arranging stones into a large medicine wheel. Two others were lashing together roughly hewn trees to make two crosses.

"What you are seeing, my dear one, is what is happening in the natural realm," the Lord said, placing a hand over her eyes. When He pulled it away, the scene had changed. The women were still in the midst of their preparations, but Pat was able to see hordes of demons dancing and chortling, flitting to and fro from woman to woman.

Then she lifted her eyes to the surrounding hillsides. Legions of warring angels in battle formation stood at ease. Several battalions of massive foot soldiers in gleaming armor of light waited patiently. A celestial cavalry stood at the ready, white stallions pawing restlessly at the air. Archers knelt in front, their bows of bronze bent and straining, awaiting the signal.

"Don't they see them?" Pat wondered. "Aren't the demons afraid?"

"Our angels are cloaked in the light that radiates from the face of God," Jesus explained. "No one will see them until it is time."

Her attention was captured by a group of large, particularly nasty looking creatures, who sat upon the rocks and supervised.

"Who are they?" she asked the Lord.

"They are Satan's Legion of Commanders," he answered. "See how small they are compared to my angels. Yet they try time and time again to engage them in battle, thinking they might win. But the battle belongs to the Lord."

"And the victory belongs to the saints of God," Pat finished happily. "Why are you showing me this?"

Jesus took her by the shoulders, making sure He had her full attention.

"First of all, you must not allow fear to overtake you," He directed. "Second, you must remember everything you have seen, because the time is coming when you will need to be able to encourage my people. Remember the number of angels and their great size compared to the ranks of the enemy."

"I will, my Lord," Pat promised.

"Good," He smiled. "Now what I am going to tell you may seem distressing, but you know that all things are not as they appear."

He turned her back around to the portal, and what she saw there made her recoil. She saw her mother and Heather being forced to kneel before what looked like Star White. But another face was superimposed on Star's.

"That demon is Yoko-Sharuhen," Jesus revealed. "She is the entity that these women believe to be their Earth Goddess and has seized total control of Star White."

As Pat watched, she observed her mother being slapped and roughly shoved to the ground.

"She just used my name," Jesus revealed. "The enemy hates my name."

The women began to paint one another's faces. Libby Brinkman was there, and two massive demons followed her wherever she went. "The one on the left is Zethar-Zebah, who is the master of abortion, and the one on the right is Bizjothjah, which means 'contempt of Yahweh,'" Jesus pointed out.

Pat viewed Libby filling a syringe, and as the worshippers lined up, she injected each one. When she withdrew the needle from each arm, a massive demon slipped into each woman's body. They then began to sway and dance. Then she refilled the syringe from another bottle and injected Heather, who fell asleep. Molly objected and pointed her finger at Libby. The Lord allowed her to hear her mother's words:

"Elizabeth Brinkman, the Lord rebukes you," Molly shouted.

Libby sneered, "I was going to allow you the privilege of sleeping through your son's agonizing death, but now I'll let you watch."

Pat wanted to weep. Jesus placed a comforting arm around her shoulders.

"Remember, victory belongs to the saints of God," He reminded her. Then with a sweep of His hand, He closed the portal.

"Now remember these names," the Lord said, placing a hand on her head. "Zethar-Zebah, Bizjothjah, Yoko-Sharuhen, Rosh-Rot, Quench-Bersha, Rezin-Rohgah, Mibzar, Desmodus, and Humtah. These are the demon chieftains with which you and your intercessors will have to deal. When you have defeated them, the desert, the church, and the town will be freed from demonic oppression. When you take dominion over them, you must call them by name. Remember their names."

Pat began to mumble, "Remember their names." Suddenly, she was once more aware of her physical surroundings. She sat up saying, "Praise the Lord! Glory to God! Get a pen someone and write these names down before I forget."

Alice scrambled for a pen, and Pat dictated the odd-sounding names.

"How do you spell these?" Alice struggled.

"It doesn't matter," Pat assured her. "I'll remember how to say them."

"Where were you, girl?" Harold said, helping her up from the floor.

"I was with the Lord, and here's what He showed me," Pat said and then described in detail what she had seen in the vision.

"So what do we do now, just sit here and pray?" Pastor Mike asked, still amazed by her revelation.

"Now we seek God's wisdom," Trish declared. Every head bowed. "Father, it says in James 1:5 that if any of us lacks wisdom, we should ask believing and you will grant it. We need your wisdom in this situation."

There was silence, and then Pastor Mike spoke out a supernatural word of knowledge. Jim, who hadn't stopped praying since the meeting started, confirmed that it was the same message he had received just moments earlier.

"As I told my servant Joshua, says the Lord, I will give you every place where you set your foot. Have I not been your commander? Then be strong and courageous. Do not be terrified; do not be discouraged, for the Lord your God will be with you wherever you go. So go. Set your foot upon the desert and take the land."

Then Jim picked up where Pastor Mike left off, "You will hear reports that there are giants in the land, but I tell you, Goliath was a giant and a small shepherd boy felled him. You are born to overcome, says the Lord. Use the name, the name of Jesus Christ of Nazareth. You will prevail. Come against the enemy, dispatching the spirits, whose names I have given you. The legions of angels cannot act until you have made the way clear. Be bold, be strong, for the Lord your God, I am with you."

They sat in stunned silence. Finally, Pastor Mike spoke.

"I believe we are to go to the desert where this unholy thing is happening," he said, jumping to his feet. "I felt the Lord tugging on my spirit, saying 'Go, go.' We can't just leave it to others this time."

"Shouldn't somebody call the Sheriff?" Sue asked logically. Just then the doorbell rang. Pat ran to the door, hoping it was her mother. Flinging it open, she stared open-mouthed at the face of Sheriff Anderson, holding his hat.

"For the life of me, Miss Pat, I don't know why I'm here," he said, stepping into the foyer.

"I do," she exclaimed, grabbing him by the arm. "Come with me."

The Sheriff looked around the room as everyone stared at him dumbfounded.

"Why, Sheriff," Pastor Mike suppressed a chuckle. "What brings you here?"

"I don't rightly know," the Sheriff shook his head. "I was headed home, and the next thing I knew I was pulling into the driveway. Is Miss Molly at home?"

"Sheriff, we need your help," Pat said excitedly. "In fact, we were just talking about you."

✝✝✝✝✝

Molly watched in horror as her son and Christine were lashed to the crosses. As they lay on the ground, the women ripped open John's shirt and began to paint his chest with strange symbols. A moan escaped as his head lolled to one side, and he began to awaken. It was like waking up after an all-night drunk, still a bit intoxicated. His head throbbed. He could hear his heart beating in his ears. Then he realized it was a drum he was hearing. Struggling, he fought to move his arms, but he was unable. He forced his eyelids to open, but they were only slits.

Lord Jesus, help me. Then he remembered. Heather and the gun. Star . . . Libby sticking a needle in his arm. Christine. *Where's Christine?* He strained to move his head. Then he heard the lilting chants and the maniacal laughter of the demon, posing as the goddess Coatlicue.

He heard Christine scream and he turned his head toward the sound. She was lying on his left, lashed to a crude wooden cross. Star straddled her struggling body and ripped open her shirt. He looked away, crying, then called out to her.

"Christine, are you okay!"

"John!" she screamed, and Star viciously slapped her, relishing the domination. The torchlight flickered on Christine's terrified face as the demon slowly painted the facing rattlesnakes of the goddess Coatlicue on her chest.

"You've always belonged to me, you know," Coatlicue crooned.

"Leave her alone," John tried to shout, but he was dizzy.

"And you, I've been waiting for you a long time," the demon spat, rising up from Christine. Taking her jar of red paint, she knelt at the top of his head, so that he was looking at her diabolic face upside down. She clamped his head between her knees so that he could not move and began to paint a coiled rattlesnake on his forehead.

"I could write 666," she leered, "but that would betray me. So I'll just draw a little picture for the benefit of these idiots." She laughed malevolently. "What does it matter? Tonight your innocent blood will complete my Master's plan. After that, what I have painted on your body won't matter."

John shuddered involuntarily. Staring up into her face, he could hardly believe that he had once loved her. But she wasn't the woman he had loved. Somewhere inside, if she hadn't already been killed by the evil thing that possessed her, was the fragile flower that was once Star. Aiming for that, John spoke.

"Star, for God's sake, are you there?" John cried, his tongue thick and his speech garbled. "Fight, Star. Fight. You can win."

He tasted blood as she slammed her fist into his mouth, mimicking him, "Fight, Star. Fight!" Her laughter rang out into the night.

Molly huddled against the rock, her feet and hands bound in front of her, with a drugged Heather lying across her lap. If only she could offer herself instead. She realized that she would willingly die for her son or Christine. In horror, she watched a fully costumed Libby, wearing a red feathered headdress, prepare the altar with a bowl of fire and water.

"Please don't kill us," Christine whimpered, now fully coherent, as the frenzied women danced around her. "Please. Oh, God, I don't want to die! Not like this. Please God."

Then she heard the audible voice of the Holy Spirit speak to her, "Though you walk through the valley of the shadow of death, fear no evil, for I am with you." Her fear began to subside, replaced by a holy anger. "You won't get away with this! The Sheriff already knows about you. We told him everything. He'll find you!"

The goddess and Libby laughed, exchanging amused looks. That's what they all said. After tonight, it wouldn't matter anyway. Once they were in power, what they had done before would be exalted. Star ripped off two long strips from John's shirt and gagged them both.

Joan and two others danced forward and pulled steel spikes from their sashes. Christine could hardly believe the sight. It was just like her dream. They laid them on the altar and backed away, bowing and chanting. Libby lifted the spikes overhead and spoke the magic over them. Then she dipped them one by one in the water bowl and waved them through the fire.

John and Christine exchanged long looks, each hoping the other would not be first and unable to comfort one another. Libby walked forward and stood between the two crosses, still lying on the ground. Lifting the spikes overhead, she began to spin and dance in a circle around John's cross. A sickening feeling rose up in his mouth. He would be first.

✛✛✛✛✛

Sheriff Anderson and two deputies pulled into the driveway of Libby and Star's home, their lights flashing. Seeing John's Jeep, the Sheriff quickly got out of the car and inspected it. Christine's purse was on the passenger side floorboard. Dr. Brinkman's red Porsche was still parked by the house.

"Let's hope this is all a big misunderstanding," he muttered to Clarence as they walked up to the door. He rang the doorbell and waited. There was no answer. He knocked on the door, but still no one came. Motioning to Clarence to go around to the back, he tried the handle and found the door unlocked.

"Anybody home?" the Sheriff called, stepping cautiously over the threshold. Dan Littleheart, the other deputy, drew his gun. "Yoo-hoo, Dr. Brinkman? Miz White?" Whispering, the Sheriff continued, "Check the dining room." Even though the lights were still on, the house appeared deserted. He poked his head into the chapel and let out a long belly sigh. "Holy hoppin' john! Looks like somebody butchered a hog in here."

"There's got to be a body somewhere," Dan whistled.

The Sheriff jumped, "Dan, how many times have I told you not to slip up on me like that? Check in back and see if Clarence found anything. Wish it was daylight."

The Sheriff flicked on the rest of the lights and walked around the stone throne, kneeling down to inspect the blood. It was already mostly dry. An empty medicine bag was lying behind the chair.

"Sheriff?" He looked up and saw Clarence standing in the doorway. "I think you better come out back. We got us a body."

The Sheriff quickly rose from his haunches and followed his deputy, who turned on his flashlight. "I thought maybe they might have hightailed it down the gully and gone out a back way," Clarence said as they approached Katona's grave. The Sheriff looked down in the dim beam. The head and part of a leg were exposed.

"Looks like a wild animal, or a neighbor's dog thought he smelled him some dinner," the Sheriff said matter-of-factly. "You must have scared him off." He shone the flashlight into Katona's face.

Dan exclaimed, "Hey, I know her! Her grandfather and my grandfather were drinking buddies. Her last name's Whitefeather. Don't remember her first name."

"Let's get the lab boys out here," the Sheriff shook his head. "Looks like somebody sliced her throat. Any sign of our missing folks?"

"Nope," Dan declared. "I went through the whole house. There was some kind of weird stuff going on in the living room. There's blood all over the place."

They all went back to the house, and Dan led the Sheriff into the living room. Furniture was in disarray, and there were wet blood stains on the carpet and coffee table. A bowl with what appeared to be blood in it had been dropped to the floor.

"Dan, you stay here and wait for the lab," the Sheriff ordered briskly. "Clarence, you come with me."

Racing out the door, the two jumped into the Sheriff's car and Clarence reached for the radio, informing dispatch that there had been a probable homicide at the Brinkman house. With sirens blaring, they headed for Boynton Canyon.

"I only hope we're not too late," the Sheriff sighed.

CHAPTER
20

In panic, Christine watched as Libby straddled the crossbeam to which John's left hand was tied. Placing a steel spike against the soft place between the bones on his wrist, she raised the steel mallet over her head and brought it down. He screamed in spite of his gag, and Molly screamed with him.

"My son, my son. They're crucifying my baby," she cried, rocking Heather's limp body, seeking comfort where there was none. "Sweet Jesus, help us. In the name of Jesus, Satan, take your hands off my son!" she screamed, her voice echoing through the canyon.

"If you don't shut up, the kid's next," Star gnashed her teeth in anger.

Christine wept bitter tears, as Libby raised the steel mallet for its second blow. Wham-ting. Steel struck against steel. But Christine could not use the name because of her gag. Mentally, she reached out to her newfound Lord Jesus and pleaded for John's life.

If somebody has to die, Lord, please take me. Don't let him be the one. Please, Lord. Don't let him die.

The hammer raised for the third time, and John again screamed as the spike finally found the wood. The air hung heavy with demons, licking their lips for the taste of blood. Desmodus rushed to lap the red liquid as it ran from the wound. The villains rejoiced at John's agony and revelled in Christine's fear.

Pat heard her mother's cry from the parking lot, and it was all she could do to keep from rushing up the hillside into the canyon. But she remembered that fools rush in where angels fear to tread. Once again she saw the battle scene of her vision. If the angels could wait for the word, so could she. She reminded the intercessors quietly about what they might see.

"Remember that we have been promised victory," she encouraged them. "It doesn't matter what we see or hear or feel. God is for us."

In silence, with no dread of the rattlesnakes which would surely be out to feed in the night, the Joshua Intercessors fanned out over the hillside.

"I can't see," Alice whispered, reaching out for Pat. Then she heard a rattle. "I can't do this!" she cried as she slipped on the loose shale and fell to the ground. Her guardian angel covered her so that she would be protected from all danger.

Looking up, Alice noticed that she couldn't hear anybody else's footsteps, even though they were only a few feet away from her. She gasped. From a glow emanating from the other side of the Kachina Woman, she could see that Pastor Mike's feet were at least two inches above the ground. She looked to her left. So were Pat's. Then she saw the angels: millions of angels on the hillsides. She blinked and they disappeared. "Thank you, Jesus, for letting me see that!" Alice softly wept into the crook of her arm.

The others had noticed that their footfalls made no sound on the rough terrain, but they didn't quite know what to make of it. They blessed God for it just the same. They all waited for the promised signal in their spirits as they surrounded the ceremonial site.

Pat cringed as she saw what looked like Libby Brinkman kneeling over her brother's right arm. Libby rested a steel spike on his wrist and raised the mallet. Simultaneously, every intercessor heard the word as clearly as if God Himself had shouted it in their ear. "Take the land!"

At that same moment, a celestial trumpet blew the charge, and the warrior angels were uncloaked. The glory of God lit up the entire canyon.

They all began marching, and Pat shouted out the first name, "Zethar-Zebah." The intercessors echoed, "Zethar-Zebah, in the name of Jesus, we bind you and cast you into outer darkness."

Zethar-Zebah screamed as he was sucked backward into a void of blackness.

The angelic battalions surged forward majestically. Swinging their weapons left and right, they stormed into the ranks of hell. Wails of torment pierced the night as demons were dispatched to oblivion. The stench of burning sulphur was heavy in the air. Kerestel soared into the sky, his sword twirling and flashing in a billion streams of white light, as he challenged demon after demon.

Pat cried out again, "Bizjothjah." The intercessors echoed the same name, "Bizjothjah, in the name of Jesus, we bind you and cast you into outer darkness."

Bizjothjah's talons sank into Libby's back, trying to hold on, but the blackness enveloped him as he was rebuked.

✛✛✛✛✛

Now permitted to intervene, Miklos drew his sword and headed straight for the startled Rosh-Rot, who stumbled backward. Miklos swung his sword with both hands, slicing a huge gash in the demon's massive chest. Rosh-Rot drew his red flaming sword and swung at the angel, who zipped out of the way.

Chasing Miklos into the air, the demon wielded his weapon overhead and slashed at his archenemy. Miklos tumbled out of reach, then whirled to face the foe.

"Take a deep breath," Miklos sang. "For it will be your last." Then he plunged his sword to the hilt, right between the demon's ribs.

At that moment, Pat called out, "Rosh-Rot." Terror filled the demon's eyes as the intercessors banished him, shrieking through the earth.

✝✝✝✝✝

Yoko-Sharuhen saw the hesitation on Libby's face as the hammer wavered in the air, poised to strike. She snatched the curved flint knife from the altar and leaped venomously onto the now useless Libby Brinkman.

"I will not be opposed," the demon roared, foaming at the mouth, as she plunged the knife into Libby's heart.

As her spirit was released from her body, Libby finally saw the real face of her beloved "Earth Mother." A split second passed as Libby realized the inescapable truth.

Suddenly, she felt as if she was being sucked into a black hole. She could feel the heat as it beat into her face. A sharp-clawed hand grabbed her ankle, drawing her down into the inky black pit. Screaming, she scrambled for a handhold, but even the sound was swallowed up. As Libby descended, it grew hotter and hotter until she felt she was melting. Red and black flames that gave off no real light licked at her. Her body was in agony.

If I could just die, she wished. Then the most horrible being she had ever seen grabbed her by the throat.

"You *are* dead," Satan cackled, "and you are mine forever!"

Jerking the knife from Libby's lifeless body, Yoko-Sharuhen turned to face Pat who, with the other intercessors, continued to advance. Steely-eyed, Pat met the demon's gaze, and she remembered its name.

"Yoko-Sharuhen," Pat shouted.

Screeching in rage, the demon launched herself at Pat. As she arched in the air, Star White's body fell to the desert floor. Pat was face to face with the reptilian countenance of a demigod of the nether world, the knife held in a taloned hand. At that moment, the intercessors intoned, "Yoko-Sharuhen, in the name of Jesus, we bind you and cast you into outer darkness." The she-devil spiraled into nothingness, and the knife clattered to the earth.

✝✝✝✝✝

Quench-Bersha lay writhing on the ground, pierced through the hip by Sandor. Pat called his name, and he was dispatched without a fight. The demons fell back to gather around their four remaining Commanders: Mibzar, Rezin-Rohgah, Humtah, and Desmodus. Rezin-Rohgah quickly took command.

"Turn and fight, you fools," he shouted. "We've come too far to retreat now. The battle is ours."

The company of demons rallied around him as he propelled himself into the heart of the battle. Kerestel, the Captain of the Host, took pleasure in facing Rezin-Rohgah, the prince of tumult.

"So, you are the one who has been meddling among the faithful," Kerestel challenged, the light from his shield momentarily blinding the prince. "Come. Meddle with me."

"With pleasure," Rezin's voice boasted. The two clashed like knights of old, jabbing and lunging at one another across the sky.

For one moment, Rezin's attention was diverted as he heard the final cry of Mibzar, coiling into the death-like womb of hades. That was all Kerestel needed. Taking off the left arm first, then the right, he plunged his sword into the gut of the prince of tumult, who spat on him with his final breath. The air was filled with the fetid smell.

The tide of the righteous swept over the floodgates of hell, banishing demon after demon into the swiftly closing rifts all over the earth. Outflanked on the right and the left, they were forced to retreat into the darkness once again.

Humtah disappeared into the caverns below, hiding behind a wall of crystal. He stuck his fingers into his ears as Pat called out his name.

"Humtah," Pat recited. The intercessors repeated, "Humtah, in the name of Jesus, we bind you . . ."

"No!" he squealed. Grabbing onto a quartz stalagmite, he felt the yawning maw of the abyss inhaling him into its neverending blackness.

". . . and cast you . . ." His fingers were slipping. "Into outer darkness." With a yowl, the lord of the place of the lizards imploded.

There was only one commander left. Desmodus, the drinker of blood, stood and faced his attackers.

"Not me," he vowed. "I will not bow to that name." With that, he disappeared where her voice could not reach him, or so he thought. As he stood in Satan's empty throne room, Pat's voice reverberated within the walls.

"Desmodus-s-s . . ." it echoed. "Desmodus-s-s-s, in the name of Jesus-s-s-s, we bind you-u-u-u and cas-s-s-t you into-o-o-o outer dark-k-k-ness-s-s-s."

A fire tore at the vampire's chest, ripping him to shreds, and thrusting his consciousness into the ever-hungering void.

✝✝✝✝✝

The throne room of hell was empty because Satan watched with the Lord Jesus and God the Father from the vantage of the Mercy Seat. The Lord of the Underworld gnashed his teeth in rage as demon after demon was dispatched into the black pit of hell.

"No," Satan roared. "I will not be defeated again!" He turned and pointed a gnarled talon at Jesus. "The earth is mine!"

"You are a defeated foe, fallen angel," Jesus reminded him sternly. "I redeemed the world when I took all of its sin to the cross with me. You cannot rewrite the Revelation!"

"Now back to your pit!" the Father ordered. "Soon, you will taste the agony of the lake of fire forever. Be gone!"

"You haven't seen the last of me yet!" Satan assured them, disappearing in a puff of smoke as Jesus and the Father smiled down on the righteous.

The angelic forces corralled the remainder of the hissing gargoyles into the last of the rifts. As a remnant stood guard, Kerestel flew into heaven and returned with a cup. Pouring one drop of the blood of Christ Jesus onto the cavernous rupture, he sealed it forever.

Pastor Mike was the first to reach John, who had mercifully passed out with the pain. There was nothing he could do until help arrived. He surveyed the carnage around him. Although no weapon had been fired, the ground was littered with dead bodies. The pastor checked each woman and saw that their bellies had been ripped open as if something had exploded from within. He covered his mouth and staggered over to Christine, who lay sobbing, still tied to the cross. He covered her with Libby's feather cape. Pulling out his pocketknife, he sawed at the ropes which held her, while softly crooning words of comfort.

Sirens wailed in the near distance as Sheriff Anderson pulled into the parking lot, and they could hear the squawking of his radio. An ambulance pulled up right behind him.

As she knelt beside her weeping mother, Pat realized that what had seemed like an eternity had actually taken only a few minutes. The air now smelled clean and fresh.

"Is my baby dead?" Molly cried, looking up at Pat.

"No, Mama, but he's hurt pretty bad," Pat pulled her mother's head to her chest and cradled it there. "It's okay, Mama. It's all over."

Jeremio wrapped his wings around Molly and prayed peace into her spirit. She stopped sobbing and noticed Star's body lying a few feet away.

"Is Heather's mother dead?" Molly asked, concerned for the now stirring teenager. With new strength, the older woman called to Pastor Mike. "Bring that knife over here, Pastor."

Harold knelt down and pulled out his Swiss Army knife. "We'll have you out of those in just a flash, Molly," he assured her, slicing right through the twine. Molly pulled Heather against her and turned to Pat. "Let's get her out of here before she sees this mess." Joanne and Trish led a groggy Heather back down to the cars.

The ambulance crew rounded the hillside and entered the circle of light cast by the bamboo torches.

"Over here," Pastor Mike shouted to the paramedics. They immediately started triage, as Pat, supporting her mother, led her over to John. It was too horrible to contemplate what might have happened.

Finally released from her bonds, Christine crawled to John's side.

"Please don't die," she whispered, tenderly kissing his freed right hand. "I love you, John. Don't die."

Pastor Mike felt the spirit of the Lord rise up on the inside of him and he spoke authoritatively, "In the name of Jesus, he will live and not die. I rebuke you spirit of death."

The paramedics looked up at him as if he were crazy, but Pastor Mike had decided long ago that pleasing God came first before pleasing men.

The Sheriff lumbered over to the grisly scene as they worked frantically to free John.

"Miss Christine," he exclaimed gladly. "You're one pretty sight."

Pastor Mike lifted Christine and helped her to the stone throne.

"I will not sit in that!" she protested.

"Fine, Christine," Pastor Mike calmed her. "We can go back down the hill."

"No, I want to stay with John," she wept.

Just then a fire engine arrived with the tools they needed to cut through the spike and release John. He had already lost a lot of blood. Quickly, they lifted him onto a gurney and charged back down the hill for the trip to the hospital in Sedona. Pastor Mike and Molly went in the ambulance with John, while Pat promised to follow with Christine.

✛✛✛✛✛

As they crossed the medicine wheel, Pat saw a movement out of the corner of her eye. Turning, she beheld a dazed Star White sitting up and staring in bewilderment at the carnage around her.

"What happened?" she asked dully. Then she saw Libby being lifted into a body bag. "Libby!" she cried. "Libby!"

Deputy Clarence Clausen reached down and gingerly picked up the sacrificial knife. Placing it in a plastic bag, he handed it to a detective and turned to Star White. He pulled out his cuffs and began to recite the Miranda Rights as he restrained the hysterical woman.

"You have the right to remain silent," he intoned, lifting her from the ground and leading her down the hillside.

+++++

The Joshua Intercessors, waiting in the parking lot, were clustered around Alice. Excited, she was telling them of the angelic forces she had seen surrounding them, and how the intercessors had walked on cushions of air.

Pat seated Christine in her car and waved to the triumphant prayer warriors as she backed out. Tomorrow was Sunday. She could thank them all then.

+++++

Pastor Mike, holding John's right hand, said "Amen," as Christine breezed into the hospital room.

"Excuse me," she said, "I didn't know you were here."

"Come on in, honey," Molly invited, her eyes twinkling. "We were just thanking God for John's healing."

She sat down in the spare chair beside his bed, where she had spent most of the last three days.

"Did you eat all of your breakfast?" Christine chided John playfully.

"Well, all but the oatmeal," he grimaced. "It was solid as a rock. The spoon stood straight up in it." Everybody laughed.

"That's okay, honey," Molly patted her son on the shoulder. "You never did like oatmeal anyway. When you get home, I'll fix a stack of blueberry pancakes for you."

"That's a deal, Mom," John licked his lips. "Can you have them ready tomorrow? I'm being discharged in the morning."

"Yea!" Christine shouted, bounding up and kissing John's still smiling mouth. Pastor Mike chuckled and winked at Molly.

"Seems like a few things have happened in the last couple of days that I'm not aware of." The pastor looked at John in mock seriousness. "Anything you need to talk to me about, son?"

"Well, Christine and I will be needing some appointments with you for pre-marital counseling," John smiled.

"I just happen to have my calendar right here," the pastor said, pulling his appointment book from his coat pocket. Flipping through the pages, he said, "How about a week from tomorrow?"

"That okay with you, Chrissy?" John asked solicitously.

"Fine with me," she glowed.

"Well, why don't we leave these two lovebirds alone," Molly said, taking the Pastor's arm. "I'll call you tonight, John. See you later, Christine."

In the hallway, Molly strolled arm in arm with her pastor.

"I have a feeling you need to talk," he remarked, giving her the opening she was looking for.

"I had an experience in the desert that I'm confused about," Molly began. She was fighting an inner battle. "I'd never thought much about the events surrounding Jesus' crucifixion. But that seems to be all I can think about lately."

"What do you mean?"

"Well, as I watched John being nailed to that cross, anger and hatred rose up inside of me until I could hardly breathe," she admitted. "I wanted them dead. All of them." She hesitated.

"That's a normal reaction, Molly."

"Normal for who?" she went on. "Is that how Mary felt when her Son hung on the cross? Did she hate them all for what they'd done? I don't think so."

"Molly, this may come as a surprise to you," the pastor counseled, "but in spite of all your redeeming qualities, you're still human, and so was Mary. We don't know what she was thinking at the foot of that cross. What we do know is that she saw her Son rise again. Just like you."

Molly felt the tears burn her eyes. "I want to forgive them," she sniffed. "I really do. But every time I think about those women and what they did, I just get angry all over again. I could have lost him forever."

"Not forever," he reminded her. "Molly, sometimes we can forgive even when we don't feel like forgiving. Forgiveness is a choice of the will. Then we ask God to work out the rest. We can release our anger to Him and ask that He wash away the hate. We can ask Him to love those people through us."

She looked at Pastor Mike with a dawning understanding. "So, I don't have to *feel* gushy and sweet before I have forgiven them?"

"No," the pastor explained. "All you have to do is say, 'Lord, I *will* to forgive those that have wronged me, and I *will* to receive your forgiveness for holding anything against them.' Then He works out the forgiveness."

"Will I ever feel it?" Molly sighed.

"Maybe, or maybe not, but what you feel doesn't matter," Pastor Mike concluded. "It's what you believe in your heart that counts."

Molly kissed her pastor on the cheek. "Thank you," she said, "for everything."

EPILOGUE

Christine tiptoed into John's studio as he added the final brush strokes to a new masterpiece. Peering over his shoulder, she was amazed at the lifelike faces that stared back at her.

"John, it's wonderful," she exclaimed. "The light is so brilliant. It's almost as if they're going to fly right out of the painting."

"It's easier to paint something when you've actually seen it," John said, standing back and putting an arm around Christine. They both stared in satisfaction at the portrait of the two guardians.

"What do you call it?" she asked, laying her head against his chest.

"Guardians of the Promise."

Christine stared at the tiny baby in the cradle between the two angels in the painting.

"I never thought of him as a promise," she teased. "More like a gift."

"A gift then, from me to you," John smiled, kissing her on the forehead.

✛✛✛✛✛

The portrait of the Indian maiden that John had so aptly named "In the Eye of the Storm" hung proudly in Molly's family room. She sat rocking, contemplating the truth in the name of the painting.

Slowly, the baby in her arms stirred and she began to sing softly, "Oh precious is the flow, that makes me white as snow, no other fount I know, nothing but the blood of Jesus."

Molly looked back up at the painting. *In the eye of the storm: that place where everything is so peaceful and so calm, that you forget the storm that's yet to come.*

"Lord God," she prayed, "make us ready for the storm to come. Come, Lord Jesus, come."

Miklos and Aaro hovered near, instructing their new companion, a small, but beautiful angel, Nelo, which meant "God is my judge."

"You are always near, when they are asleep and when they are awake, all the days of their life," Miklos explained.

"And you can't always stop them from falling down," Aaro continued, "or they'd never learn to walk."

"I know it sounds hard," Miklos was saying, "but you'll get used to it. We'll be right there with you."

"Buck up, Nelo," Aaro encouraged. "We've been given one of the greatest assignments of all. We are the guardians of the Promise."

✛✛✛✛✛

A golden shaft of light illuminated the gray in Pastor Mike's hair as he leaned back in his desk chair contemplating the events of the past few weeks. As close as he was to his Lord, he still didn't quite understand.

"Why?" he asked the seemingly empty room. "Why didn't we see what was happening in our own town? Why didn't you warn us?"

Once more the Lord intervened by the inner witness of the Holy Spirit, leading Pastor Mike to open his Bible for the answer. The still small voice instructed him to turn to 2 Peter 2:1–12 and 3:3–13 (NKJV). This is what he read: "But there were also false prophets among the people, even as there will be false teachers among you, who will secretly bring in destructive heresies, even denying the Lord who bought them, and bring on themselves swift destruction.

"And many will follow their destructive ways, because of whom the way of truth will be blasphemed.

"By covetousness they will exploit you with deceptive words; for a long time their judgement has not been idle, and their destruction does not slumber.

"For if God did not spare the angels who sinned, but cast them down to hell and delivered them into chains of darkness, to be reserved for judgment; and did not spare the ancient world, but saved Noah, one of eight people, a preacher of righteousness, bringing in the flood on the world of the ungodly; and turning the cities of Sodom and Gomorrah into ashes, condemned them to destruction, making them an example to those who afterward would live ungodly; and delivered righteous Lot, who was oppressed by the filthy conduct of the wicked (for that righteous man, dwelling among them, tormented his righteous soul from day to day by seeing and hearing their lawless deeds)—then the Lord knows how to deliver the godly out of temptations and to reserve the unjust under punishment for the day of judgement, and especially those who walk according to the flesh in the lust of uncleanness and despise authority. They are presumptuous, self-willed. They are not afraid to speak evil of dignitaries, whereas angels, who are greater in power and might, do not bring a reviling accusation against them before the Lord.

"But these, like natural brute beasts made to be caught and destroyed, speak evil of the things they do not understand, and will utterly perish in their own corruption . . . knowing this first: that scoffers will come in the last days, walking according to their own lusts, and saying, 'Where is the promise of His coming? For since the fathers fell asleep, all things continue as they were from the beginning of creation.'

"For this they willfully forget: that by the word of God the heavens were of old, and the earth standing out of water and in the water, by which the world that then existed perished, being flooded with water.

"But the heavens and the earth which now exist are kept in store by the same word, reserved for fire until the day of judgment and perdition of ungodly men.

"But, beloved, do not forget this one thing, that with the Lord one day is as a thousand years, and a thousand years as one day.

"The Lord is not slack concerning His promise, as some count slackness, but is longsuffering toward us, not willing that any should perish but that all should come to repentance.

"But the day of the Lord will come as a thief in the night, in which the heavens will pass away with a great noise, and the elements will melt with fervent heat; both the earth and the works that are in it will be burned up.

"Therefore, since all these things will be dissolved, what manner of persons ought you to be in holy conduct and godliness, looking for and hastening the coming of the day of God, because of which the heavens will be dissolved being on fire, and the elements will melt with fervent heat?

"Nevertheless we, according to His promise, look for new heavens and a new earth in which righteousness dwells."

As Pastor Mike finished reading the Scripture, he understood. The truth of God's Word burned like an unquenchable flame within his very body, soul, and spirit. God *had* warned the inhabitants of Sedona, as well as the rest of mankind, in *His Word.*

In a loud clap of thunder, the voice of the Lord filled the room. "Tell my people that which has been revealed unto you."

"Yes, Lord, I will do as you have commanded," Pastor Mike declared. "And I will give all the glory to You, Lord God . . . who was, and is, and is to come," he cried, with tears trickling down his face.

Next to the praying Pastor Mike stood Chioke, his guardian angel, whose hand was ever ready on a flaming, two-edged sword as he cautiously gazed about the glory-filled room.

"He comes sooner than man could ever imagine," Chioke declared. "The Lord God Almighty is at hand."

Authors' Note

This novel was not written to make you afraid of the dark or to look for demons under every rock. There is no doubt that our enemy, the devil, prowls like a roaring lion, seeking whom he may devour. But darkness cannot exist in the presence of the light. When you worship the Lord, giving Him your praise in thanksgiving, He draws near to you, manifesting His glory and power through His Holy Spirit. God inhabits the praises of His people, and when you lift up the name of Jesus and exalt Him, the devil runs and hides like the defeated foe he is.

Unfortunately, many people have taken spiritual warfare to an extreme, giving the devil more credit than they do to Jesus. You don't have to yell and scream at the devil all day to make him run. Take authority over the enemy, then turn your back on him and begin to praise God. Get your mind off the enemy, and keep your mind focused on the Lord. It's vital to your physical and spiritual welfare to be God-conscious instead of devil-conscious.

You can dwell in God's peace all your days, despite the devil's howling in the circumstances of your life. If you don't know Jesus as your Lord and Savior, if you've never experienced the love and peace of God, then we invite you to pray this prayer:

"Heavenly Father, I confess that I've walked my own way far too long. There have been times when I've been alone and afraid, not knowing where I would spend eternity. I want to spend it with you. It says in Romans 10:9 (KJV), 'That if thou shalt confess with thy mouth the Lord Jesus, and shalt believe in thine heart that God hath raised him from the dead, thou shalt be saved.' Then in Romans 10:13 (KJV), it says, 'For whosoever shall call upon the name of the Lord shall be saved.' Father, I do believe Jesus died for my sins and that He was raised from the dead and now sits at your right hand. I confess that He is my Lord and my Savior. I am saved! Thank you, Father!"

Peace be unto you!

ANGEL NAMES

NAME	MEANING
Aaro	Hebrew—From Aaron—Enlightened
Chioke	Nigerian—Gift of God
Delta	Fourth Letter of Greek alphabet—"D"
Feodor	Slavic—From Theodore—Gift of God
Goyo	Greek—From Gregory—Watchful
Heronim	Old English—From Harold—Powerful Army
Icon-El	Greek—Image, Hebrew—God
Issa	Swahili—God Is Our Salvation
Jeremio	Hebrew—From Jeremy—May God Raise or Exalt
Kerestel	Hungarian—From Christian—Anointed One
Lenis	Hebrew—from Lena—Sleep
Miklos	Hebrew—From Michael—Who Is the Lord
Monchi	Spanish—From Moses—Saved
Nelo	Hebrew—From Daniel—God Is My Judge
Pesach	Hebrew—From Pascal—Of the Passover
Sandor	Greek—From Alexander—Defender of Men
Wardar	Old German—From Howard—Protector of the Soul
Yoel	Hebrew—From Joel—The Lord Is God

DEMON NAMES

These names were chosen to reflect the demons' characters and tasks using several baby-name books (some out of print) and the Biblical Index of the Open Bible, Expanded edition, New King James Version.

NAME	MEANING
Acish	Serpent Charmer
Bizjothjah	Contempt for Yahweh
Darkon	Scatterer
Desmodus	Drinker of Blood
Hormah	Devoted to Destruction
Humtah	Place of Lizards
Ishma-Ithma	Desolate—Bereavement
Jabez	He Makes Sorrowful
Kinah	Lamentation
Koz	Thorn
Mibzar	Stronghold
Mizzah	Fear
Nahash	Serpent
Nod	Wandering Exile
Ozem	Anger
Piteous-Cull	Wretched Scavenger
Pocheroth	Binder
Quench-Bersha	To Extinguish with Wickedness
Rezin-Rohgah	Prince of Tumult
Rosh-Rot	Chief of Decay
Shashak	Assaulter
Shemed	Destruction

Shicron	Drunkeness
Shiphishion	Abundant Ruin
Shuham	Depression
Tartak	Hero of Darkness
Tilon	Scorn
Vaizaitha	Son of the Atmosphere
Yoko-Sharuhen	Female Abode of Pleasure
Zaham	Foul
Zethar-Zebah	Sacrifice Victim

About the Authors

Barbara Scott is currently a full-time student at Rhema Bible Training Center in Broken Arrow, Oklahoma. She holds a B.A. degree in English from Missouri Southern College and a certificate in Film Production from the Mass Media Institute at Stanford University. Formerly, Barbara has worked as a free-lance writer and as a newspaper reporter and editor. Before rededicating her life to God, Barbara served as editor of *Eck World News*, the international magazine of the New Age cult Eckankar.

Carrie Younce is also a full-time student at Rhema Bible Training Center and plans to join her husband in the ministry upon completion of her studies. She has attended numerous classes and seminars to sharpen her God-given writing talent. She writes children's books and designs Christian greeting cards. Carrie is involved in the counseling and healing ministries and has spoken on a variety of subjects from God's Word.